Dani Taylor was beginning to occupy his thoughts far too often—and all because of their close proximity. Or so Brendan wanted to believe.

He had enjoyed his day alone and didn't realize how late it was until he heard a car on the gravel road. A few minutes later he heard not one, but two car doors slam.

Curious, he walked toward the parking area. The first person he saw was Dani, looking as beautiful as she had when she'd left that morning. Standing on the other side of the car was a young girl. She carried a backpack and wore baggy clothing.

When she saw him, she said, "Hi, Uncle Brendan. Remember me?"

The voice was familiar. So was the face. "Jodie?" He crossed swiftly to her, wondering if this teenager could possibly be his niece.

Shyly she opened her arms for his embrace. He pulled her close and gave her a hug. It was then he discovered that Jodie had definitely changed since the last time he'd seen her.

She was pregnant.

ABOUT THE AUTHOR

Award-winning author Pamela Bauer chose northern
Minnesota as the setting for *Babe in the Woods* because it's a
place she fell in love with twenty years ago when she and her
husband became summer residents of a cabin on one of
Minnesota's ten thousand lakes. Today they still enjoy roasting
marshmallows over an open fire and listening to the call of
the loons in summer. And during winter they trek through the
woods on snowshoes and fish through a hole in the ice. Is it
romantic? Ask a Minnesotan and you'll more than likely get
the answer, "You betcha!" says Pamela, who treasures those
moments "up North."

Books by Pamela Bauer

HARLEQUIN SUPERROMANCE
605—I DO, I DO
670—MERRY'S CHRISTMAS

HARLEQUIN AMERICAN ROMANCE
668—THE PICK-UP MAN
718—MAIL ORDER COWBOY

BABE IN THE WOODS
Pamela Bauer

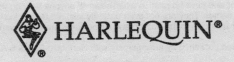

HARLEQUIN®

TORONTO • NEW YORK • LONDON
AMSTERDAM • PARIS • SYDNEY • HAMBURG
STOCKHOLM • ATHENS • TOKYO • MILAN • MADRID
PRAGUE • WARSAW • BUDAPEST • AUCKLAND

ISBN 0-373-70792-4

BABE IN THE WOODS

Printed in U.S.A.

A very special thank-you to Barbara Schenck and Andie Sisco for helping make this book possible.

PROLOGUE

SHE SAT ALONE on the bus-stop bench, sandwiched between a school backpack and a canvas gym bag. She wasn't waiting for the bus. Bus rides took money. She was simply resting. Her feet ached. So did her back.

It was the baby's fault. She used to be able to walk for miles without stopping. Now she could barely manage a couple of blocks before she'd either get tired or felt the need to relieve herself. She glanced around in search of a gas station or restaurant, knowing it wouldn't be long before she'd have to use the washroom.

Her stomach rumbled with hunger. She reached for the backpack. Instead of schoolbooks and paper, it held an odd assortment of things—makeup, CDs, a tattered issue of *Seventeen* magazine and half of a cheeseburger, the remainder of her lunch. Lunch had been an extravagance she couldn't afford, but when she'd walked by those golden arches, the temptation had been too great to resist. Even cold, the burger tasted good. She ate slowly, savoring every bite, knowing she probably wouldn't get anything else to eat for a while.

When she'd finished, she gathered her meager belongings together. It was time to move on. If she didn't keep walking, she wouldn't make it out of the city before dark. If she wanted to keep to her schedule, she needed to leave Minneapolis today.

She pulled a frayed map from a pouch on her back-pack. Opening it carefully, she studied the blue and black lines and sighed. She hated traveling on the high-way. A train would have been less hassle and much easier.

The baby inside her kicked and she glanced down. "Don't worry. I'm not going to hop a train." She patted her stomach as she spoke. "I just said it would be eas-ier."

But then, everything had been easier before she'd gotten pregnant. Walking, sleeping, eating. If only she could turn back the clock and erase the last eight months. Again the baby kicked.

"I'm sorry. Really I am." Her voice was barely a whisper as tears rose in her throat. "It's not that I don't want you. It's just that I don't know what to do with you."

She needed help. Someone who knew what she should do. Someone she could trust. She carefully folded the map and put it away. Then she pulled out a wad of tissue. Gently she peeled away the wrinkled lay-ers until she uncovered the silver locket. She opened it to look at what was hidden within the oval frame. It was a tiny picture of a bride and groom.

"You said you'd always be there for me," she mur-mured as her fingers traced the filigreed edges of the locket.

Then she snapped it shut, buried it once more in the wrinkled tissue and put it away. She slung the backpack over one shoulder, the gym bag over the other, and set out on her journey.

CHAPTER ONE

DANIELLE TAYLOR SAT ALONE at the glass-topped patio table in the shade of an umbrella. Her suit was still damp from her morning swim in the kidney-shaped pool. Not a morsel of her breakfast—a dish of fresh strawberries, an applesauce muffin and a glass of guava juice—had been touched. Her eyes focused on the photograph lying beside her plate.

It was a black-and-white snapshot of a log house nestled between tall, majestic pines. Tacked to one of the trees was a sign that said The Last Place On Earth. There were no people in the photo, just a couple of cabins by the lake. She knew that the lake was in a wilderness thousands of miles from the traffic-jammed freeways of Southern California.

Dani had looked at the photograph often during the past few days, troubled by the feelings it evoked whenever she held it in her hands. Why did it have the power to make her ache with an unfamiliar longing? It was just a picture of a place she'd never seen, built and owned by a man she'd never known, in a part of the country she'd never visited nor had any desire to visit.

Until now. And all because of one legal document. In the blink of an eye, everything had changed. Suddenly her uncomplicated life had become a complex puzzle, her mind preoccupied with getting answers to questions she would never have ventured to ask until a week ago.

She'd been looking forward to summer. School was out. She had survived another year of teaching French and English and coaching soccer at the Marchand Academy for Young Women. There would be no more impudent thirteen-year-olds, no high teas with the parent-teacher association, no pleas to the school board for new textbooks. At least not for the next three months.

As much as she enjoyed teaching, Dani needed the time away from her job that summer vacation afforded. Ever since taking the teaching position at the elite private school, she'd spent the summers at home on her father's estate in Montecito. It was a way to recharge her batteries, to see her friends, to spend time with her father whom Dani knew had been lonely ever since her mother's death six years ago. And this summer she had a wedding to plan.

Only, in the week she'd been home, she'd been alone for six of the seven days. Although she could have picked up the phone and called any number of friends, she hadn't. She couldn't. Seeing friends would have meant explanations. She didn't want to have to explain how she was feeling to anyone.

It was painful enough to discover that her fiancé had been unfaithful. To see pity in the eyes of friends was something she couldn't have stood at the moment. Which was why she'd shut herself away in the Spanish-style house. She needed the comfort of the place she'd called home all her life.

Except she hadn't found contentment, but rather disappointment.

"Dani?"

A shiver raised the hairs on her back of her neck. She knew without even turning around who it was.

"What are you doing here?" she asked flatly, refusing to look at her ex-fiancé.

In white shorts and a lemon yellow polo, Matthew Wellington looked every inch the tennis pro he was. "We need to talk, Dani," he said, then grabbed a wrought-iron chair and pulled it close to hers, placing his lean, trim figure in her line of vision.

"No, we don't." She swallowed with difficulty.

"Look, I made a mistake, but I've promised you it won't happen again. Why won't you give me a chance to prove that?" He reached for her hand, but she quickly snatched it away.

"Go away, Matt. Please."

He ignored her plea. "Why don't you get dressed and come with me to the club? We'll play a few games of tennis, have lunch." He gave her an engaging grin, the one he used whenever he wanted to persuade her to do something she didn't want to do. Before this summer, it would have had Dani forgiving him just about anything. Now it only made her feel sick.

"I can't," she answered, running her fingers through her short blond hair.

"Can't or won't?" He sounded a bit churlish.

"Both."

This time, instead of reaching for her hand, he lifted her chin with his fingers. "If I didn't think you loved me, I could be hurt by that." He gave her a look that could make most women swoon.

Dani swooned over no man. Never had, never would. Matt's conceit only strengthened her resolve to move forward with her life—alone. "I'm not saying it to hurt you, Matt." She pushed her chair back so that his hand fell away from her face. "Look, I have to get dressed. I have an appointment with Edward Collins."

"Edward? Why not call my dad and have him come here?"

Ever since Dani could remember, Howard Wellington had been coming to the house on a regular basis and bringing Matt with him. It was one of the reasons she and Matt had become so close—they'd spent a good deal of their childhood together. Besides being her father's attorney, Howard was her father's best friend, and everyone who knew the two families expected that one day they would be related through marriage.

"I think it's best if I see Edward," she said coolly.

His mouth tightened. "So now because we're having problems, you're going to punish my father?"

"Your father is my dad's attorney, not mine," she reminded him. "I'm not punishing him. Edward is his partner. And we're not having problems, Matthew. We've broken up."

"Don't say that," he pleaded, placing his hands on the arms of her chair so that she couldn't stand.

She looked pointedly at his hands. "It's the truth. Now you're going to have to let me get up. I told you I have an appointment."

Reluctantly he backed away. "Why do you have to see Edward when your dad handles everything for you?"

Law firms and corporate boardrooms were foreign territories to Dani. She had made it perfectly clear that the family business didn't interest her. Anything of a legal nature was handled by her father, which had suited Dani just fine.

Until now.

"I have some legal matters I need to take care of personally," she told Matt, rising.

"You're not still angry at your dad because of that stuff about your grandfather's estate, are you?"

"No, I'm not," she answered honestly. She had never been one to harbor resentment, and the truth was, right now she wasn't sure what she was feeling.

"Well, you sound angry."

She placed her hands on her hips and glared at him. "And how should I sound, Matt? I come home for the summer thinking I'm going to be planning my wedding. Instead, I'm trying to figure out what to do with a resort I've inherited from a man I didn't even know existed."

"You could be planning a wedding." Again he gave her that roguish grin.

"No, I can't," she stated firmly.

He looked at her with hurt in his eyes. "Dani, don't do this to me."

She paid no attention. "You're going to have to excuse me, Matt. I really do need to get ready for my appointment with Edward." She started to walk away, but he stopped her with a hand on her arm.

"Does your father know what you're doing?"

"No, but if he were here, I'd tell him. It just so happens he's not," she answered curtly.

Matt shook his head. "I don't understand why you're so upset over all this."

"Matthew! How would you feel if your father tried to sell your inheritance without your ever finding out about it?"

"I don't think your father had any intention of doing that." When he saw her eyes flash, he quickly added, "He probably just thought he was taking care of business for you—as usual. It's not like you're going to do anything with some run-down resort in the boonies, is it?''

The more he said, the more annoyed she became with him. "Just forget it. You wouldn't understand."

Like her father, Matt did not give up easily. "You have to admit he's been a pretty good father to you, Dani. I mean, there aren't many schoolteachers who drive a Porsche. Hell, you have a big trust fund—you don't even have to work."

Dani made a sound of exasperation. "This isn't about money!"

"What are you saying? That it's one of those *girl* things guys don't understand?"

"It's something you and my father don't understand," she said impatiently. "You sound just like him."

"I'll take that as a compliment. He's a smart man."

She could only stare at him in disbelief. He *was* just like her father. How come she hadn't noticed it before now?

"What you need is to have some fun. Come play tennis with me." The cajoling grin was back.

"No."

He ran a finger along her jaw. "Come on, Dani. Do it for me."

"No." She brushed his hand away. "Look, everything's changed, Matt. *I've* changed." And without another word, she hurried inside, not once glancing back.

"WELL, LOOKEE WHO'S HERE!" The gray-haired man behind the cash register gave Brendan Millar a welcoming grin. Then he leaned over the checkout counter and hollered toward the back of the store, "Vera, put another burger on!"

"How did you know I was hungry, Pete?" Brendan reached out to shake the man's bony hand as the familiar aroma of hamburger sizzling on the grill teased his taste buds. Because it was the only market in Hidden Falls, Minnesota, Pete's Place served as a grocery, drugstore, hardware store and restaurant all rolled into one. To the 232 residents of the town, it truly was—in every sense of the word—a convenience store.

"They must be working you long hours at the hospital. You look tired," Pete noted, giving Brendan the once-over.

Brendan fidgeted under the close scrutiny. "I could use a little peace and quiet."

Pete chuckled. "Well, we both know you'll get that at The Last Place on Earth. It's still peaceful there. Now Cedar Lake—that's another story. Ever since they opened that new lodge, there's a constant parade of Jet Ski machines in the summer and snowmobiles in the winter. They come up from the cities, you know. You should see the traffic that goes through here." He shook his head. "Vera and I can hardly keep up."

"I thought you two were going to retire." Brendan reached for a red plastic shopping basket.

"And do what? Twiddle our thumbs? This place is what keeps us young." Pete glanced affectionately at aisles cluttered with boxes. "Besides, we'd be foolish to quit now. Business is good. That's why I had that thing installed." He nodded toward a refrigerated case at the entrance to the store. In it was an assortment of canned and bottled beverages, including mineral water.

Brendan opened the door and pulled out a six-pack of soda. "This is great. Now I know where to come when I need a cold one."

"Earl put one in at the gas station, so I figured I

might as well, too.'' Pete leaned closer and said in a near whisper, ''Those city folks want that fancy bottled water. They'll pay a buck-fifty a bottle for it.''

''Have to give the customers what they want,'' Brendan said with a knowing grin.

''Should I put onions on that burger?'' a woman's voice called out from somewhere in the back of the store.

Pete looked to Brendan, who shook his head.

''No onions,'' Pete shouted back, then asked, ''you got a list of what you need? I can put it together while you have your lunch.''

''If you're busy, I can get the stuff myself,'' Brendan offered, but the store owner dismissed him with a flap of his hand.

''That's my job.''

''It's nice to see some things never change,'' Brendan said with a grateful smile, then pulled a scrap of paper from his pocket and handed it to Pete.

''It's easier for me since I know where everything is.'' The older man peered at the list through reading glasses perched low on his nose. ''You go say hello to Vera and get your burger. She's going to be tickled pink to see you, Father.''

''Pete, why don't you call me Brendan this summer?''

The old man looked a bit taken aback by the request but said easily, ''Sure thing.''

''Thanks.'' Brendan grinned, then worked his way through the maze of cereal boxes and soup cans, the word *Father* echoing in his thoughts.

It was a title of respect—and one Brendan hadn't earned yet. He was on his way to the resort known as The Last Place on Earth, not because he was a seminarian on vacation from his ministerial work at the hospital, but because he needed to decide whether to continue studying to become an ordained priest.

Instead of counseling the sick and the injured as a clinical pastoral educator this summer, he would be spending time alone. Reflecting. Meditating. Soul-searching. Trying to decide if he was ready to commit his life to the priesthood.

Andrew Lawrence, his student master, didn't believe he was and had suggested he take some time away from the seminary. Although Brendan had argued that he was prepared to take his final vows, he also knew that Andrew's reservations weren't without merit. Brendan would be the first one to admit he'd been restless lately. What he didn't know was why. Andrew thought it was unresolved anger; Brendan didn't dispute that possibility.

A man didn't live the life he'd led and not have anger inside him. Suffering either made one bitter or better. He was better—or at least he'd thought he was until questions had been asked that he couldn't answer. Questions that had inevitably led to doubts in both him and Andrew.

One thing Brendan did know was that anger could be a positive force if directed against the injustices of this world. As a child growing up in a city where street gangs warred nightly, he'd watched a man channel frustration into positive work in a neighborhood where kids like himself hardly stood a chance of surviving. Father Joseph Dorian had been the only male role model Brendan had ever known, guiding him through his turbulent youth, showing him that good could come out of anger.

Every time Brendan thought of his mentor, a feeling of nostalgia washed over him. If anyone had told him when he was growing up that one day he would reflect fondly on his childhood, he would have laughed aloud. Living in the inner city and having only one goal—staying alive—was hardly the stuff childhood dreams were made of.

Brendan often wondered how different his life would have been had he grown up in a neighborhood where drug transactions didn't take place in the house next door and gunfire didn't keep children from falling asleep at night. What would it have been like to be able to ride a bike and not have to worry about its being stolen right out from under you? To go to a school where they didn't lock the students inside once the bell rang. To shop in a store that didn't have bars on its windows.

But then, had he not grown up in the inner city, he would have missed out on having a remarkable man like Father Joe in his life.

Brendan had been tempted to drive the 250 miles to Minneapolis to tell his mentor of his conversation with Andrew. It would have been so natural to seek solace at the church on North Fifth Street. It was the place to which he'd always run when he was a boy. Father Joe had always been there—to listen, to advise, to console.

But this was different. Although the church had been a refuge in the past, Brendan now felt as if he was running away from it, not to it. There was only one place where he could go and truly be alone. The Last Place on Earth at Sacred Lake.

When he reached the alcove in the back of the store, seven of the eight bar stools lining the eating counter were unoccupied. The lone diner was a man wearing bib overalls, a faded blue T-shirt and a baseball cap bearing the name of a seed company. Cooking at the grill was a tiny woman who barely measured five feet tall. A hair net covered white curls tinted blue from a shampoo rinse. Glasses as thick as pop-bottle bottoms framed a face that had only the slightest hint of wrinkles. She appeared frail, yet Brendan knew that was deceptive. A stronger, more energetic woman he'd never met. When she saw Brendan, a wide grin revealed perfectly straight false teeth.

"You're back!" Vera leaned across the counter and raised her cheek so he could brush it with his lips. "Are you my hamburger with no onions?" she asked excitedly.

Brendan grinned as he sat down. "Is it too late to ask for cheese?"

"You got it." She wiped off the counter in front of him with a wet rag, then set silverware and a napkin at his fingertips. "It's so good to see you! We didn't think any of the priests would be at Sacred Lake this summer." Like her husband, Vera treated the seminarians as if they were members of the clergy.

"There aren't going to be any priests. Just me." It was his way of reminding her that he hadn't been ordained.

"You here for the week?"

"Actually I'm here for the summer."

"You're not working at the hospital?"

"No. I'm going to take care of the maintenance at the resort until the new owner decides what to do with it," Brendan answered, aware that the other diner, a local farmer named Wayne Boggs, could hear every word of their conversation.

The blue eyes behind the glasses widened. "You have to tell me everything you know. There've been plenty of rumors floating around about what's going to happen to The Last Place on Earth.''

Knowing that everything he said would be repeated to the other 229 citizens of Hidden Falls, Brendan said, ''I'm afraid I don't have the answer to that one. You probably know more than I do.'' Actually, the lawyer who'd hired him had said that the new owner had no intention of coming to Minnesota and that the property was expected to be put up for sale in the near future.

''I hear Wilbur left the place to his granddaughter.''

Brendan nodded. ''I heard.''

''That was a shock,'' Vera admitted. ''No one even knew he *had* a granddaughter, although I suspect Louella Hortense may have known.''

''He was a quiet man.'' Brendan didn't tell them that Wilbur Latvanen had confided in him on more than one occasion the circumstances of his relationship—or the lack of one—with his granddaughter. Whenever Wilbur had spoken of her, a wistfulness had transformed the normally gruff voice. ''Someday she'll come and she'll like it here,'' Brendan had often heard him say.

Now that Wilbur had died without ever seeing that day, Brendan could only hope that the old man had been wrong, that she wouldn't come to Sacred Lake. What Brendan didn't need was his new landlord in his face. He needed solitude—and an occasional visit to Pete and Vera's for a burger and fries.

Wayne Boggs spoke up. ''Someone said there's talk of her dividing up the land and putting up time-share condominiums.''

Vera shuddered. ''That would be a real shame. It's so peaceful out there.''

''If she's from California, she probably doesn't know what peace and quiet is.'' The farmer mopped up his eggs with a piece of toast. "It's no wonder she doesn't want to come up here."

Vera shook her head disapprovingly. "She probably wouldn't fit in with the rest of us, anyway. Still, I hate to see Sacred Lake get taken over by tourists."

"It'd mean more business for you and Pete," Brendan said.

"We got more than we can handle now," Vera declared with a click of her tongue. A regular visitor to Hidden Falls for the past three summers, Brendan knew that even though the tourists brought in much needed revenue to their community, the local residents valued their privacy and quiet way of life.

"The way they keep building stuff around here, pretty soon we'll have a fast-food restaurant and a shopping mall," Wayne predicted grimly.

"I hope not. We couldn't compete with that." Anxiety put little lines across Vera's forehead.

"I don't think you need to worry," Brendan reassured her. "What makes Hidden Falls attractive to outsiders is its isolation. People come to this part of the country to get away from ringing phones and electronic gadgets. You have what everyone wishes they could get back to—a simple life."

"We'll see if the little lady from California agrees with that," Wayne said skeptically.

"Most of the land around Sacred Lake has been declared a natural wildlife area," Brendan said. "I don't see how anyone's going to be able to build on that property."

"Money talks," Vera stated uneasily, dividing her attention between her two customers and the food on the grill.

"You're right about that, Vera," Wayne said.

"And from what I hear, even without Wilbur's estate, this little gal has plenty of it," she added, waving her hamburger turner for emphasis.

"Yeah, and don't forget what happened to the Voyagers National Park. Parts of that wilderness area now have motorboats and snowmobiles racing across them," Wayne reminded them.

"We've all seen it coming," Vera said. "One by one the area lakes are being developed. I'd always hoped that Sacred wouldn't follow like the rest of them. I'm afraid that one day there won't be any wilderness left."

Sacred Lake was twelve miles from Hidden Falls, yet the residents considered it a part of their community, just as they did the other four lakes in the region. Although Hidden Falls was small, it had the only post office within a fifty-mile radius. Located in one of the most remote areas of Minnesota, it also had telephones and electricity. Pete and Vera, who lived in an apartment above their store, often opened their door to cottage owners who didn't have such services.

"At least Wilbur was smart enough to appoint Lou Hortense as executor of his will. She'll keep an eye on things," Wayne proclaimed, then held up his cup for Vera to refill with coffee.

While Brendan ate his hamburger, Vera and Wayne continued to talk about Wilbur Latvanen and his granddaughter, but he only half listened. Although he cared about the future of Sacred Lake, the subject foremost on his mind was his own fate. As Vera and the other folks in Hidden Falls fretted over the possibility this could be the last summer for the resort known as The Last Place on Earth, he wondered where he would be come September. As for Wilbur's granddaughter, it really didn't matter to him what her plans were for Sacred

Lake. By the time any decisions were made, he'd be gone.

THE DAY AFTER DANI visited Edward Collins, Robert Taylor returned. Although her father claimed to have finished his negotiations in San Diego and was ready to come home, Dani suspected his early return had more to do with the changes she was making in her life. She had no doubt that Matt's father had called him and told him of her visit to the law firm.

Her suspicions were confirmed when minutes after arriving home he led her by the hand into his study. He gave her a hug, kissed both cheeks, then said, "Now what's all this nonsense about you going to see Edward?"

"I would hardly regard visiting an attorney as nonsense," she answered, pulling away from his grasp.

"No, but it's something I've always taken care of for you." He walked over to the sideboard and poured himself a Scotch. "What was so important it couldn't wait until I got back?"

She pulled the photograph from her pocket. "This."

"The property in Minnesota." There was a hint of resignation in his voice.

"It's not just property. It belonged to my birth family." *Birth family.* They were words she had seldom used. For twenty-six years she had only wanted to be Robert and Sharon Taylor's daughter. Except for a brief period when she was twelve and had fantasized that her birth parents were either celebrities or royalty, she'd been content with not knowing them.

"Danielle, we've been through all this," her father said on an impatient sigh.

"No, we haven't. You told me what *you* planned to

do with my inheritance.'' She tried to keep her voice even.

He sat down on the leather sofa and patted the cushion. ''And what is it you want to do?''

She sat down beside him. ''I'm not sure, but I know I can't just sell the place without seeing it. I might want to keep it.''

''And what would you do with a resort in Minnesota?''

He made her feel like a fool for even considering keeping the place. ''I don't know. Maybe I'll invite some friends to visit. Everyone's always looking for a new place to go.''

Her father laughed. ''There's no indoor plumbing. Do you honestly think your friends would find that amusing?'' He was silent for several moments, then said, ''Are you upset about your quarrel with Matthew? Is that why you're doing this?''

''It's more than a quarrel, Dad. We broke up. There isn't going to be a wedding.''

He looked disappointed. ''I'm truly sorry to hear you say that. Matthew's a fine young man.''

''Who has a problem with fidelity,'' she retorted. She could feel her temples beginning to throb. ''Look, I don't want to argue with you about Matthew. I know you and Howard thought we were the perfect match, but it's not going to happen.''

''That doesn't mean you have to go to some backwoods resort in Minnesota. Danielle, be practical. The place is primitive.''

''It's not primitive. It's rustic.''

He nearly choked on his Scotch.

''So it's lacking a few conveniences,'' she said airily.

''We're not talking conveniences, Dani. It's necessities—like the clear stuff that comes out of a shower-head and the little current that runs through wires so you can see after dark.'' He gave a sarcastic chuckle.

"You're not going to change my mind," she said stubbornly.

"Well, if lack of conveniences doesn't stop you, what about the isolation? I can't picture you out in the middle of nowhere by yourself. You're a people person. Not to mention it isn't safe to be there alone." Worry caused his thick eyebrows to nearly meet.

"I won't be alone. There's a priest staying in one of the cabins."

"A priest?" Robert lifted both eyebrows.

"Yes. Apparently Mr. Latvanen let members of the clergy use the other cottages on the lake as some sort of retreat. Edward's arranged for one of them to do the maintenance for the summer, so you needn't worry about me. I'll be in good hands."

"What about the bears and other wildlife? They named their basketball team the Timberwolves for a reason."

She folded her arms across her chest. "You ought to know better than to try and scare me."

"You're serious about this, aren't you?"

"Yes. I think it'll be fun. I'm going to go hiking in the woods and have picnics by the lake."

He snorted. "You can sure tell you've never been to northern Minnesota."

"Why?"

"Because if you spend any time outdoors, you're going to get eaten alive. Don't forget your mother and I lived there when we were first married. We had so many mosquito bites we looked like we had chicken pox. And they also have biting black flies." He shuddered at the thought.

She clicked her tongue. "You can buy a lotion that repels them."

"Better buy a case of it."

She ignored his attempt at humor. "It looks serene," she said, gazing once again at the picture.

"Appearances can be deceptive," he reminded her. "Wouldn't it be easier to send someone out there who can give you a report on the situation?"

"I can't do that."

"Why not?"

"Because…" She trailed off, unsure how to tell him it wasn't just the land drawing her to Minnesota, but curiosity about her birth family. "I can't."

"This isn't about the land, is it?" her father said perceptively. "You want to find information about your birth family."

"I never knew them," she said quietly.

"I didn't think you wanted to. You never asked about them except that time when you were in seventh grade and thought they might be movie stars."

"You knew about that?"

"Your mother told me."

"I'm sorry. I didn't want to hurt you."

He placed a hand on her shoulder. "You didn't hurt me. Your mother and I adopted you at a time when records were kept private. However, we knew that the time might come when you would want to search for your birth family."

"But now that will never happen. My birth parents are dead."

"Then why go to Minnesota?"

She didn't answer that question. She couldn't, because she really didn't know the answer. "I'm leaving tomorrow."

"Tomorrow?" She could see he wasn't happy with her announcement.

"I'm going to do this, Dad," she said firmly.

He shrugged. "Suit yourself, but don't say I didn't warn you."

Dani didn't need any warnings. It wasn't her physical well-being that motivated her actions. It was her emotional state. It demanded that she go to The Last Place on Earth and see for herself how her birth grandfather had lived and maybe even discover what had happened to the rest of her birth mother's family.

A sense of melancholy washed over her. Robert and Sharon Taylor had been wonderful loving parents who'd made her feel as if she were the most special child in the world. And except for that brief period when she was twelve, she hadn't found it necessary to search for her birth family.

Now it was too late to look. All she had was a chunk of land called The Last Place on Earth and a restlessness that compelled her to search for answers to the questions that burned inside her.

She looked at the photograph again. She would go to Minnesota and, hopefully, when the summer was over, she'd understand why a man she'd never known left her this legacy.

CHAPTER TWO

BRENDAN HAD ONLY ONE STOP to make after he left Pete's Place. He needed to see Louella Hortense, the executor of Wilbur's will.

Louella's cabin was on a tributary of the river that created the falls for which the town was named. At sixty-seven, she was as physically fit as most women half her age and not afraid of hard work, or so Wilbur had often told Brendan. Brendan believed it, for whenever he visited Louella, she was usually tackling some strenuous project—chopping wood or replacing a board in the porch.

A retired park ranger, Lou had spent a good deal of her life in the Boundary Waters Canoe Wilderness befriending and helping people. No stranger to primitive conditions, she and her husband had operated a ranger outpost with propane- and solar-powered buildings. After the death of her husband, she'd returned to her roots—the tiny town of Hidden Falls. She lived in her cabin alone, but often had the company of her childhood friend, Wilbur Latvanen.

When Brendan turned into her driveway, he caught a glimpse of her through the trees. She was on a ladder with a hammer in her hand. At the sound of his Geo Metro, she turned and waved. As soon as he had the car door open, two huskies came running toward him.

"What are you doing up there?" he called as he

headed for the log cabin, a dog panting on either side, licking his hands.

"Need to fix the shingles that came loose during the storm last week," she answered.

"Want any help?"

"Nope. A couple more whacks and I'm done," she answered. He watched as she pounded the roof several more times, then climbed down the ladder. He held the base of it for her. As soon as she reached the bottom rung, she proclaimed enthusiastically, "Hot damn, it's good to see you!" She gave him a bear hug, then pushed him back to arm's length. "Let me look at you." She gave him a thorough appraisal. "You've got shadows under your eyes. Have you been pulling extra duty at the hospital again?"

"Only when they need me." He paused to pet the larger of the two huskies. "You took Rex."

"The new owner didn't want Wilbur's dog, so…" Louella didn't bother to finish. Instead, she said, "I don't suppose those circles under your eyes are the reason you're staying the whole summer instead of a week?"

"Same old Lou. Never one to beat around the bush, are you?"

"Shortest distance between two points has always been a straight line, hasn't it?"

Brendan grinned.

"So why *are* you here for the entire summer? They kick you out of the seminary or something?"

"Or something," he replied, wondering just how much he should tell her.

"Did you leave for good?"

"I haven't exactly left. I'm just taking the summer off to do some thinking."

"Sure you are."

He shifted uneasily under her scrutiny. "Now what does that mean? You know I've wanted to be a priest since I was eight years old."

"So what's the problem? You miss women?"

That produced a laugh. "No, it's nothing to do with women."

"You sure?"

"Yes." He looked out at the quiet stream. "I'm not sure what's missing, but something's not right."

"Then you're doing the right thing taking some time to think it over. You know what Wilbur would say if he were here."

Brendan nodded. "There's nothing like peace and quiet to help a man get his head straight."

"It sounds as if you'll have that. The last I heard, the only person you're going to see is a real-estate appraiser. Supposed to be around next week."

"Then the new owner's selling the place?"

Louella shrugged. "Who knows? I had to send a set of keys out to some law firm in California." She waved a hand in the air. "Come. Let's get something to drink and we'll talk."

"I don't want to put you to any trouble."

She grabbed him by the arm and led him up the steps to the porch. "It's no trouble. Besides, it isn't often I have an excuse for a beer. You know I'm not one to drink alone."

Brendan took a seat on a pine chair and admired the view from her porch. A gray heron stood as still as a sentinel on a log at the river's edge, watching for a sign of his dinner. Within seconds, he swooped and flew away, a fish clasped in his bill.

"Here we are." Louella returned with two bottles.

She gave one to Brendan, then sat down in the chair beside him and took a long swallow. "Ah. There's nothing like a cold beer on a June afternoon, is there?"

Brendan nodded his head in agreement.

"Too bad Wilbur's not here to have one with us," she said wistfully.

"He always enjoyed a cold one on a summer day, didn't he?" Brendan remarked.

Her sentimental smile faded. "Did you know he was on his way here when it happened?"

"No."

She nodded soberly. "It was snowing and he was worried I'd get stuck here, so he was coming over to get me and take me back to his place. As if it'd be any less treacherous getting out of *his* place." She sighed.

Brendan leaned forward. "Lou, you're not feeling responsible, are you? I mean, he could just as easily have had the heart attack sitting in his rocker at home."

She looked off into the distance. "I know that. It's just that...I miss him."

He reached over to cover her hand with his. "I know. I do, too."

She smiled at him and patted his hand with her other one. "People thought he was a crotchety old thing, but he had a marshmallow for a heart. He would have done anything to help me."

"You were a good friend to him, Lou."

She sighed again, then chuckled. "He and I were a lot alike. Two stubborn old fools is what he called us." She took another long swallow of her beer. "I should have moved in with him. He needed someone to take care of him."

"Lou, are you saying that the two of you...?"

She flapped her hand dismissively. "Naw. It wasn't

like that. But I could have helped him take care of the place.''

''And what would you have done with this?'' He gestured with his beer bottle at the log cabin. ''It's too nice to leave vacant.''

She looked around with an appraising glance. ''Yeah, it's nice. Too quiet, though. I miss the ranger station. The people.''

''Well, you can come visit me anytime you want.'' He stood to leave. ''Just make sure you bring some beer.'' He gave her a wink and started for his car.

''Hey—aren't you forgetting something?''

Puzzled, he turned around.

She dangled a set of keys. ''You're going to need these.''

He grinned as he held out his hand.

''I don't suppose you could take Rex for a few days, could you? I'm going to visit friends on the North Shore, and one dog is about all I can handle in the car.''

Brendan looked at the husky. He could swear he saw a plea in the animal's eyes. ''Sure, I'll take him.''

''I opened up all the cabins, including Wilbur's. Aired them out just in case you fellas showed up this summer,'' she told him, walking him to his car. ''You'd better use cabin number two. It's got clean linens on the bed.''

''Thanks, Lou.''

''Everything looks the same, but I should warn you— the generator hasn't been run since Wilbur's death.''

Brendan nodded. ''I brought plenty of candles.''

''We'll do some fishing when I stop by to get Rex.''

''I'd like that.'' He gave her another hug, then climbed into his tiny car.

"Watch out for deer," she called as he backed out of the drive with Rex trying to climb onto his lap.

"Down, boy," Brendan commanded, but the dog's front paws remained on his lap all the way to the cabin.

THE LOCATION OF Hidden Falls in the northern part of the state made it directly accessible only by car or bus. The closest airport was in Hibbing, which meant flying first to the Minneapolis/St. Paul airport, then catching a connecting flight on one of the small commuter planes. Since Dani avoided planes in which she couldn't stand, she opted for flying into the Twin Cities, then renting a vehicle to drive the remaining 250 miles. This allowed her to stop at the Mall of America and buy the necessary clothes and supplies she'd need for the wilderness.

Now, armed with packages containing sweatshirts, hiking boots, a powerful flashlight and insect repellent, she climbed into her rented Ford Explorer and began her journey. On the passenger seat beside her was a map highlighted in yellow. According to Edward Collins, all she had to do was follow the yellow road and it would take her straight to The Last Place on Earth.

As the sun sank into the horizon, she realized she'd spent more time than she'd intended at the mall, which meant she'd be arriving at the resort after the sun had set. Long after the sun had set, judging by the distance still remaining on the map.

Not that it mattered what time she arrived. She already had a key to the main house and it seemed likely that the other person at the resort would be asleep. Although she didn't know any priests personally, she couldn't imagine that someone who was at the resort to meditate and pray would be up late. Besides, he had his own separate cabin, which according to Edward, was a

short distance from the main residence. She would have
preferred to have no men in her life this summer, but a
celibate one, well, that she could handle.

After stopping for a bite to eat in the small town of
Cloquet, Dani found herself on a country road where
the only light came from the twin beams of her headlights. The longer she drove, the more apprehensive she
became about finding the resort.

It was after midnight when she passed through Hidden Falls. Nothing stirred in the small town, not even
the trees. It was as still and quiet as a picture, and except
for a neon sign advertising beer outside a bar and a
mercury-vapor lamp in the service station's parking lot,
everything was in darkness.

"So much for getting groceries," she muttered to
herself.

In a blink, the town was gone and she was once more
on the dark highway. She slowed, looking for the turnoff to Sacred Lake. According to the map, it was at a
junction marked by an old railroad boxcar beside the
road not far past Hidden Falls.

Only, in the dark it was nearly impossible to see what
was beside the road. Just when Dani thought she must
have missed her turn, there it was, marked by a small
faded green sign that read Sacred Lake 10 Miles.

As the Explorer bounced along the rutted gravel road,
she shuddered at the prospect of having to drive that far
on such a rough surface. She slowed even more, wondering what she would do if another car came toward
her, for the road barely looked wide enough to allow
one car to pass, let alone two. Large trees lined the road,
giving her the sensation of driving through a tunnel.

Finally she came to a yellow sign with a large black
arrow pointing to the right. She knew she was almost

there, for on the directions was a note saying that once she came to the bend in Sacred Lake Road, she only had another mile to go.

Fog settled on her windshield, clouding her vision. Turning on the wipers only smeared the smattering of insects that had collided with the glass, making it even more difficult to see. She squirted her window-washer fluid and watched the wipers struggle to clean the glass. Just as it cleared, a deer leaped out of the woods in front of the Explorer, then froze in the headlights. Dani slammed on the brakes and turned the wheel, sending the vehicle skidding off the gravel road. By the time she came to a stop, her heart was palpitating, her mouth dry. She looked back, but the deer was gone.

Dani switched on the four-wheel drive and shifted the car into reverse. She could hear the wheels spinning, but the car didn't move. She reached for the flashlight and climbed out. Mud oozed through the toes of her sandals.

"Geesh, why didn't I change into those boots?" she moaned, stepping onto higher ground. She flashed the light on the underside of the vehicle and saw the reason the car wouldn't move. It was hung up on a stump.

Automatically she reached back inside for her cell phone, dialing the eight hundred number of the road service. It was then she noticed the "no service" indicator light. She was out of range of the cellular service.

She tossed the phone onto the leather seat. "Great. Now what do I do?"

She looked around and saw nothing, not even the twinkling of a light in the distance. Just blackness. Dani looked up at the sky. "Where are you, Mr. Moon, when I need you?" she asked rhetorically.

She had no choice but to retrieve one of her suitcases

from the back of the car and start up the road, flashlight in hand. Several times she turned around, wondering if she heard footsteps behind her. Of course not. There was no one on this road in the middle of the night. And the occasional rustling she heard in the trees was just the sound of the forest residents. Squirrels, birds, raccoons.

Before she'd left home, her father had told her that campers often banged pots and pans together to keep the bears away. Since she had no pots or pans, she made the only noise she knew how to make. She sang church hymns.

She was on "Amazing Grace" when she stopped suddenly. A skunk entered the beam of her flashlight, pausing to stare at her. She stood frozen to the spot until the striped creature ran back into the woods. Then she sang with more vigor.

She was cold, her feet were wet, and she needed to go to the bathroom. None of which could be rectified on this dirt road. Well, the last could have been, but she preferred to keep her shorts on and not expose her backside to any creepy crawly things. She could wait.

Although Dani's eyes had adjusted to the night, she was still amazed at how dark it was. Her flashlight cut a lonely beam of light through the blackness as she dragged her suitcase on wheels over the gravel road.

Then out of nowhere came a huge barking animal. It tackled Dani, and just as she was expecting fierce jaws to close on her throat, she felt only the slathering of a wet tongue all over her face.

"Down!" she commanded several times, but to no avail.

A sudden whistle had the dog sitting obediently on

the ground. Then she heard a man's voice. "What's going on out here?"

Dani squinted as a beam of a flashlight shone in her face. She held up her hand to shield her eyes. "That...that animal attacked me."

He slowly moved the light up and down her figure as he scolded the dog. "Rex, you lady-killer. When are you going to learn not everyone wants a taste of that tongue of yours?"

Dani shone her own beam on the man that went with the voice. "Craggy" was a word she had often heard used to describe certain male faces, but until tonight she hadn't known what that meant. Dark hair, dark eyes, a nose that looked like it had been broken more than once and at least a three-day growth of beard. She lowered the light and noticed that he wore a ratty pair of blue jeans and an even rattier flannel shirt that was open in the front. He looked as if she'd gotten him out of bed. The only question in her mind was where was that bed located? In a tent in the woods?

He ruffled the dog's ears, saying, "Rex is harmless." His voice was a bit gruff, confirming her suspicion that she'd awakened him. "Although I can't say the same thing for some of the local wildlife."

She glanced anxiously over her shoulder. "Do you mean bears?"

"The bears are just as afraid of you as you are of them. It's the bobcats you need to watch out for."

She shuddered. "Bobcats? You mean as in wild-cats?"

"Yes. Which is why you shouldn't be out walking at this time of night. It's nearly two in the morning. What are you doing here? Are you lost?"

"Is this the road to The Last Place on Earth resort?"

"Yes."

"Then I'm not lost." She shifted her purse to her other shoulder.

"You were on your way to the resort?"

"Yeah. My car is stuck in a ditch just up the road a ways. I had to swerve to avoid hitting a deer and I ended up in a muddy ditch, so if you would be kind enough to let me use your phone, I'll call for a tow."

"I'm afraid that's not possible."

The hair stood up on the back of Dani's neck. Here she was in the dead of night in the middle of nowhere with a perfect stranger who didn't exactly look like a Good Samaritan. She remembered the first rule of her self-defense classes. *Don't take a victim's posture. Stand tall and act confident.* She straightened her shoulders.

"I know it's an inconvenience, but I really have no other option. I tried my cell phone, but I'm out of range of the closest carrier." She tried to sound more self-assured than she was feeling at the moment. "I'll pay you for your trouble."

He shook his head. "You're misunderstanding me. You'd be welcome to use my phone if I had one. It's just that I don't have one. Sorry."

Her apprehension turned to fear. Who was this man with the wolflike dog? Edward Collins said Wilbur Latvanen had had no neighbors. Dani wondered if he was a vagrant camping illegally on the estate.

"And even if I did have a phone, there are no twenty-four-hour service stations around here. You're going to have to wait until morning to get someone to tow you out," the stranger explained. "If you want, I'll get my car and give you a lift to one of the nearby towns. You should be able to get a motel room for the night."

"That won't be necessary. I told you—I'm going to The Last Place on Earth. I'm sure I'm within walking distance." She started down the road with her suitcase.

He followed her. "You are, but the resort isn't open to the public."

"I'm not the public. I'm the owner." She saw no point in withholding the information.

He stopped walking. "You're Wilbur's granddaughter?"

She stopped, too. "Yes. I'm Danielle Taylor. And you are...?"

"Brendan Millar. I was hired to take care of the place for the summer."

The priest? So she should call him Father Millar? Dani was speechless. There was nothing reverential about the man at her side. Quite the contrary. So it took her a few seconds to realize that he had extended his hand to her. "Oh! Of course. It's nice to meet you," she told him, giving his hand a brief, but firm tug.

"I wasn't expecting you," he said as they started down the road once more.

"My attorney was supposed to notify Louella Hortense that I was coming."

"She's out of town for a few days."

"Then you didn't get any advance warning." She wondered if he'd have shaved had he known of her arrival.

They walked for several minutes in silence before he asked, "Were you singing hymns back there?"

"Yes."

"I thought so."

He didn't comment further, and Dani added, "I was trying to scare away the bears. My father said they don't like noise."

His only response was a deep chuckle.

She could feel insects buzzing around her head. "What are all these bugs I keep swatting?"

"Probably mosquitoes."

"I thought they only bit for an hour on either side of sundown."

Again he chuckled. "Not in Minnesota."

She slapped at her thighs for the umpteenth time. "I wish I had my insect repellent. I left it in the car. Aren't they bothering you?"

"Mosquitoes like certain scents better than others," he answered.

Dani wondered if that meant she used too much perfume.

"We're almost there," he told her. He flashed his light at a sign on a post with the words Last Place On Earth painted across three boards. She recognized it from the photograph. "Watch your step," he warned. "There's a hill here. Maybe you ought to give me your hand."

She placed her hand in his and found his grip surprisingly gentle and warm, yet firm enough to be reassuring as he led her down a slight incline. He flashed his light at a log building and said, "That's the big house. The guest cabins are off to the right. I'd better come inside and show you where everything is."

She reached into her purse for the keys to unlock the door.

The scent of cedar greeted them as they stepped into the house. He set his flashlight on the table, reached into his pocket for a book of matches and lit a kerosene lamp suspended from a hook on the wall. Wide pine timbers lined the vaulted ceiling, and one whole wall was taken up by a stone fireplace. A large braided area rug covered most of the wood floor.

None of the furniture matched. The high-backed sofa was a colonial-style plaid with wood trim. Across from it were two chairs—one an oversize leather recliner, the other a wooden rocker. There were several tables, all with big thick candles in the center.

"Here's the bedroom." He walked toward the back of the cabin and shoved open a door. "You can see the kitchen's over there." He gestured toward the opposite end of the house.

She saw a stove and refrigerator in the shadows and nodded.

"Everything's been closed up, so the place smells a little stale," he told her, opening a window at the front of the house. "And I'm afraid there are no clean linens on the bed."

"It's all right. I'll manage," she said. He walked into the kitchen, then took out the matches again and lit another kerosene lamp.

For the first time, there was enough light to allow Dani to get a really good look at the Reverend Millar. A little shiver of shock trembled through her. Even with a jaw that hadn't been shaved in several days, he was more than ruggedly good-looking. He didn't have classically handsome features, but it was a strong face, and his eyes... She had to look away when she realized she was staring at him.

He spread his hands. "As you can see, Wilbur was rather old-fashioned. Quite a departure from the accommodations you're used to, I'm sure."

She thought she might have detected a hint of criticism in his remark, but she refused to be intimidated.

"I don't suppose there are many people who are used to going without electricity nowadays, are there?"

His face remained blank. He glanced at her overnight bag. "Do you plan to stay awhile?"

She answered honestly. "I'm not sure how long I'll be here."

"I hope you brought some suitable clothes. If you're going to wear shorts after dark, you're going to get eaten alive by the bugs."

He sounded like her father, and what she didn't need was another man giving her a lecture on how to dress. "I know what to expect. My lawyer gave me a detailed report of conditions here at the resort."

"And yet you still came," he marveled.

Was he laughing at her or was her fatigue making her a bit sensitive? "I wanted to see the place."

"Well, here it is." The dog, who'd been left outside, whined. "Should I let Rex in? He was Wilbur's dog."

"Has he been staying with you?"

He nodded. "Louella Hortense has been taking care of him, but I'm dog-sitting in her absence. This *is* his home."

"I wish I could keep him here, but I'm allergic to dogs."

"Then I guess he'll stay with me." There was something about the way he looked at her that had Dani wanting to ask him for identification. Certainly no priest would be running his eyes up and down her legs in appreciation. Then she realized how ridiculous her thoughts were. He was curious about her. Nothing more, nothing less.

"If you want to leave now, I'm sure I'll be fine," she told him, taking a friendly approach instead of a suspicious one.

"First I'd better show you where the outhouse is. You do know there's no indoor plumbing other than the pump at the sink?"

She nodded.

"Bring your flashlight." She followed him outside to a small wooden structure. He shone his light on a crescent-shaped opening near the top of the door. "The reason it's called the half-moon," he explained, then pulled the door open and gestured for her to enter.

Go quickly and hold your breath. The advice her best friend had given her when they'd gone camping as children echoed in her head. Dani put one foot inside and paused. No noxious odors assaulted her senses, only a strong chemical smell that reminded her of the disinfectant used at the school where she worked.

She didn't realize she'd hesitated until he said, "It's not as bad as it appears. Just don't look down the hole."

She allowed the door to bang shut behind her. Unsure what to do with the flashlight, she set it on the floor, its beam shining upward. The opening in the bench had a regular toilet seat on it and the lid was down. As quickly as possible, she relieved herself, embarrassed that the man outside could hear her. It sounded like water pouring into an empty bucket.

But that wasn't the worst of it. Mosquitoes were attacking her. She slapped at her thigh, then her ankle, her neck, her arm. They were everywhere. She needed to get out and get out fast. She barely had her shorts zipped when she raced outside clutching the flashlight beneath her arm.

"See? It wasn't so bad, was it?" he said.

"The mosquitoes are awful," she replied, swatting her arms.

"Well, you might want to forgo the perfume while you're here."

She hurried on ahead of him and back into the house. "Where do I wash up?"

He led her over to the kitchen sink, which had a pump attached to it. "You're lucky you're in this house. You have indoor water."

He grinned, and Dani felt her insides do something funny. She was still having trouble believing he was the priest who was going to be right next door to her, doing maintenance at the resort. He pumped the handle several times until a stream of water poured from the spout.

"Wilbur had one wash basin for dishes, one for hands." He pointed to the two enamel bowls sitting on the counter.

Dani dug inside her suitcase for a bar of soap and a towel. "This is it? The only washroom facilities?" she asked as she washed her hands in the basin.

"There's a sauna out back with a shower."

"A shower?"

"It's only cold water, but you can make it lukewarm by hauling boiling water and adding it to the cisterns. That takes a while so Wilbur usually filled the tanks with cold water in the morning, then waited until late afternoon for the sun to warm them."

"There must be a way to bring plumbing into the house," she said, wiping her hands.

"Plumbing's not the problem. It's the electricity. Unless you have that, you're not going to be able to pump the water through those pipes."

She eyed the two appliances. "But there's a stove and refrigerator in here."

"Both gas operated." Her face must have shown her disillusionment for he said, "This isn't the Ritz."

"I didn't realize it was going to be quite this rustic." She met his gaze, and something in their deep brown depths sent another little tremor through her.

"There's a motel about twenty-five miles from here."

Dani had the distinct impression that he expected she wouldn't be able to live without all the modern conveniences. Well, she was going to have to show him how wrong he was.

"Thank you for your help. I'm sure I'll be just fine now."

The look he shot her was dubious. "I'm the second cabin down on the right if you need me."

She nodded and again thought how unlike a priest he looked. He had buttoned his shirt and tucked it into his jeans, but he still had that sleep-tousled look.

"What's this?" She pointed to a shelf on the wall. It held a radio with a microphone beside it.

"That's the CB—citizen-band radio. It was Wilbur's telephone."

"Maybe if I get on now, I can connect with someone who'll be able to get a tow truck out here first thing in the morning."

"I doubt anyone in Hidden Falls has a CB on at this time of night," he told her. "We can try in the morning, but you're probably going to want to go to town anyway, so it'll be easier if I take you in my car."

Dani wondered if perhaps he was offering out of a sense of duty. "I don't want to inconvenience you."

He shrugged. "It's no trouble. I have to go to town myself. It'll save you some time."

She didn't see much point in arguing. "Then I'll ride with you. I'll pay you for your trouble, of course."

His eyes narrowed. "You don't need to pay me."

"All right. Thank you."

"You're welcome."

Dani sensed an undercurrent of tension in the room, which she found surprising. Why should there be any uneasiness between them? If it was because he was unhappy that she'd disrupted his solitude, she would assure him first thing in the morning that she wouldn't trouble him again.

However, Dani wasn't sure that *was* the reason for the tension between them. If she didn't know better, she would have thought he looked uncomfortable because she was a woman and he a man. But he was a priest, so that was ridiculous.

As soon as he was out the door, she turned the lock. A chill traveled down her arms, and she chased it away with a brisk rub. She was all alone in a house with no plumbing or electricity, and the only other human within ten miles was a man who wanted to be left alone. Had coming here been a mistake?

She picked up the kerosene lamp and made her way to the bedroom. Everything looked foreign to her. Even though Wilbur Latvanen was no longer alive, she felt as if she was invading his privacy. Several prescription bottles sat atop the dresser. On the nightstand beside the bed was a book by Carl Sagan with a small reading light attached to the cover. But it was the photo protruding from under the book that caught her attention. It was a picture of a woman and a little girl wearing matching red-and-green-plaid dresses and smiling at the camera. Apart from the difference in age and the girl's missing front tooth, the pair were nearly identical. Obviously mother and daughter. *Her* mother and grandmother?

Dani was struck by a pang of something indescribable. She swallowed back the lump in her throat that suddenly seemed as big as an apple. Why *had* she come to this place? What could she possibly learn about this family called Latvanen that would make any difference in her life?

They were questions she couldn't answer. At least not now. She was too tired. What she needed was sleep. In the morning she'd try to figure out why this man who read about the mysteries of the universe and pumped water by hand should want to leave her his entire life's work.

WITH REX AT HIS SIDE, Brendan walked back to his cabin in the dark. He was not happy. For the first time in months, he'd fallen asleep that night without the usual tossing and turning.

Then Rex had barked. The dog only did that when a stranger was near. To discover that the stranger was someone who wanted to share his piece of solitude was disturbing enough. But the fact that it was Wilbur's granddaughter only made it worse. He sure didn't need to baby-sit a spoiled California girl who, because she had nothing better to do with her summer, had come to claim her inheritance.

It annoyed him that she was even interested in the place. All those years Wilbur had written to her and she hadn't once responded. Now because there was money involved, she was here to check out her property.

What kind of woman drove through the north woods at two o'clock in the morning wearing shorts and sandals? She deserved every mosquito bite she'd gotten on those legs—those perfectly shaped legs. It had been a long time since Brendan had paid any attention to a woman's legs, but this particular pair was hard to miss. Especially when she wore such short shorts.

He shook his head to clear away the disturbing thoughts. What was wrong with him anyway? Just because he was no longer in the seminary didn't mean it was time for his hormones to revert to adolescent status. So Danielle Taylor was one beautiful, shapely woman. So what?

A slight distraction. That's all she'd be. That's all he'd *let* her be.

Well, at least she wouldn't be staying long. He'd give her a couple of days of running to the half-moon and she'd be gone. Which would suit him just fine. He didn't need the distraction, no matter how slight.

Later, as his lay in bed, he heard his mother's voice in his head. *Ah, Brendan, you're going to grow up and be a good priest, just like Father Joe.* How many times had he heard that?

Brendan punched his pillow and muttered to himself, "I'm not so sure, Ma."

CHAPTER THREE

DANI DECIDED TO SLEEP in a T-shirt and jeans in case she needed to get up during the night and make a trip to the outhouse. Besides, she hadn't wanted to climb under the covers of the four-poster for two reasons— there were no linens on the mattress and there were still traces of mud on her feet. In the morning she would have Father Millar show her how to use the shower. Until then, she had to be satisfied with a quick splash of cold water after removing her makeup. Then she'd stretched out on the bed with a knitted afghan for comfort.

She didn't sleep very well. She attributed her frequent awakenings to all the scratching sounds—mice probably or some other small creature scrambling across the roof. At any rate, she was relieved when daylight poured through the plate-glass windows.

After a quick wash at the sink, she changed into a fresh pair of shorts and T-shirt. Then she went back into the kitchen and scraped the mud from her sandals into the sink. After slipping them on, she glanced around. Maybe she could make herself a cup of coffee.

In the light of day, it was easy to see that Wilbur Latvanen had been a carpenter. She assumed he'd done the intricately carved cornices edging the cabinets and the spindles trimming a plate rail that ran the length of one kitchen wall. A wooden bread box sat atop the counter, while a coat tree stood guard beside the door.

The cupboards were well stocked with cans of beans, soup, vegetables and fruits. Good—there was a canister of coffee, and sitting on the stove was an old-fashioned navy blue coffeepot, similar to one she and her father had used on a camping trip into the mountains. It wasn't long before was having her regular morning dose of caffeine.

She looked around for a clock, but found none. When she went to get her watch from the nightstand in the bedroom, she was shocked to see it was only six-thirty. Then she realized that it was actually eight-thirty, Central time.

As she walked through the living room, she noticed that the fireplace mantel was lined with miniature wooden covered wagons. And scattered around the house were wooden animals—deer, moose, squirrels—all whittled, she deduced, by Wilbur Latvanen. Spread across the thick pine coffee table was an assortment of magazines—*Popular Mechanics, In-Fisherman, Newsweek.*

During the night, she thought she'd detected a faint hint of pipe smoke. Now she knew why. Beside the oversize recliner was a large amber ashtray with a pipe tipped on its side. Next to it was a humidor of tobacco.

Dani opened the draperies covering the front windows and gasped at the sight that greeted her. The lake, so perfectly still it gave her the impression of a gigantic mirror, reflected a landscape of evergreens and blue sky. If this was what Wilbur Latvanen had awakened to every morning, it was no wonder he'd loved this place.

Dani slid open the patio door and stepped out onto the wooden deck. The air was as quiet as the lake, refreshingly clean smelling, yet with a hint of the scented pines that grew in such abundance. At the water's edge were sections of dock piled one on top of the other. Beside them was a small fishing boat turned upside down. So it appeared that Wilbur Latvanen had been a fisherman, too.

Following the path that led from the cabin to the shore, she walked down to the lake, surprised by the water's clarity. No weeds lined the bottom, no lily pads floated on the surface.

"Good morning."

Startled, Dani turned to see Father Millar coming toward her, the husky at his side. Gone was the stubble that had darkened his jaw last night. Without it he was downright good-looking. A bit embarrassed by the direction of her thoughts, she glanced away as she replied, "Good morning. I was just admiring the lake. I can't believe how clear the water is."

"That's because there's been no motorcraft on it. Your grandfather wouldn't allow it."

"So no one uses the lake?"

He shook his head. "Not very often. There's no public access. Your grandfather owned all the land with the exception of the section that belongs to the state. He allowed people to launch small fishing boats, but never any with motors."

"There's no law against motorboats, is there?"

"No." His eyes narrowed. "You're not thinking about bringing one here, are you?"

She could see the idea was distasteful to him. "Actually I hadn't thought about it before now."

"Your grandfather was quite adamant about not allowing motors on the lake. He was an environmentalist and wanted to keep the lake as healthy as possible. He believed it should be a sanctuary for birds and fish alike.''

She sensed a warning in his tone, as if he expected she didn't have any concern for environment. Consequently her own voice sounded rather curt when she asked, ''What about swimming? Is that allowed?''

To her surprise, he cracked a smile. ''The aquatic life doesn't mind sharing the pond with us human fish.''

She kicked off a sandal and dipped in a toe. ''The water's cold.''

''It's supposed to be. That way, after you've had a sauna and washed away all the impurities, you can jump into the water and close your pores.''

''So it's true that people take a sauna, then jump in the lake?''

''The Finns around here do.''

''Was Wilbur Finnish? I wondered about his last name—Latvanen.''

''Yes. If you have any doubt, take a look at his sauna.''

''Would you show it to me? I'd like to clean up before we go into town—or are you in a hurry to leave?''

''No, but it takes several hours to heat the sauna properly. If you want, you can take a shower. There's water in the tanks, but it won't be warm until this afternoon,'' he warned.

''I'm a lot hardier than I look,'' she said.

He simply shrugged and, with Rex running ahead, led her around the side of Wilbur's house to a building that was actually closer to the lake than any of the cabins.

''There's very little light inside, just enough to be able to see,'' he told her as he opened the door. ''You sit here." He gestured to the wooden benches lining the walls. "The higher the bench, the warmer it is."

"That's the stove?" she asked, motioning toward a wood-powered heater that had rocks piled on the top.

He nodded. "Once the rocks are hot, water can be ladled on them from the bucket there on the floor. That creates steam heat, which adds to the temperature."

"Then after you get hot, you run and jump into the lake?"

"Or take a shower next door, whichever you prefer. In the winter when the lake is covered by ice, it takes a little effort to chop a big enough hole."

"But some people do it?"

"Only the hardiest of the hardy." He opened the door leading to the other side of the building. "Over here are the changing room and the shower. In a true Finnish sauna, bathers leave their clothes in here."

Dani noted the hooks protruding from the wall. "Where's the shower?"

Brendan took her out a second door to a small closet-size room with a showerhead protruding from the ceiling.

"I don't get it," Dani said. "You told me there wasn't any plumbing at the resort."

"There isn't. Follow me." He led her outside to the back of the building and directed her to look up. Two large washtubs sat on the roof. He explained how both drained into pipes that ran through the roof to the showerhead inside.

"How did he fill the tubs with water?" Dani asked.

Brendan pointed to the hill behind the building. "Notice how close the roof is to the top of the hill?" She followed the direction of his gaze and saw steps carved into the earth. "Wilbur brought kettles of water from the house, then climbed those steps and poured it in. As I said, cold water if the sun was out, hot water if not.''

''Must have taken a lot of kettlefuls.''

''Quite a few. You learn to take very quick showers if you don't want to be exhausted by the time you're done filling the tanks. If you soap up first, you'll be surprised how fast you can finish. Of course, you can always bathe in the lake if you don't want to haul the water—or wait for it to rain.''

His tone was polite, yet she sensed he didn't want to show her how to use anything at the resort. Again she had the feeling he resented her presence, and she could only surmise it was because he'd expected to be alone the entire summer.

''Thank you for explaining all this to me,'' she said in an equally polite tone. ''I'll get my things and take a shower so you can get to town.''

When she started to walk back to the house, he stopped her. ''I've already filled the tubs for you.'' Before she could thank him again, he added, ''I figured since I'm the maintenance person around here, I should probably take care of it.''

She nodded. ''I appreciate it, but in the future it really won't be necessary. I can do it myself.''

He shrugged. ''Whenever you're ready to go to town, just let me know. I'll leave Rex here since you're allergic to him.''

And that's that, Dani thought. Determined not to keep him waiting, she quickly showered and dressed, amazed at how little time it took to get ready when she didn't have to worry about applying makeup and blow-drying her hair.

She found Brendan waiting for her by a dark blue Geo Metro. As she climbed into the passenger seat, he said, "I saw your Explorer while I was out walking this morning. You were right. It's caught on a stump."

In a matter of minutes they were at the spot where the Explorer had gone off the road. The ditch Dani had skidded into was actually a spring feeding into the lake. Another couple of feet and she would have landed in the water. She shivered at the sight of her vehicle hanging so precariously close to the lake's edge.

He must have seen her shudder, for he said, "This is a not a road for high speeds."

The words sounded like a reprimand. "I wasn't speeding," Dani returned sharply. "I told you before. I had to swerve to avoid a deer."

"You have to expect wildlife around here. That's why you need to slow down. Besides, this is a gravel road. It's easy to lose control of a car."

If he hadn't been a man of the cloth, Dani would have been tempted to say something sarcastic. But he was, so she held her tongue even though she found it extremely annoying that he should be so patronizing.

"Why were you driving so late at night?"

"In case you've forgotten, I flew in from California," she reminded him. "By the time I arrived in Minneapolis, rented a car and stopped for a few necessities, it was already dark."

At that point she saw him glance into the Explorer and eye the shopping bags, which only made her more defensive.

"Then I had to drive a good portion of the journey on poorly lit, two-lane highways that had curves with posted speed limits sometimes as low as twenty-five."

"Roads are dark at night in this part of the country. You'd have been wise to stay overnight in Minneapolis and make the journey first thing in the morning," he said with irritating logic.

"Yes, well, hindsight is twenty-twenty." She knew she sounded churlish, but she couldn't help it.

In the close confines of the Geo, she could smell the scent of his shaving cream—a lime menthol. She cast a quick sideways look at him and noticed he had a small scar on his right jaw. A scar, a slightly crooked nose and a pair of eyes that could make a woman feel as if he were looking into her very soul. It was an unsettling combination.

He wore a long-sleeved chambray shirt and a pair of khaki shorts. The feet working the clutch and brake pedals were encased in hiking boots. He could easily have been mistaken for a wilderness guide instead of a priest.

In the daylight, Dani could see that the road she'd traveled last night was every bit as narrow as she'd imagined. Except for patches of sunlight that cut through the densely forested roadside, a canopy of green arched over the gravel road. At no point did they encounter another vehicle and she was reminded of just how isolated The Last Place on Earth actually was.

When they reached the paved county road, she realized how lucky she was to have found the turnoff to Sacred Lake in the dark. Even in daytime, the sign was barely visible.

"Is there a towing service in Hidden Falls?" she asked, uncomfortable with the growing silence.

"Earl Husker should be able to help you," Brendan answered. "He runs the service station."

"Is there a phone in town?"

"Several public ones. You can either use the one at Earl's or you can stop at Pete's Place."

"And who's Pete?"

"He and his wife, Vera, run the grocery store. Except they don't just sell groceries, but hardware, books, magazines—a little of everything. That's where most of the summer people go when they need stuff," he answered.

"Then I guess I should go there," she said. "I need groceries."

The Geo turned onto the main street of Hidden Falls. Smack-dab in the center of town was a glass-fronted brick building with the words Pete's Place on a sign beside the door. Next to it was the Dew Drop Inn, which Dani gathered was a bar. The only other business establishments in town seemed to be the agricultural co-op and Earl's Service Station across the street. A smattering of houses could be seen on intersecting streets.

"Vera cooks breakfast if you're hungry," Brendan told her as he slowed to a near crawl.

"I'd like that," she said, feeling hunger pangs.

Brendan pulled in between two pickup trucks parked on the main street. Dani noticed he didn't take his keys from the ignition when he climbed out of the car.

"We'll talk to Earl first and get the tow lined up. Then you can stop in at Pete's, have some breakfast and get what you need."

Dani had little choice but to agree. She followed him across the street into the service station, which also housed the Laundromat. Next to the vending machines for soda and snacks were four coin-operated washers and dryers.

No one was behind the counter so they walked through to the garage. A car was up on the hoist and a man in mechanic's coveralls was under it looking at the tires.

"Hey, Earl. How's it going?" Brendan called out.

The mechanic ducked under the wheels and came out

to greet them. "Well, I'll be. How have you been, Father?" he asked, wiping his hands on a dirty oil rag.

Dani saw a glimmer of discomfort cross Brendan's face at the greeting. It was quickly replaced by a smile.

"This is Danielle Taylor, Earl. She has a Ford Explorer in the creek that runs into Sacred," he told the older man, who was eyeing Dani curiously.

"Took the corner too fast, did you?" Earl said with a knowing grin.

"Actually I swerved to avoid a deer."

"That was probably the smart thing to do. It's easier to tow you out of a ditch than replace a fender."

Dani couldn't help but shoot a small glance of triumph at Brendan Millar. *See, I wasn't reckless. I was smart.* To Earl she said, "I tried using the four-wheel drive, but the frame's caught on a stump. Do you think you can help me?"

"I have to finish putting brakes on this car first. Promised I'd have it done by noon." He used the sleeve of his coveralls to swipe at the perspiration on his forehead. "I could probably get out there right after lunch."

Dani had hoped to have her wheels back long before then, but apparently it wasn't to be. "That would be fine."

"What were you doing over at Sacred anyway?" the mechanic asked.

"I was trying to find The Last Place on Earth," she replied.

He rubbed his chin thoughtfully. "You don't look like a real-estate appraiser," he said.

"I'm not." Dani could see no reason to try to keep her identity a secret. "I'm the new owner."

The man's jaw dropped and he exchanged looks with Brendan, who nodded in confirmation. It took Earl a couple of moments to recover before he said, "Well, ain't that something. No one expected you to come here."

"I know I caught a few people by surprise," she said, glancing at Brendan as she spoke.

"Well," Earl went on, "I'm pleased to meet you. Your grandfather was a decent man."

"That's nice to hear. I never had the chance to know him," she said frankly.

He pointed his oil rag at Brendan. "You talk to this fella here. He can tell you all about your granddaddy."

Maybe he could, but would he? Dani wondered. She met Brendan Millar's gaze and knew any such information would only be given grudgingly.

"I'd better get back to work if I'm going to get that Ford out of the creek for you. Did you leave the keys in it?" Earl asked.

Dani shook her head. Apparently, in a town the size of Hidden Falls, no one worried about car theft. She reached into her purse and pulled out her heart-shaped key ring. "Would you like me to pay in advance?"

Earl waved a hand. "Naw. We'll settle up when I come out there. So what are you gonna do with the place?" he asked boldly. "Sell it?"

"I haven't decided," she answered honestly, aware of Brendan's interest in her reply.

"Myself, I can't see why anyone would want to live without plumbing and electricity." Earl chuckled. "The joke around here is that although your granddaddy invited the priests to come stay for a relaxing visit, the true purpose of the visit was to do penance." He looked at Brendan and said, "Sorry, Father."

"Having spent the night there, I can relate to that," Dani said with a grin.

Brendan spoke up. "For some of us, the simplest things in life are the most precious."

Earl tugged on his ear. "I don't know. A hot shower can be pretty precious to me."

"It's all a matter of perspective," Brendan answered amiably.

"Good thing you have that attitude if you're going to spend the entire summer there."

His words reminded Dani of her situation—even though she and Brendan weren't under the same roof, they were the only two people staying at the resort. She didn't want tension between the two of them. No reason it should be there anyway. They could peacefully co-exist without ever seeing one another if they had to.

As they left the service station and headed for the grocery store, she decided to clear the air. "Are you annoyed that I showed up at the resort?"

He didn't break stride. "It's your place, not mine."

"That doesn't answer my question. I know you thought you'd have The Last Place on Earth to yourself this summer, but surely it's a big enough place that the two of us can keep out of each other's way. Once I get my car back, you'll see very little of me. You'll be able to meditate without having to worry about my interrupting you."

"I'm not just meditating," he said somewhat irritably, holding the door open for her to enter Pete's Place. "And I think we need to set the record straight about something. I'm not a priest."

Dani didn't understand. Edward Collins had said he was a priest. Earl had called him Father. Before she could ask him to explain, her hand was grasped by a stranger.

"Welcome to Pete's Place. I'm Pete. I hope Brendan

here has been taking good care of you," the grocer said with an affectionate grin.

"WHY, SHE'S NOT AT ALL what I expected," Vera remarked to Brendan while Dani used the rest room.

Brendan didn't want to say that she was not what he'd expected, either, but thought it would be best not to comment on Danielle Taylor. She hadn't even been here twelve hours and already he was feeling as if she'd invaded his life. He should have realized, however, that Vera was not about to let the subject drop.

"She's a pretty little thing, isn't she?" Vera said. "I expected she'd be wearing all sorts of heavy makeup and have those press-on fingernails and dangling gold chains." She set a cup of coffee down in front of Brendan. "She's actually quite normal-looking. I can see the resemblance to Bridget Latvanen. I bet other folks'll notice it, too. How long's she planning to stay?"

Brendan shrugged. "She hasn't said." This was something that worried Brendan. If it was simply a fleeting visit to scope out the place, he could tolerate her presence for a few days. But if she decided to stay for any length of time, he would have to leave. He wasn't going to baby-sit a full-grown woman.

And she was definitely a full-grown woman. As the woman in question made her way toward the eating counter, Brendan couldn't help but notice just how lush her curves were. She'd taken off the loose denim overshirt she'd been wearing to reveal a ribbed-knit, melon-colored sleeveless top that left little to the imagination.

Brendan wondered if she even wore a bra, for her nipples poked through the fabric in a most provocative way. He experienced an involuntary arousal that had him averting his gaze, concentrating on the coffee cup in front of him. As she sat down on the stool beside him, he caught a tantalizing floral aroma. She must have just applied the perfume since he hadn't noticed it when they were in the car. Who was she trying to impress? Pete? Just another reason to feel antagonistic toward her.

Then she said, "Vera, I really like that hand lotion you have in the rest room."

"It's called Romantic Treasure," the older woman said, obviously pleased. "One of the summer people sent it to me for my birthday. I thought it would be nice to leave it in there for customers to use."

So he had Vera to blame for her smelling so sweet. Not that he could blame her for putting hand lotion in the ladies' room.

"So what can I get you for breakfast?" Vera asked the two of them.

Brendan saw Dani examine the plastic-coated menu, then request oatmeal and whole wheat toast.

"And what about you, Brendan?" Vera looked expectantly at him. "What do you want?"

I want my peace and quiet restored. I want this woman to be gone. I don't want this woman sitting next to me smelling like a flower garden. "Uh... Just coffee for me," he said. "I had something to eat earlier."

Normally Vera would have fussed over him and insisted that he at least have a roll or a doughnut, but not today. She was too interested in Wilbur's granddaughter. Brendan thought that was actually a good thing. He didn't want to be included in their conversation. He would sit and meditate while the two of them chatted.

Only he found he lacked the concentration to do so. No matter how hard he tried to shut them out, he kept hearing the melodious voice of Dani Taylor. There was a huskiness to it that didn't make it deep, but rather soft. He liked the cadence of her speech. Even though she had no accent, there was something distinctive about her voice.

"We didn't expect you to show up this summer, what with you living in California and all. We figured you probably have a job that wouldn't make it easy to take time off." Vera's probing was not very subtle, Brendan thought with amusement.

"Actually the timing worked out well," Dani responded. "You see, I'm a teacher and I'm off for the summer break."

A teacher? That surprised even Brendan. "What do you teach?" he asked.

"French and English. At the Marchand Academy for Young Women."

"A private school," he said.

"Yes. I also coach the soccer team."

That would account for her looking so athletically fit, Brendan thought.

She straightened her shoulders. "We took first place in our conference this year."

Vera gushed all over that statement, complimenting her on such a grand achievement. "So you're here to rest, too, then," Vera continued. "I was a schoolteacher for twenty-two years before we moved here, and I know what summer vacation means. A chance to have some peace and quiet." She smiled broadly, then looked at Brendan and added, "You two have something in common. You're both looking for peace and quiet."

Brendan didn't want to think he had anything in common with Dani Taylor. Nor did he really want to hear any more about her personal life.

"I think I'll check out the book rack," he told Vera

and Dani as he stood. Despite walking to the other end of the store, he could still hear their conversation.

"If you make up a list of things you need, Pete will gather them for you," Vera told Dani in response to her inquiry about food. "Although we're small, we do stock quite a variety of things."

"Where do you go to get things you don't carry?"

"Either Hibbing or Chisholm. They've got those discount warehouse grocery stores there. How long do you plan to stay?"

Brendan's ears perked up, waiting for her answer. It was long in forthcoming. He figured it was because she was chewing a bite of toast. Finally she answered, "I plan to stay most of the summer."

Brendan's spirits sank. This was not good. He could not have this woman around for the entire summer. He'd come to The Last Place on Earth to ponder the most important decision of his life. He needed solitude, not distraction. And Dani Taylor was definitely a distraction.

"Then you plan to open the resort?" Vera asked the question on the tip of Brendan's tongue.

"I'm afraid I don't have the experience to do that, but of course, Brendan can stay."

"Gee, thanks," he mumbled under his breath, causing Pete to look at him quizzically.

"That's very generous of you," Vera said to Dani, once more complimenting the intruder.

For she was an intruder. At least that was how Brendan was coming to regard her. She was pushing her way right into the hearts of the people of Hidden Falls. First Earl. Now Vera.

"Okay, Dani, tell me what you need." Pete walked

to the back of the store, a shopping basket in his hand, a big grin on his face. She'd won him over, too.

Together, the three of them composed a shopping list while Brendan browsed in the paperbacks. No one paid the least bit of attention to him; they were too busy helping Dani decide whether it would be easier to clean her pots and pans if she used vegetable oil or cooking spray. The longer they talked, the cozier they became. Brendan thought that if they got any friendlier, Vera would be doing Dani's laundry for her.

"Now if you find it's too much of a hardship getting in to Earl's to use the washer and dryer, you can come here anytime and use mine," he heard her tell Dani.

"Why, thank you. That's so sweet of you."

"And Pete here is a crackerjack mechanic. I know you've got Brendan to take care of the place this summer, but if you have any problems he can't solve, you come get Pete. He'll fix you up right quick."

Brendan peered over the book rack, expecting Pete to give Vera one of his "Don't get me into this" looks that had become a regular sight whenever Vera volunteered his services without consulting him first. But to Brendan's surprise, the older man simply grinned and nodded agreeably.

"Anytime you don't want to disturb Brendan, you just come get me. I'll take care of you." He gave Dani a fatherly wink.

"Thank you. You're very kind. I'm going to see Louella Hortense later this week. She should be able to fill me in on all the details about the resort," Dani told them.

That suited Brendan just fine. The less he saw of Danielle Taylor the better. And Lou was the person she needed to see anyway. She had all the legal information on the resort. He was just the handyman. And it would be wise for him to remember that.

BRENDAN GOT HIS WISH to be left alone. As soon as Earl pulled the Ford Explorer out of the creek, Dani disappeared down the gravel road. Brendan was left to read and contemplate in the serenity of the lake setting. As he sat on a lounge chair near the shore with Rex stretched out at his feet, the only noises he heard were the chirping of birds and the buzz of insects.

He moved to the cabin after a while and, despite his efforts not to think of Dani, found himself listening for the sound of her tires on the gravel road. He wondered where she'd gone. Lou was still away, so it couldn't have been there.

As the sun began its descent and there was still no sign of her, he figured she must have gone to Hibbing to do some shopping. Although he could hardly see why she would have to buy anything. Between the packages she'd had in her Explorer and the ones he'd carried out from Pete's Place, there surely couldn't be anything else she needed. He didn't know why he should even be concerned about her. He told himself he wouldn't have been if she hadn't been Wilbur's granddaughter.

He glanced at his watch. Darkness was settling in. He'd give her another half hour. Then he'd get in his Geo and take a ride down the road—just to make sure she hadn't had another mishap. She could have run out of gas, or had a flat, or taken a curve too fast and skidded into a ditch.... He reached for his keys and was about to leave when he heard a car rumbling along the gravel road. In a matter of minutes, headlights lit the area behind Wilbur's house.

Brendan knew he should stay put in his cabin. There

was no point in having any contact with the woman. She was back, safe and sound. Where she had been or with whom was none of his business.

Nevertheless, something inside him had him commanding Rex to stay, pushing open the screen door and walking toward the headlights. Before he reached them, the lights were extinguished. Brendan heard a car door slam.

Even in the darkness, he could see enough of Dani to know she was still wearing shorts. A windbreaker covered her arms, but her legs were bare. His heart did a peculiar little dance, which he quickly attributed to relief that she was back safely. He didn't want it to be anything else. In each of her hands she carried a shopping bag filled with packages. While he'd been worrying that something horrible had happened to her, she had merely been shopping.

"Have a good day?" he drawled.

She paid no attention to his sarcasm. "Mmm-hmm. It was quite nice, thank you."

When she started toward the house, he took the shopping bags from her hands. She didn't protest. She pulled a tiny flashlight from her purse and lit the way for him. Once they were inside, he set the packages on the kitchen table.

"Doesn't look like you had any trouble finding something to do," he said, eyeing the assortment of packages on the table.

"I went souvenir shopping." She opened a small bag and pulled out a hand-painted ceramic loon. "Look. Isn't this pretty? I'm going to send it to my dad for his desk."

Brendan didn't miss the fact that she said she was going to *send* it. Not take it back with her.

"And look at these. Aren't they cute?" Out of another bag, she removed a set of candles whose holders were sections of birch. "And I bought dozens of postcards and even a couple of T-shirts for my friends. I like this one." She held up one with a picture of a giant mosquito and the slogan, Minnesota State Bird.

Brendan's irritation dissolved. He'd thought she'd been shopping for herself when in reality she'd been buying gifts for family and friends.

"I bought something for myself," she told him, pulling a battery-operated lamp from a cardboard box. "I don't like using the kerosene lamp in the bedroom," she explained.

He nodded. "Well, I'm glad to see you got back all right."

"Oh, yeah, no problem. You were right. If you drive slowly, the road's not bad even in the dark." She began cleaning up the mess from the packaging.

"Since there's only the two of us here and there's no phone, it might be a good idea to have some sort of buddy system—you know, so I can tell whether I should come looking for you," he said, trying to sound pragmatic.

She looked surprised. "Were you worried about me?"

He shrugged. "'Concerned' would be a better word. You didn't say how long you expected to be gone, and after what happened last night..." He let his words trail off, feeling a little uncomfortable with the emotions she aroused in him.

"I'm sorry. I suppose we *should* keep each other posted as to our whereabouts. It just makes sense in a wilderness like this," she said thoughtfully.

"Good enough." He found himself reluctant to leave.

However, she made no offer of anything to drink and he really had no reason to stay. "I'll say good-night if you don't need any more help."

"No, go ahead. I'm fine...and thank you...again." She smiled almost shyly, making Brendan feel as if he'd just received a shot of adrenaline. He was almost out the door when she called, "What about the shower? We should probably set up a schedule since there're no locks on the doors." She actually looked embarrassed.

"I'm usually up by seven. Do you want to use it at eight or would you rather wait until the afternoon when the water's been warmed by the sun?"

"Eight is fine. I'll heat water if it's too cold."

"Fair enough." He was halfway down the steps when she stopped him again.

"By the way, what did you mean when you said you're not a priest? I thought the resort was only used by the clergy."

"And seminary students."

"You're studying to be a priest?"

"I was."

"Oh, I see."

He doubted she did and he really didn't feel like explaining his situation. In fact, he thought it was safer if he didn't.

She folded her arms across her chest. "Well, just in case I don't see you in the morning, I have an appointment at ten and I probably won't be back until after dinner."

Brendan wanted to ask her with whom she had the appointment, but he knew it was better not to get any more involved with Danielle Taylor than was absolutely necessary. As he walked back to his cabin, he knew he should be relieved. He would have tomorrow to him-self—complete solitude, no distractions.

But on the following morning, there was one major interruption. It occurred during his breakfast. He'd been for his morning walk, showered and now was just fin-ishing his usual breakfast, a sugar-coated cereal in the shape of dinosaurs. He was in the middle of a mouthful of T-rexes when he heard Dani scream.

He dropped his spoon and went running toward the big house. By the time he got there, all he saw was Dani's backside as she went streaking into the lake, completely nude. She dove beneath the surface and came up not far from shore, keeping all her body sub-merged except for her neck and head.

"What's wrong?" Brendan shouted.

"There's a bat in the shower," she shouted back. "Will you get me my towel from the changing room?"

He did as she requested, dangling it from his fingers at the water's edge.

"Just leave it, please," she called.

Again Brendan did as he was instructed, walking back to his breakfast of sugar-coated dinosaurs. Resist-ing the awful temptation to turn around and sneak a peek at Dani's naked figure.

When he'd finished, he took a broom over to the sauna and shagged the bat outdoors. Then he walked over to Dani's place and knocked on the door. When she opened it, she was completely dressed and had her purse and keys in hand.

"I just wanted to let you know the bat's gone," he told her, noting that, like yesterday, she wore no makeup or jewelry the way she had the first night he'd seen her. There was a wholesomeness about her that made her look as if she fit right in with the locals.

"Thank you. I'd just finished soaping up when it started making those screeching sounds." She shuddered. "I decided it would be better to take an ice-cold bath in the lake than be in the same room with that thing."

"That's the first time I've ever heard of a bat getting in there. I'll climb up on the roof later this morning and see if there's an opening that allowed him to get in."

"At least you won't have to haul water for your shower tomorrow. I didn't use what I brought." She glanced at her watch. "I'd better go if I'm going to make my appointment."

Instead of shorts, she wore a long, floral-patterned skirt and a vestlike top. The slight curl in her short blond hair made it bounce as she walked toward the Explorer. Brendan thought it was a good thing she'd be gone all day. She was beginning to occupy his thoughts far too often—and all because of their close proximity. Or so he wanted to believe.

He did enjoy his day alone, although it went much too fast. He didn't realize how late it was until he heard a car on the gravel road. Must be Dani, he thought, but when Rex began to bark, he wasn't sure. A few minutes later he heard not one, but two car doors slam.

Curious, he walked toward the parking area, leaving the husky at the cabin. The first person he saw was Dani, looking as beautiful as she had when she'd left that morning. Standing on the other side of the Explorer was a young girl wearing baggy clothing. She carried a backpack and a gym bag.

When she saw him, she said, "Hi, Uncle Brendan. Remember me?"

The voice was familiar. So was the face. "Jodie?"

He crossed swiftly to her, wondering if this teenager could possibly be his niece.

Shyly she opened her arms for his embrace. He pulled her close and gave her a hug. It was then that he discovered Jodie Fisher had definitely changed since the last time he'd seen her.

She was pregnant.

CHAPTER FOUR

"I FOUND HER WALKING on the gravel road," Dani told Brendan.

"I went to the seminary and they said you were spending the summer here," Jodie explained.

"How did you get here?" Brendan wanted to know, although he had the feeling he wasn't going to like her answer.

"I hitchhiked."

Brendan's stomach clenched at the thought. The idea of a pregnant teen accepting rides from strangers was enough to put fear into any adult's heart. He could see from the look on Dani's face that she shared his feelings.

"It's a long way from north Minneapolis," he said.

"It took me four days. I wouldn't have come except I didn't have any other place to go...and you told me if I ever had a problem, I could always come to you." Jodie sounded almost childlike.

Brendan knew there'd been plenty of trouble in his niece's life. During the past ten years, she'd come to him with problems that ranged from needing help with her homework to getting arrested for stealing food. Considering the instability of her home life, it shouldn't have surprised him that pregnancy was now one of the problems. Yet it still left him feeling as if someone had knocked the wind out of his sails.

Jodie misread his silence. "Look, if you don't want me here, just say so."

Brendan slung his arm around her shoulders and gave her a reassuring squeeze. "Hey, this is your uncle Bren. Of course I want you here. You just took me by surprise, that's all. It's been a long time, hasn't it?"

She smiled weakly. "I didn't want to bother you. I thought I could figure stuff out by myself—like I usually do, but..." Her voice trailed off uncertainly.

"It doesn't matter," Brendan said, keeping his arm around her. "You're here now."

Dani spoke up. "Why don't we all go inside? Jodie's going to need something to eat and a place to sleep. And it'll be much easier to talk without being attacked by mosquitoes."

Brendan could see the schoolteacher in Dani taking charge. Before he could say another word, she was treating Jodie like one of her students, ushering her into the house and seating her at the kitchen table.

As she lit a kerosene lamp, Dani said, "The good news, Jodie, is that you've made it to The Last Place on Earth. The bad news is that we don't have electricity or running water."

"Didn't you pay your bills?"

"The power hasn't been shut off," Brendan answered for Dani. "There aren't any lines servicing this area."

"You mean people actually live in a place where they can't get electricity? That's *weird*."

Brendan didn't miss the smug look Dani threw his way.

Jodie looked around curiously. "I guess that's why there's no TV, huh?"

"Nope, no TV."

"But you got a toaster."

"There's a gas-powered auxiliary generator we can use if we need it. You can plug in appliances and use them for short periods of time," Brendan explained.

"Why didn't you tell me that?" Dani asked.

"Because it's noisy," he answered. "If you're in desperate need of an electrical appliance, I'll get it going for you."

Jodie picked up the backpack she'd set on the floor beside her, then unzipped it and pulled out a frayed stack of envelopes tied together with a shoelace. "Look. I kept all the letters you wrote me," she told Brendan. "That's where I got the address for the seminary. Like I told you, I went there first and they said you'd be staying here for the summer."

He could see it wasn't a very big stack and wished he'd written more often. But Jodie had been a part of his past—the part that involved Caroline. And after his wife's death, he'd gone back to college then made the decision to enter the seminary. His life had taken a very different direction, and although he'd never lost contact with Jodie, he could count on one hand the number of times he'd seen her since Caroline's death seven years ago.

Now she sat across the table, looking at him as if he had the key to world peace. And all he could wonder was how he was going to help her when he hadn't found any answers to his own dilemma.

"Are you tired?" he asked, noting the dark smudges beneath her eyes.

"Mmm-hmm, but you don't have to give me your bed, Uncle Bren. I can crash on the couch or even the floor. I'm used to it."

Dani spoke up before Brendan had the chance.

"Don't worry about it, Jodie. We've plenty of beds here. First, though, I'm going to make you something to eat. I know what it's like when you're traveling. You never get to sit down and eat a decent meal. Am I right?"

"I am a little hungry," Jodie admitted.

Brendan knew it was an understatement. He appreciated Dani's handling of the situation. Instead of sounding patronizing, she was managing to put Jodie at ease.

"I need to use the bathroom," Jodie said, looking around nervously.

"I can take you," Dani offered, reaching for her flashlight.

"Take me?" She wrinkled her face.

"To the outhouse," Brendan interjected. "No running water means no indoor plumbing."

"Oh." She shrugged. "It's all right. I can go by myself."

Brendan took the flashlight from Dani. "How about if I point you in the right direction?"

Jodie didn't protest. While they were gone, Dani went to work in the kitchen. By the time they returned, chicken noodle soup was simmering in a pot and a cheese sandwich was grilling on the stove.

"Something smells good," Jodie said, sniffing appreciatively.

"You can wash up over here." Dani pumped water into one of the enamel basins and set a liquid soap dispenser next to it.

Brendan didn't miss the way the girl's eyes glanced hungrily toward the stove. He wondered how long it had been since she'd eaten.

"I love grilled cheese sandwiches," she gushed as

Dani set the food in front of her, then filled a tall glass with milk.

In a matter of minutes, the sandwich was gone, prompting Dani to ask, "Would you like another?"

"If it's not too much bother...?"

"Not at all." Brendan watched Dani make a second sandwich and drop it in the frying pan. "What about you, Brendan? Would you like one?"

He shook his head. "No, I'm fine."

"Am I supposed to call you Father?" Jodie asked, fixing her uncle with a puzzled look.

"No, just call me Brendan."

"Good," Jodie responded. "'Cause no offense or anything, but it kinda freaks me out to think of you as a priest. You know, seeing as you were married to Aunt Caroline and all. And you're, like, way too cool to be someone who runs around in robes all day."

The spatula clanged against the frying pan and Brendan's gaze met Dani's startled one. He'd planned to tell Danielle Taylor as little as possible about himself. Despite her obvious effort to act unmoved by Jodie's comments, how could she not be curious?

"I haven't been ordained, Jodie," he said. "I've only studied to be a priest. But even if I had taken my final vows, I wouldn't be wearing robes around the resort."

His niece took a long drink of milk, then wiped her lips with the back of her sleeve. "Good," Jodie said again. "'Cause I didn't come here so I could see a priest. I coulda talked to Father Joe if I'd wanted that."

Brendan noted the sag to her shoulders and knew it would be better not to broach the subject of her pregnancy until she'd had a good night's sleep. "You've had a long journey. Why don't you get some rest and we'll talk tomorrow?"

Jodie nodded in agreement.

When the girl had finished eating, Dani once more took charge. "Why don't I heat some water and you can freshen up a bit? If you need a nightgown, I have one you can borrow."

"I better not. I might stretch it and ruin it," Jodie answered.

"No chance of that. It's actually an extra large T-shirt I use for a nightgown." The two of them disappeared into the bedroom, leaving Brendan to wonder what he would have done with his niece had Dani not been here.

As soon as Jodie had everything she needed, Dani reappeared carrying fresh linens. She reached for the key ring dangling from a nail on the end of the set of kitchen cupboards. "I'm going to put her in cabin number one."

While Jodie washed up, Dani and Brendan went to the cabin. Each of the cabins consisted of a bedroom and a sitting room with a kitchenette. While Dani's flashlight beam panned the room, Brendan pulled a book of matches from his pocket and lit the kerosene lamp on the small table.

"There aren't any mice in here, are there?" She continued to run her flashlight beam along the floorboards.

"Why do you ask?"

"I thought I saw something scurry across the floor when we came in."

"This is my fourth summer here and I've never seen any," he answered honestly. "If you want, I'll see if Wilbur has some mousetraps lying around."

"I think Jodie would appreciate that."

Brendan expected to see fear in her eyes, but there was none. Just concern. He was having to amend his first impression of her. Maybe she wasn't as self-centered as he'd originally thought. She was, however, still rich. And beautiful. More than a distraction. He sighed and went in search of the traps.

WHEN BRENDAN RETURNED, Jodie was with him. She'd pulled on a flannel shirt over the T-shirt Dani had given her. Her bare legs showed just how thin she was. Dani felt a rush of sympathy for the girl with her drawn features and dark circles under her eyes.

"I'll slip this behind the sofa just to make sure you don't have any extra guests," Brendan told Jodie as he bent over the back of the threadbare sofa with a mousetrap in hand.

"What's on that?" Dani asked.

"Peanut butter."

"Mice like it better than cheese," Jodie stated with the voice of experience. "Though you can put just about anything on it and they'll eat it. We've even caught them with peanut shells."

Jodie's observation made Dani wonder about the kind of living conditions the girl had had. "Hopefully there's only one in here and you won't be bothered by it," she said reassuringly.

Jodie shrugged. "Mice don't bother me. What I really hate are cockroaches 'cause they'll climb in bed with you. In this one place where we used to live, we had to put cotton in our ears when we went to sleep so they wouldn't get inside."

Dani felt for this young woman. She'd endured things she, Dani, had never even had to *think* about.

"There are no roaches here," Brendan stated firmly. "So don't worry."

Dani saw Jodie sniffing the air curiously. "It smells good in here."

"That's the cedar. It's an aromatic wood. It keeps the cabin from getting musty when it's not in use," Brendan explained. "I'm going to run back and get another mousetrap just in case there's more than one of them hiding in here, okay?"

Jodie nodded, then followed Dani into the bedroom. She set her backpack and gym bag at the foot of the bed and looked around. "This is nice."

"It's small, but the bed's comfortable," Dani told her, setting a flashlight on the nightstand. "I'll leave some bottled water for you in the kitchenette in case you get thirsty. Would you like me to leave some fruit for you, too?"

"No, I'm full." Jodie slipped off the flannel shirt, and Dani saw for the first time just how far along the girl was. She still felt unsure about leaving the teenager alone in the cabin.

"If you want, I can make up the other bed and stay here with you."

"I'm not afraid, if that's what you're worried about," Jodie said a bit gruffly, as if insulted that anyone would think she couldn't take care of herself.

"No, I know you're not afraid, Jodie. I just thought you might like to have someone nearby in case… something happens." Her eyes focused on the girl's enormous stomach.

"You mean with the baby?"

Dani nodded.

"It's not due for another month."

"Then you've seen a doctor?"

"Once. Some guy at a free clinic."

Dani knew that one visit was not enough. Prenatal

care was just as important as what happened to the baby after it was born. Jodie looked undernourished. "Did he give you any vitamins to take?"

"He gave me a prescription, but I never had it filled."

"You're not smoking, are you?"

"Uh-uh. I had to quit. It made me throw up."

One point in her favor, Dani thought.

Jodie wobbled slightly and dropped onto the bed, rubbing her thighs with the palms of her hands. Dani thought she was simply tired, but asked, "Are you okay?"

"Yeah, it's just that sometimes my legs go a little numb. I think it's 'cause the baby's so heavy." She slid between the covers. "This feels good. The pillow's soft." She sank farther into the bed, inhaling deeply. "The sheets smell good, too. Whoever owns this place must be rich."

Dani didn't comment.

Jodie yawned and said, "I'm so tired I probably won't wake up until tomorrow morning."

Dani smiled. "But that's what you want, isn't it?"

"I usually have to get up and go to the bathroom a couple of times—because of the baby," she explained.

"Then maybe I *should* stay here with you. It's no fun going alone to the half-moon in the middle of the night."

"It's all right. Beats going in the woods," Jodie said sleepily, and yawned again.

Dani realized that to someone who'd spent the past four days on the road, even rustic conditions were better than no shelter at all. She walked to the doorway and said, "You need to get to sleep, so I'll go. I'll leave

my house unlocked just in case you need me for anything, okay?''

"Mmm-hmm. Say good-night to Uncle Brendan for
me, will you?''

"Sure." Dani carried the lantern into the other room.
Brendan was sitting in the dark at the small table in the
kitchenette, staring out at the moonlit night. "Jodie said
good-night.''

"She's asleep?''

Dani nodded. "Just about.''

As they stepped outside, he said, "Thank you for
everything you did tonight. You were very good with
her.''

The sincerity in his voice warmed her. "I think beneath that tough exterior is a frightened little girl." She
kept her voice low, unsure if Jodie might still be awake
and overhear.

"I'll see what other arrangements I can make for her
tomorrow.''

"She's welcome to stay here for a few days.''

"You don't mind?''

She placed her hands on her hips. "No. That cabin
was just sitting empty anyway.''

"All right." He turned in the direction of his cabin.

"Wait. Could we talk about this?''

"You mean Jodie?''

She nodded. "Why don't you come inside the house
and I'll make us some coffee?''

He shrugged. "I'll pass on the coffee, but if there's
something you want to discuss, I'll come in for a few
minutes.''

He followed her into the log home, and they sat down
across from each other at the kitchen table. Dani decided to pass on the coffee, too.

"So, what is it that's bothering you?" he asked.

"I'm not bothered, exactly. Concerned would be a better word."

"About Jodie."

She nodded. "She told me she hasn't had any prenatal care."

"Considering her situation, that doesn't surprise me," he said.

"What *is* her situation?"

He sighed. "You know those statistics you always hear about one in four children growing up hungry? She's the one of four."

"Where are her parents?"

"Good question." He leaned back in his chair and sighed. "Look, this is not a simple case of a teenage girl getting pregnant and running away from home. This particular teen doesn't *have* a home."

"Are you saying she's a street kid?" Dani asked, although considering the girl's appearance, she was afraid she already knew the answer.

"Jodie has spent most of her life being bounced between foster homes and her mother. Her father was never part of the picture," he replied. "Unfortunately it's resulted in her often ending up on the streets rather than in any sort of family structure."

"And now she's pregnant with no place to call home." Dani pushed a stray wisp of hair away from her face. "Do you think her mother knows she's going to have a baby?"

"Probably, but I don't expect Jodie will get much support from that direction. Linda Fisher spends most of her time trying to stay out of detox."

"Then you aren't going to call her?"

"I'm not sure it would accomplish anything other

than to let her know her daughter's safe...and that's presuming we could find her.'' Dani got the impression he didn't think that was very likely. "Alcoholism has a way of robbing people of their sense of responsibility."

There was one question nagging at Dani's mind. "Is she your sister?"

"No. Jodie's my niece through marriage. She was only six years old when I first met her—just a tiny thing." He smiled wistfully. "She was the flower girl at my wedding. Her mother was Caroline's sister." He shook his head reflectively. "It seems like a long time ago. So much has happened since then."

Dani knew he wasn't simply talking about Jodie's life. "If there's anything I can do to help, let me know. I work with teens every day, so I'm familiar with the problems they face on a day-to-day basis."

"You didn't come here to take care of a pregnant teenager."

Dani leaned forward, her elbows on the table. "No, and I didn't expect a priest to question the reason for my being here."

He looked her squarely in the eye and said, "And I told you, I'm not a priest."

Not with that look in your eye, you're not. Dani shifted uneasily as a current of excitement rippled through her. Those penetrating dark eyes made her wish she had a cup of coffee in front of her. She needed the distraction.

But at last he broke eye contact. He pushed his chair back and got up to leave. "I appreciate your concern for my niece."

"But you don't need my help," she said in resignation. She rose, too. "I don't know what your plans are for her, but she needs to see a doctor as soon as possible.''

"I've worked with people at the local hospital. I should be able to get her in to see someone tomorrow." He started for the door.

"If you want me to go with you, I can. Jodie might be more comfortable if there's another woman present when she does see a doctor," she told him, tracing his steps.

"I'll ask her."

"And after the doctor? Then what?"

"I'm not sure," he admitted. "I can probably get her in to speak to someone at an adoption agency, as well."

"What makes you think she's decided to give the baby up for adoption?" It surprised Dani that he assumed Jodie had already chosen that option. She knew that all too often pregnant teens chose to be single mothers.

"I don't know that she has." He paused at the door to face her. "All I know is that she's sixteen and very pregnant."

"And that's why I want to help if I can."

She could see by the look on his face that he was reluctant to accept that help.

"Tell me something," she said. "What do you think Wilbur would have done if he'd been here and Jodie showed up on his doorstep?"

"He would have fed her and given her a place to stay," Brendan replied confidently. "Why?"

"Because as the benefactor of his legacy, I'd like to think he would be pleased with what I'm trying to do."

"Isn't it a little late to start worrying about earning his respect?"

There was no mistaking the criticism in his voice.

Ever since she'd arrived at the resort, he'd treated with her a coolness that she'd attributed to his disappointment in not having the place to himself. Now she could see that wasn't the case.

She stiffened her back. "Considering I didn't even know he existed until a few months ago, I really didn't have much say in the matter, did I?"

"He told me he'd written to you several times, but you never wrote back."

She frowned. "I never received any letters from him."

His eyebrows slanted skeptically.

"I didn't get any letters," she repeated, then decided it was better to drop the subject. What good would it do to argue about something that couldn't be changed? At least now she understood Brendan's attitude toward her. He thought she'd ignored Wilbur Latvanen while he'd been alive, then rushed to Minnesota to claim her inheritance after his death.

An uncomfortable silence stretched between them until finally Brendan said, "It's late. If I'm going to take Jodie to the clinic tomorrow, we'll need an early start."

"I can make her breakfast in the morning," she offered. "You're welcome to come, too, if you like."

"I'll meet you after breakfast," he told her, then disappeared into the darkness.

Later, as Dani climbed into bed, her gaze swung to the picture on the nightstand. Two women—her birth mother and her grandmother. Why now, after twenty-six years, did she want to know their stories? Because she'd inherited their personal belongings? Because her grandfather had apparently tried to contact her but had been unsuccessful? Or because she'd met Jodie, a pregnant teen facing the adoption decision?

She'd come to The Last Place on Earth to find answers. She just didn't expect there'd be so many questions.

BRENDAN LAY ON HIS BUNK staring up at the ceiling. A sliver of moonlight shone through the window, creating just enough light to allow him to make out the pattern of wood on the beamed ceiling. If he thought he'd had trouble sleeping a few weeks ago, it was nothing compared to his restlessness tonight.

It was bad enough sharing his solitude with Wilbur's granddaughter, but now he had the responsibility of his pregnant niece. She'd come to him for advice. He had no right to be counseling anyone this summer, not when his own life was a jumbled mess. How could he possibly deal with a sixteen-year-old girl with an unwanted pregnancy?

Yet maybe it wasn't an unwanted pregnancy. Maybe he'd jumped to the wrong conclusion. For all he knew, Jodie may have planned to have a baby. He hadn't really had a relationship with her in the past seven years—except for the occasional letters exchanged between the two of them.

And, of course, the time he'd had the criminal charges against her dropped. She'd been thirteen, stealing food to eat. Thanks to Father Dorian's testimony, Brendan had been able to convince the store owner that Jodie wasn't a teenager who needed to be taught a lesson. She needed a stable home life—just like so many of the kids on Fourth Street did.

He knew all about that for he had walked in shoes similar to Jodie's. Only he'd had Father Dorian to keep him from ending up in trouble. Jodie didn't have a mentor. She had no one but herself to rely on. If only Caroline hadn't died, they might have been able to be the parents Jodie so desperately needed.

He pushed aside the thoughts of his wife. Years of discipline had taught him to block out her memory. There was no point in thinking about what might have been. Caroline had died. He had returned to college then entered the seminary after graduation. Jodie had survived a childhood riddled with pain and disappointment.

Now she had come back into his life. The question plaguing him was why now? Why now when he needed to be alone? He had come to The Last Place on Earth hoping to find answers. All he had found so far were complications. Instead of being alone, he was sharing his solitude with two women—one who expected him to have all the answers, the other who only made him realize how few answers he really had.

What bothered him most was that in a few short days, Danielle Taylor had stirred emotions in him that he'd successfully managed to keep at bay for eight years. He was supposed to be deciding whether or not to take his final vows as a priest, not imagining what it would be like to hold her in his arms.

Self-discipline was what he needed. It was what had helped him survive the streets. It was what had guided him through the painful period following Caroline's death. And it was what he needed if he was going to enter the priesthood.

Self-discipline. His ability to practice it seemed to be slipping out of his reach. There was no way he could afford to allow a woman like Dani to play with his emotions. The answers he sought were out there, just waiting to be discovered. He only hoped his emotions didn't get in the way of finding them.

CHAPTER FIVE

BECAUSE BRENDAN had worked as a clinical pastoral educator at the hospital in Hibbing, he managed to get an appointment for Jodie the following afternoon with one of the doctors on staff. While Dani made breakfast, he used Wilbur's CB radio to contact the ambulance dispatcher, who in turn relayed the request to the receptionist at the clinic.

While Dani prepared breakfast, Jodie sat at the kitchen table staring out the window. "The way the sun hits the lake, it looks like there are diamonds on it," Jodie said, sounding rather awestruck. "I've never been at a lake resort before. Does it cost a lot of money to stay here?" She looked at her uncle for an answer.

"You'd have to ask Dani that question. She's the owner," Brendan replied.

"This is your place?"

"Mmm-hmm. I inherited it." Dani placed a plastic bottle of syrup on the table. "It's not really a resort. The only people who use the cabins are the priests from the local seminary. They come here to pray."

"They don't pray the whole time they're here," Brendan corrected her.

"What do they do?" Jodie.

"The same thing other people do at a resort. Swim, take walks, do a little fishing."

"It sounds like a vacation to me."

"It is. Priests need time away from work, too." As Dani set a plate of pancakes on the table, he said to her, "You look surprised."

"No, it's just that I was told the resort was like a retreat. I didn't realize the priests used it for recreation," she answered honestly.

"So how come there aren't any other priests here now?" Jodie asked, spreading butter over her stack of pancakes.

"The resort isn't officially open," Brendan replied.

"But *you're* here."

"Your uncle is going to take care of the place for me this summer," Dani explained, filling Brendan's cup with coffee.

"What happens to it in the winter?" Jodie asked Dani.

"That's what I need to figure out. My home's in California. When the summer ends, I have to go back to teach school."

"Everyone in town expects you to sell the place," Brendan said.

Including you, Dani thought. "I haven't made that decision," she said, sitting down across from Jodie.

"Then why is a real-estate appraiser coming to look at it?" he countered.

"That was my father's idea, not mine." She reached for the syrup and poured a liberal amount on her pancakes. "I came here for the summer to see what the place was like before I made any decisions."

"I don't know why anyone would want to live in Minnesota if they could live in California," Jodie said dreamily. "I heard it's always warm and there's so much stuff to do." She sighed. "I've never seen the ocean. I think it'd be really cool to live there." Then she looked at her uncle and asked, "If Dani sells the resort, where will you go?"

"He doesn't have to go anywhere," Dani answered before Brendan had a chance to reply. She turned to him and said, "You do realize you can stay the entire summer?"

"Are you going to stay all summer, Uncle Bren?"

"I'm not sure," he answered.

Dani wondered if he was simply being cautious or seriously thinking of not staying the full three months. "I thought you'd planned to stay until the end of August."

"Plans change," he said cryptically.

"You mean because I came?" Jodie looked at him with an anxious frown. "You don't need to worry. I'm not going to be a bother to you. I just need a little help and then I'll be gone."

"You're not a bother," Brendan assured her. "But I need to know what kind of help you want."

Dani noticed that Jodie was slow to answer.

"I was hoping you could help me find my boy-friend," she finally said after swallowing a bite of pancake and washing it down with some orange juice.

"Is he missing?" Brendan asked.

"I haven't seen him in over three months. Dusty's in a band and they travel a lot, you know, playing gigs at bars and stuff. I've been moving around so much lately that I don't think he knows where to find me anymore."

"Does he know you're pregnant?"

"Yeah. And he's happy about it. He says he's going to take care of me and the baby."

"Yet you don't know where he is," Brendan said with a lift of one dark brow.

"No, but he's gonna come back." The anxiety in her

eyes belied the confidence in her voice. "You'll find him."

Brendan waited a beat. "What makes you think I can do that?"

"You found my mother that time she went to Wisconsin."

"And if I find this guy, what then?"

She fidgeted nervously, then boldly stated, "Then I'll move in with him."

Brendan took a sip of his coffee. "And until then?"

"I was wondering if it'd be all right if...if I stayed here for a while," she said in a tiny voice. "You said there are two empty cabins. I won't be any trouble. I could help out around here. You know, cook and make beds and stuff." She looked eagerly to Dani, who felt her heartstrings being pulled.

Brendan also turned to Dani. "Would it be all right if she stayed?"

"Actually I wouldn't mind the help or the company." Her answer produced a grateful smile from Jodie and a guarded look from Brendan, who continued to press his niece for answers.

"And what happens if you don't find this guy?"

"You mean about the baby?"

"Yes," he said quietly.

She shifted on her chair. "When I went to the free clinic, they sent me to this counselor. He told me I could do one of three things—have an abortion, give the baby up for adoption or keep it."

"Since you're eight months pregnant, that leaves only two options, right?"

She nodded. "My friend, Shawna, told me we could move in with her and she wouldn't charge us any rent. She's got two kids of her own, so she said it wouldn't matter if there was one more in the apartment.'' Dani noticed that Jodie was no longer eating but pushing her food around on her plate. ''My friends say I'm stupid if I give it up. They say I'll live to regret it.''

''Jodie, this isn't a decision for your friends to make. It doesn't matter what any of them think or say. You are the one who's going to be responsible for this child, not them,'' he stated firmly. ''Only you know what's best for you. What's best for the baby.''

The way she was chewing on her lip led Dani to believe she wasn't convinced that what Brendan said was true. ''That's why I came to see you. You've always been the one person who's never made me feel stupid when I've been in trouble.''

''You're not a stupid person, Jodie,'' he said sincerely.

''Well, I feel really dumb getting myself into this mess.'' Her voice broke and she sniffed back tears.

''Every one of us finds ourselves in a mess now and then. But there's always a way to straighten it out. We just have to figure out what it is,'' Brendan said calmly.

Dani could see what it was that Jodie responded to in Brendan. He had a quiet inner strength that came across as confidence. It made you believe him when he said things could be fixed.

Brendan pointed at her plate. ''First of all, you need to finish your breakfast. Then you should go to the clinic, talk to the doctor and take it from there, okay?''

Jodie scowled. ''I hate going to the doctor.''

''But it's important. You want your baby to be healthy, don't you?''

''Yeah, of course.''

''Good. We'll go after breakfast. Okay?''

She gave him a reluctant nod. ''Okay.''

"Mr. Millar? The doctor will see you now."

Brendan followed the nurse to a corner office of the clinic. He took a seat in one of the two chairs in front of the desk. After a couple of minutes, a large man in a white lab coat entered the room. "Brendan. It's good to see you." He greeted him with an outstretched hand. "I hear you're not working at the hospital this summer."

"No, I'm not." He didn't care to elaborate, but Dr. Fred Sellers had been a longtime supporter of his and he felt he owed him some kind of an explanation. "I've taken a sabbatical from my work to take care of a few things."

"Is Jodie one of those things?" The doctor sat down, dropping a manila folder on his desk.

Brendan shook his head. "She wasn't until she showed up on my doorstep last night. She told you she's my niece, didn't she?"

The doctor nodded. "I take it she ran away from home."

"She hasn't exactly had a place to call home."

"It sounds to me as if she thinks you can change that."

Brendan sighed. "The last time she stayed with me she was eight years old. I'm not sure I know what to do with a sixteen-year-old."

"Well, she definitely needs someplace to go." Sellers opened the manila folder and glanced at the contents. "Looking at the results of her exam, I'd say she could use someone to look after her until the baby comes."

"She's all right, isn't she?"

"Her blood count is low and she hasn't been eating the right kind of foods, but considering she hasn't had any medical care in the past six months, she's doing pretty well. If I'm going to deliver the baby here, I'd like to get a copy of her medical records from the clinic she used in Minneapolis.'' He closed the folder and leaned forward. "Do you think she'll have the baby at the hospital here in town?"

"At this point, I'm not sure what arrangements can be made. I told her she could stay with me for now, but you and I both know that The Last Place on Earth is no place for someone who's pregnant.''

"The conditions are rather primitive.''

Brendan nodded. "I'll check with Social Services here and see if we can't get her into a group home.''

The doctor grimaced. "From what I hear, they're continually full. What about a foster family?''

"It's an option, but we both know there's a shortage there, too. Jodie said she's eight months pregnant. Does that mean I have three or four weeks to find her a place to live?''

"I'd say the sooner she gets settled, the better. In the meantime, I've prescribed some supplements she should take and I've given her some reading materials on prenatal care. These last four weeks are the time when the baby gains its weight. She really needs to eat properly.''

Brendan nodded again.

"She should be examined once a week now until she delivers the baby, but if she's going to be staying with you for a few days, I'd like to run a couple of tests.''

"What kind of tests?" Brendan asked.

"An ultrasound for one—just to be sure there's nothing wrong with the baby.''

"You think there could be?''

"No, but since she hasn't had any prenatal care up to this point, it's a good idea to assess the health of the fetus by monitoring its movements. We'll also be able to take some measurements that'll help us date the pregnancy."

"When do you want to do this?"

"Can you bring her back tomorrow?"

BRENDAN WOULD HAVE preferred to wait to discuss Jodie's future until the three of them got back to the cabin. What he didn't need was for Danielle Taylor to become any more deeply involved with his niece. Jodie may have wanted her company for this visit to the clinic, but he hadn't been happy about it. And he really didn't want her to be a part of any decisions concerning what happened next.

Unfortunately Jodie liked Dani. Brendan saw how quickly Wilbur's granddaughter had earned his niece's trust. It puzzled him that Jodie would open up to someone who came from such a different world. Like Brendan, Jodie had lived in the poorest part of town, unable to buy new clothes and unsure whether she'd have anything to eat the next day. Dani, on the other hand, wore designer jeans and no doubt ate in five-star restaurants.

"I don't see why I have to go back to the clinic tomorrow. I feel fine," the teenager complained as Brendan drove his Geo onto the highway. She sat in the front passenger seat while Dani sat in back, an arrangement Dani had insisted on since Jodie needed the room to stretch her legs.

"Ultrasounds are pretty common nowadays," Dani answered. "I'm sure they just want to check out the baby."

"Dr. Sellers said it wouldn't hurt," Jodie admitted. "And the nurse took me to this room and showed me what the thing looks like."

"That's good. Now you don't need to worry about it," Dani said.

"The doctor said I'm supposed to go for a checkup every week until the baby comes, but I don't see the point. I mean, Jasmine DeSantes never even went to the doctor the entire time she was pregnant, and she had her baby without any problems."

"Who's Jasmine DeSantes?" Brendan asked.

"One of my friends. Or at least she was until she got sent to Chicago to live with her grandparents."

"Why wouldn't you want to go for a checkup?" Dani asked.

"You've never had a baby, have you?" Jodie said in a knowing voice.

"No."

"Then you don't know what they do to you. Ohmigosh, Dani, it's gross!" She turned around in her seat. "They make you get up on this table and lie on your back with your feet up in these metal things. The nurse called them stirrups—"

Dani cut her off. "Jodie, it's probably better not to talk about this in front of your uncle."

"Oh! Sorry, Uncle Brendan. I didn't mean to embarrass you."

"You didn't embarrass me, Jodie. It's just a little more information than I need to know."

"Well, I just thought I should warn Dani."

His eyes met Dani's in the rearview mirror and he saw a flicker of amusement.

"Thank you for the warning, Jodie. You and I can continue this conversation later."

They traveled in silence, but it didn't last long. Brendan could see Jodie fussing with the prescription bottle they had picked up from the pharmacist.

"Damn, these pills are gigantic!" She held the bottle up to the light. "Oops. I guess I shouldn't swear in front of you. Forgive me, Father," she said with an impish grin.

"You didn't swear, and I would really appreciate it if you didn't call me Father. I'm your uncle," Brendan corrected her.

"Okay," she said docilely. Again she turned to Dani. "How am I supposed to take these pills? They're, like, monster-size. Look at them."

"They're probably coated so they go down easier," Dani responded.

"I don't see what difference it makes, my taking them now. I mean, I only have like another month to be pregnant."

"If the doctor says you better take them, you should probably take them," Dani answered.

"I guess," the girl answered sullenly.

The rest of the trip was accomplished with little conversation. Dani could see that Jodie was tired and suspected she dozed off several times. When Brendan parked the car outside the resort, however, Jodie was the first one out.

Dani noticed that she left the bag of handouts the doctor had give her on the front seat. "Aren't you going to take your reading material?"

Jodie dismissed it with a wave of her hand. "Oh, I know all that stuff already," she said, and headed for the half-moon.

Dani reached into the car and picked up the pamphlets. "She really should read these."

Brendan held out his hand. "I'll give them to her."

"No, it's all right." She held them close to her chest.

"I'll do it. It's probably easier for her to discuss this stuff with a woman."

"You don't need to take on that responsibility."

"I know I don't *have* to."

Brendan stared out at the lake for several moments, as if composing his thoughts. "It's a difficult situation. *She* can be difficult."

"I'm a teacher, Brendan. I've had experience with difficult teenagers."

"Pregnant ones?"

"Yes, and it seems to me that Jodie needs someone to be a friend more than anything else right now."

"And you want to be that friend?" As he had so often in the past, he gave her a skeptical glance.

"Yes. Why should that bother you?"

He shrugged. "It doesn't *bother* me," he lied. "I just don't think you should feel obligated toward my niece because she showed up at your resort."

"I don't feel obligated. I *want* to help. Jodie's trying to act like she's okay, but I think under all that tough talk is a frightened little girl."

"And with darned good reason," he said soberly. "She has no place to live, no job and no family to fall back on. How will she take care of an infant?"

"There must be agencies that can help her."

He chuckled sardonically. "Like they've done so far? Maybe you haven't read about recent budget cuts, but I can tell you, every day the number of those agencies decreases and their resources diminish. That's mainly the reason she's homeless now. Adoption may be her only choice."

"I doubt that it's necessarily the only one," Dani said stiffly.

"Well, it's the one I intend to discuss with her."

"She may want to keep her baby. I've been around enough teens to know that raising a child while you're still in school is not the stigma it used to be. Lots of them do it."

"You think she should keep the baby?" he asked in disbelief.

"I didn't say that," Dani argued. "I just think both sides of the issue need to be discussed—adoption and keeping the baby."

He shook his head. "I can't in good conscience advocate her raising a child. I hope you won't encourage it, either."

Before Dani could respond, Jodie returned. "I need to get a glass of water so I can take one of those horse pills."

Dani stretched out an arm. "Come inside with me and I'll get you a snack, too."

"What about you, Uncle Bren? Hungry?"

"No. You go ahead. I have some reading I want to do." He glanced at his watch. "How about if we cook dinner outside tonight?"

"Dani, too?"

There was the slightest of hesitations before he said yes. Jodie might not have noticed, but Dani did. He would have preferred not to have Dani join them for dinner. But she guessed his religious training prohibited him from saying so. And she wasn't about to let him off the hook.

"Gee, that sounds like fun. Thanks."

AT THE SOUND of a horn honking, Brendan put down his book. Another interruption. Not that it mattered. He had been reading for more than an hour and had turned only a handful of pages. His brain didn't want to absorb theology on a summer afternoon. It wanted to be outside where Jodie and Dani were wading in the crystal-clear water that lapped the sandy shore.

In the quiet summer air, he could hear faint echoes of their laughter and Rex's barking. More than once, he'd risen from his position on the sofa to lift a corner of the curtain and glance enviously at their frolicking figures.

They looked carefree, although they were anything but. Again the horn honked, and Brendan slid his feet into a pair of sandals and headed outside. Coming through the pine-bordered walkway was Lou. Rex rushed to greet her, slathering her with his tongue.

In her hand she carried a small insulated cooler. Brendan reached her about the same time Dani did.

"You must be Wilbur's granddaughter," she said to Dani, who was wiping her hands on her shorts. "I'm Louella Hortense."

Brendan could see the surprise in Dani's eyes.

"How do you do," she said, shaking the woman's hand.

Lou gave her a thorough appraisal. "If you aren't the spittin' image of your grandmother."

"You knew her?"

Lou nodded. "She was blond—just like you. And she had the same blue eyes. She was Norwegian."

"I thought I was Finnish."

"Well, yes. Your grandfather was Finnish." She sighed. "Oh, how he'd have loved to have met you."

"I'm sorry that never happened," Dani said sincerely.

"I have a message for you." She looked at Dani and said, "You're supposed to call your father. Pete said it was rather important. I didn't get any response when I tried the CB."

"We've been outside," Dani explained.

"Pete told him it would take me awhile to deliver the message and he said just to make sure that you call him back today."

"Thank you. It was good of you to drive over here," Dani said politely.

"I had to come for Rex." She patted the dog affectionately. "But I wanted to come over and introduce myself anyway. I figured you'd want to talk to me, and my place is kind of hard to find. Brendan probably told you I've been away. Went hiking with a couple of the fellas over at Superior National Forest. That waterfall at Pigeon River is almost as beautiful as the one here in Hidden Falls. Have you seen the falls yet?"

She shook her head. "They sound lovely."

"I'll take you over there if you like. There are some wonderful hiking trails if you enjoy that kind of thing."

"Lou's a retired park ranger," Brendan explained. "Anything you want to know about this area, just ask her." Just then, Jodie came walking toward them. He hastened to introduce them to one another. "Lou, this is my niece, Jodie. Jodie, this is Louella Hortense."

"Hi," the girl said guardedly.

Lou wasn't as reticent. "You look as if you might need my help before long."

Jodie gave her a puzzled look.

"I'm a trained midwife. If that baby of yours starts to come, give me a call." She looked at Dani and Brendan. "I've delivered seventy babies thus far."

"That's quite an accomplishment," Dani said. "Sorry, I should have offered sooner, but would you like something to drink?"

"I brought my own." Lou held up the cooler. "You drink beer?"

Dani nodded. "Sure."

"Then let's sit and have a cold one." She marched over to the picnic table and straddled one of the benches, then pulled out three beers. "What about something for Jodie?"

"I'm not thirsty."

"Why don't I get the lemonade?" Dani said, ignoring Jodie's shrug of indifference and heading for the house.

"I have to go to the bathroom," the teenager announced, then slunk off.

"She's pretty," Lou whispered to Brendan when they were alone.

"I guess it's true what they say about pregnancy putting a bloom in a woman's cheeks." Brendan deliberately misunderstood her.

She poked him in the arm. "I wasn't talking about your niece and you know it—although Jodie's not bad-looking, either. Wilbur would have been tickled pink if he'd met Dani."

"Maybe," Brendan allowed himself to say.

Lou twisted the cap off her bottle and took a swig. "You didn't tell me you had a niece coming to see you."

"I didn't know."

"Uh-oh. So much for your solitude, eh?"

"It doesn't matter. That was ruined when Ms. California showed up," he said dryly.

"She's pretty enough to be a beauty queen. She sure does look like her grandmother, Lillie," Lou commented.

"What happened to Wilbur's wife? He never did talk about her."

"It's a sad story. One day, she was perfectly healthy, the next, she was deathly ill. I wasn't living here at the time, but from what I understand, some sort of virus struck her heart."

"How old was she?"

"I think around thirty. I often wonder if she hadn't died, maybe Wilbur and Bridget might have had a better relationship. He didn't know how to deal with many of the problems an adolescent girl has."

At the sound of Dani approaching, Lou changed the subject.

"So what do you think of the place?" she asked Dani, sliding a beer across the table in her direction.

"It's beautiful." She glanced out at the lake. "So quiet and peaceful."

"That's what your granddad liked about it. He thought the lake should have been named Tranquillity. I have a letter for you from him." She reached into her backpack and pulled out a buff-colored envelope. "I also have a stack of information on the resort. If you're interested in seeing it, you can come over."

"I'd like that. Then you can tell me what I need to know about this place. If I'm going to stay for a while, I'd better learn where everything is and what needs to be done."

"You're going to stay?" Lou looked as surprised as Brendan was.

"For the summer anyway. Maybe you can tell me who I need to contact to get some improvements done."

"What kind of improvements?" Brendan asked suspiciously.

"Just the conveniences of water and power. I've traveled to Third World countries with more facilities than this place. Even if the power company doesn't come out here, there's got to be a way of getting electricity and running water into the cottages. They have it in mountain cabins that are hundreds of miles from anywhere.''

"You can get it here, but it'll cost a pretty penny," Lou said.

"It would be worth it to take a hot shower without having to haul water," Dani mused. "Lou, you must know the names of some reliable contractors around here.''

"Well, sure, but it would probably be a good idea to read the letter your grandfather left for you before you do anything," Lou suggested.

Puzzled, Dani opened the letter and read it. As her eyes scanned the paper, a frown creased her forehead. When she'd finished, she folded it back up and tucked it into the envelope.

"He doesn't want me putting running water into the shower or the house."

Lou and Brendan exchanged glances, but Lou just said, "Let's not worry about it at the moment. You're going to want to make some changes—that's only to be expected.''

Brendan knew there was more to it than that. Wilbur had specifically requested that the resort retain its rustic charm. Modernization had been a dirty word for the retired carpenter. The closer to nature, the better, he'd always believed.

"I don't want to do anything that might create problems," Dani told Lou.

Just her presence was creating problems, Brendan thought.

"Come over to the house and we'll go over everything." Lou gave her hand a pat of encouragement. The longer the executor of Wilbur's will stayed, the friendlier she became with Dani. By the time she left, they were on a hugging basis.

It didn't surprise Brendan. There was something about Dani—the way she smiled, the warmth in her voice—that encouraged people to come closer. That was fine for the folks of Hidden Falls, but it was something he couldn't allow to happen to him. Not if was going to come to a carefully considered decision regarding the priesthood. Unfortunately, though, he was attracted to Dani, and the only thing he could do was hope he had the self-discipline not to act on it.

CHAPTER SIX

THE PUBLIC PHONE at Pete's Place was at the front of the store. Although Dani would have preferred to talk to her father in privacy, it was better to stand out in the open at Pete's Place than in the back of Earl's noisy garage.

While Brendan and Jodie sat at Vera's counter waiting for hamburgers, Dani used the opportunity to make her call. The only other person at the front of the store was Pete, who discreetly busied himself pricing cans.

Dani punched in the numbers on her calling card and dialed her father's beeper. While she waited for him to return her call, she stared out the window at the slow trickle of traffic that ambled through the tiny town.

"Couldn't get through?"

She glanced at Pete and shook her head. "I had to leave him this number so he could call me back. It should only take a minute."

"Not a problem. Take your time."

Dani smiled gratefully, then turned her gaze to the phone, willing it to ring. It didn't. Several minutes later, Vera's voice rang out, "Burgers are done."

Pete looked at Dani. "Why don't you go sit down? I'll come get you if he calls."

Dani nodded. "Thanks." She returned to the counter where three hamburger baskets sat in a row. She took her place on a stool in front of one of them, poured a dollop of ketchup onto her hamburger and took a bite. She hadn't eaten more than a couple of French fries when she heard the phone ring. "I bet that's for me," she said, dabbing at her lips with a napkin.

As she hurried to the front of the store, Pete held out the receiver.

"Thanks." She gave him a grateful smile, then took a deep breath. "Hi, Dad. How are you?"

"Terrible. I can't believe you haven't called to tell me you arrived safely. What are you trying to do? Give me an ulcer?"

"There's no need for you to worry about me. I'm perfectly safe."

"Safe? You're in the middle of a wilderness two thousand miles away where there's no electricity or running water."

"Trust me, Dad. I'm a lot safer in Minnesota than I'd be in California."

"When are you coming home?"

"I just got here," she said.

"You have to be home for the picnic next week. After all, you are the boss's daughter."

Dani needed no reminders. She was discovering that was part of the reason she was at the resort. She had always been Robert Taylor's daughter to the rest of the world when she really wanted to be just Dani.

"I'm sorry, Dad, but I can't make the picnic this year."

The silence was so loud Dani wanted to bang the receiver back on the hook. Whenever her father was angry, he went silent. In the past, that silence had been her signal to make peace with him. Only this time she wasn't going to agree with him simply to avoid conflict.

Finally he said, "I can tell by your tone of voice it

won't do me any good to argue with you.'' He exhaled a long sigh and said, ''I've put Art Cashen in charge of helping you get things settled up there.''

''Dad, I don't need Art Cashen. I can take care of it.''

''Someone's expressed an interest in developing the place into a time-share resort. I put Art in charge of the project,'' he said in his usual take-charge manner.

''Project? I don't want it to be a project.'' She glanced nervously toward Pete who was waiting on a customer nearby.

''You will when you hear how much money you can make from developing that lakeshore.''

She turned so that her back was to the counter. ''Look, Dad, I really don't want to talk about this right now.''

''Matthew said you have some crazy idea in your head that you might want to keep the place.''

''I haven't made that decision yet.''

''What do you mean *yet?* You live and work in Southern California. Why would you want to keep a place in Minnesota? Surely you can see how impractical that would be.''

''No, I can't, and I would appreciate your remembering that it's my choice to make, not yours.''

''I've always taken care of business for you, Dani. I haven't done wrong by you yet, have I?''

''No, but this is different.'' She took a deep breath. ''I need to take care of this myself.''

''Matthew's worried about you. He thinks you're going to get eaten by a bear.''

''Better a bear than a rat like him,'' she said dryly.

''Aren't you being a little hard on him?''

''No.'' She looked at Pete again. ''I really should get

going, Dad. I'm at a pay phone here. Please don't worry about me. I'm fine. Really.''

"How do I get ahold of you if I need to speak to you? There must be a better way than having to call there and have the grocer relay the message to this Hortense woman.''

"No, there honestly isn't.''

She could hear his sigh of impatience. "I hope Matthew's right.''

"Right about what?'' she couldn't resist asking.

"He doesn't expect you can make it more than a week without running water.'' Robert chuckled softly.

"Matthew's wrong, and I really don't care what he thinks,'' she said rather childishly, although she knew that her father and Matthew had every right to think she'd see the conditions at the resort, then turn around and come home. At one time in her life, she might have done so, but not now.

After she'd said goodbye, she regretted her immature response. Especially when she turned around and saw Brendan leaning against the checkout counter not three feet away. She wondered how much of her conversation he'd overheard.

"I need to use the phone,'' he told her when she glared at him.

"Be my guest.'' She walked to the back of the store and once more sat down to eat.

"Your food's probably cold. Would you like me to make you another burger?'' Vera asked.

Dani shook her head. "No, this is fine.'' Her appetite had disappeared anyway. She made small talk with Jodie and stuffed the remains of her cold hamburger into her mouth. Her conversation with her father had truly unsettled her.

Men. She didn't want to be around any of them at the moment. Not her father, not her ex-fiancé and not Brendan Millar. She could still see that look on his face as she'd hung up the phone. It had been disapproval. He didn't like her very much—that much was evident.

Maybe it was better that way. The less their paths crossed the better. He was just a man hired to do the maintenance on the resort. There was no point in trying to prove anything to him. Certainly not her worth as a woman. It would be better if she avoided being with him as much as possible.

THAT WAS EASIER SAID than done when you were the only two adults within ten miles. And when the only contact either of them had with the rest of the world was the CB radio in Dani's kitchen.

A couple of evenings later, when Lou radioed with a message that a Father Dorian in Minneapolis had found Jodie's mother and wanted Brendan to call him first thing in the morning, Dani had to relay the information to Brendan.

She ripped the paper off the notepad and headed for his cabin, flashlight in hand. She knew it was none of her business what transpired between him and his niece, yet she couldn't help but be concerned about the teenager.

When she got to his place, he was sitting in a chair by the window, reading. She thought he might have noticed her flashlight beam or heard her footsteps on the wooden steps, but he didn't glance up from his book until she knocked on the screen door. Then he looked surprised to see her.

"Is everything all right?" he asked as he held it open for her.

She stepped inside. "I'm sorry to disturb you, but I have a message from Lou." She handed him the piece of paper.

He read it, then folded it in half and slipped it into his pocket. "Thank you. I appreciate your bringing it."

If she'd expected him to invite her to sit, she was in for a disappointment. He simply stood with his arms folded, waiting for her to leave.

Nevertheless she managed to get a good look at the interior of the cabin. It was similar to Jodie's, only his had blue drapes instead of green. Judging by the contents, he lived very simply. Lots of candles were burning, but she didn't see any crucifixes or other religious items in the room. She glanced at the book he had placed facedown on a small table. The title was *How to Tie Your Own Flies*. It took her a moment to realize that it was about fishing lures.

"I'd offer you something to drink, but it is rather late," he finally said.

Dani knew she should take the hint and go, but she didn't. "Lou said Father Dorian had located Jodie's mother."

"I expected he would. She's from the old neighborhood." He didn't elaborate and, judging by the set of his jaw, wasn't going to.

"I guess I'm a little surprised you looked for her."

"Just because a woman has problems doesn't mean she doesn't care about her daughter. All I did was send a message that Jodie is safe."

"Then you're not thinking about sending her home?"

"That would be like jumping from the frying pan into the fire," he said grimly. "As I said, she has no home."

Dani wasn't naive enough to believe there weren't any teenagers living on the streets with no real place to call home, but she didn't want that to be Jodie's reality. "Is someone looking for the father of her baby...this Dusty?"

"I've got someone working on it, but from what I know of the kid, I doubt he'll surface anywhere. It's highly unlikely he's going to accept his responsibility as a father."

"If you don't know the boy, how can you make that judgment?"

"Because Father Dorian does know him. I'd say Jodie's chances of getting any kind of support from him are next to none. Don't you think if he wanted to be in the picture, he would at least let her know somehow where he is?"

"So Jodie shouldn't be counting on any help from him."

He shook his head. "She's on her own and she's going to have to make some decisions about her life as well as the baby's."

"She's looking to you to help her with those decisions."

"And I will, but I'm her uncle—my vision is biased. That's why she needs to see a professional. I made an appointment with someone in Social Services. Hopefully she'll be able to get into a group home. Another alternative would be foster care."

"But you said she always runs away from those situations."

He shrugged. "There aren't a lot of options when you're sixteen and pregnant. Decisions have to be made and we both know she can't stay here indefinitely."

Dani knew what he said was true, yet she couldn't help but wonder if more couldn't be done to help the teen. Jodie was frightened and lonely. More than anything, she needed to be with people who cared about her. Yet no one seemed to be out there for her except her uncle. And he, well…he only wanted to see her put in a group home.

Dani knew she was becoming emotionally involved with the teenager. The minute she'd set eyes on the girl, in fact, she'd felt a bond with her. At first she'd thought it was because she was like a stray puppy in need of some tender, loving care. But now Dani was beginning to question if there wasn't more to it. For no matter how hard she tried to dismiss the thought, she wondered if her own birth mother had been a young woman just like Jodie.

"When is this appointment with Social Services?" she asked.

"Tomorrow, after she's finished at the clinic."

"When she's done, do you think there'll be time for some shopping?" she asked.

He looked at her as if she'd just sprouted horns. "Shopping for what?"

"Clothes."

"With what? She has no money."

"I know that, but I do have money and I can afford to get her a few things to wear while she's pregnant." She felt her shoulders stiffen.

"I don't see what the point is in buying her clothes when she's eight months pregnant."

"Because she needs them. You've seen her wardrobe. I thought I'd get her some new tops—big, baggy shirts she'll be able to wear after the baby's born. I want to help in any way I can."

"Why?"

"Why?" she repeated. "I wouldn't expect a priest to question a gesture of kindness."

"You forget. I'm not a priest." He paused, then added, "Yet."

"That's the problem—I often do forget." It wasn't meant to be a provocative statement, but suddenly the room was charged with tension. She shifted from one foot to the other as an awkward silence built. She noticed everything masculine about him—the shadow of a beard on his jaw, the Adam's apple on his throat, the well-defined muscles beneath the T-shirt. And those hands, so large and capable-looking, as if he would be able to hold on to a woman. He was one very attractive man. How awful to waste all that on the priesthood.

She mentally shook herself. What was she doing fantasizing about a man who was choosing to be celibate the rest of his life?

"Well, will you let me take Jodie shopping?" she asked, getting back to the subject at hand.

He shrugged in resignation. "If that's what you want to do."

"It is." She shoved her hands into the back pockets of her jean shorts.

He still looked like he wanted to say no. But to Dani's relief, he only said, "I'll take my mother's advice and not look a gift-horse in the mouth."

She thought she saw a hint of a grin and her heart skipped a beat. "Good."

He tugged on his ear as he said, "And I know Jodie would probably rip off a layer of my skin if I turned down such a generous offer on her behalf."

This time when he smiled, there was no stopping the thumping of her heart. Brendan Millar, should he choose, could win over any woman's heart with such a simple gesture. Dani said good-night and quickly left before her thoughts strayed in a direction best left not traveled.

BETWEEN THE TESTS at the hospital, the visit to Social Services and the stop at the mall, Brendan, Jodie and Dani spent nearly the entire day in Hibbing. By the time they returned to Sacred Lake, Brendan had had more than enough of Dani Taylor's company.

The woman was driving him to distraction. It was bad enough that she wore shorts that revealed the slender length of her leg, but her knit top conformed to every lush curve. With her bright blond hair and trendy sunglasses, she was the object of many men's attention as she walked down the street.

She was the kind of woman, he was sure, who could make any man's life a three-ring circus. She'd certainly created a commotion in his quiet life. First the car in the creek, then the nude dip in the lake. Any hope he'd had that she'd keep to herself and leave him be had been dashed the minute Jodie appeared at the resort. Dani was determined to be friends with his niece.

When they arrived back at The Last Place on Earth, Dani suggested they eat dinner together, since it was silly for each of them to eat alone. Brendan declined her offer of chicken on the grill. He had no intention of making mealtime a communal event. He'd come to the lake for solitude and meditation. So far he'd had little of either.

A short while later, he had to remind himself of this fact when he heard laughter coming from the beach. He glanced out his window and saw Dani and Jodie splashing about in the water. Apparently a swimsuit was one of the articles of clothing she'd purchased for his niece.

He loosened the collar of his shirt. It was hot today

and the water did look inviting. Only one thing stopped him. Dani's bikini. It was two tiny pieces of cloth tied together with strings. At least that was how it looked from where he stood. It was pink and black, and the longer he watched Dani frolicking in the water, the more power it had to make his skin turn red.

Irritated by his reaction, he stepped away from the window and busied himself in the kitchenette, rummaging through his stock of canned goods for anything that appeared the least bit interesting enough to open for dinner. He found nothing. He wasn't hungry. Not for food.

He quickly squelched such thoughts. Celibacy had not been a problem for the past three years. So why was it now he suddenly felt as if a sleeping giant wanted to be awakened? Because he no longer was in the seminary and there was no reason for him to be celibate?

The laughter continued to tinkle temptingly, sending images to his brain that were better left to another man's imagination. He wiped his brow, wondering if the humidity had climbed or if the temperature was warmer than the thermometer outside his window indicated. Finally, when he could no longer bear to think of the cool water outside his front door while he was suffering from the heat indoors, he changed into his swim trunks and grabbed a towel.

He approached the water as if he were walking up to the Communion rail. When Jodie saw him, she waved.

"Hey, Uncle Bren. Come on in. The water's great."

He let his towel drop to the sand, kicked off his sandals and waded in, trying not to notice that Dani, floating stomach down on an inflated raft, looked like a water goddess. She paddled toward him.

"There's another raft on the deck. You just need to

blow it up," she told him as he waded into the deeper water.

"It's all right. I'm fine," he told her, although he was anything but fine.

He was getting hot and bothered by a pair of breasts that looked as if they were going to fall out of the bikini top. She'd propped herself up on her elbows, totally unaware of the view it gave him. He quickly dove under the water, needing the cold to temper the automatic physical reaction to her near nakedness.

When he surfaced, Jodie was beside him. "I thought you said the water was great," he barked, shaking the water from his head. "It's freezing."

"You'll get used to it. Get a raft to float. It's warmer that way."

"I just came in for a quick swim," he told her as Dani floated toward them. He pushed off, swimming away from the shore. He swam until he was out of breath. Then he flipped onto his back and propelled himself toward the sandy beach, staring up at the puffy clouds that dangled like cotton balls in the sky.

When he touched bottom again, he stood. He would have gone ashore, but Jodie called after him, "You're not going in already, are you?"

"I said it would be a quick swim."

"But we were just going to play Frisbee. It's more fun with three."

Brendan looked at Dani, who'd slid off her raft and was wading toward the shore. She was just as sexy from the rear as she was from the front. Her swimsuit rode up her cheeks exposing another sensuous curve. At the shore, she stooped to pick up the Frisbee. Automatically she tossed it in Brendan's direction, yelling, "Catch!"

He had no choice but to grab the airborne disk.

"Over here," Jodie called.

Out of practice, he tossed the Frisbee, only to have it glide over her head.

"Uncle Bren!" Jodie yelled in reproach.

"I'll get it," Dani shouted, swimming toward the floating disk. With the ease of an experienced swimmer, she quickly cut across the water. "Jodie, you stay in the shallows so you don't have to exert yourself, and Brendan and I will take the deep water," she instructed, apparently assuming he was willing to play.

"Are you sure this is such a good idea? I mean, she is eight months pregnant," he said.

"Don't worry, Uncle Bren. I asked the doctor about swimming and he said it's really good for me because it's exercise, but there's no resistance to my muscles. I'll be fine." She clapped her hands. "Throw me the Frisbee."

After a few tosses, it was obvious that Dani had the most accurate throw, so she was the one designated to send it sailing through the air to Jodie. Jodie then flipped it to Brendan, who tossed it back to Dani.

Brendan had decided he'd toss the Frisbee a few times, then make his departure. To his surprise, however, it was Jodie who called a halt to the game and not because she was tired, but because she was hungry. It was only as Brendan glanced at the sky that he realized the position of the sun. It was sinking toward the horizon.

As they dried themselves, Dani asked, "Are you sure you don't want to have dinner with us?"

Brendan draped his towel around his shoulders and tried not to notice the delectable body standing before him. "Thank you for the offer, but I'll just grab something on my own."

Dani shrugged. "If you're sure..."

He wasn't. Not for one minute. But it was wiser to keep his distance from this lovely blonde—at least until he could get his libido under control.

"I'll see you in the morning," he said, then quickly headed for his cabin. He hadn't taken but a few steps when there was a commotion unlike anything he'd ever heard before. He turned to see Dani shaking her foot while Jodie screamed.

"Uncle Bren, come quick! Dani's got something gross on her foot!"

It didn't take long for him to see the reason for her grimace.

"I think it's a bloodsucker," Dani said, trying to pull the wormlike creature from her foot.

"They're called leeches," Brendan told her.

"Oh, yuck!" Jodie jumped back a foot. "That's disgusting. You should have told us there were leeches in the lake before we went swimming."

"We were in there a long time and this is the only one that managed to attach itself to anybody," Brendan pointed out, kneeling to look more closely at her foot.

"It won't come off." Dani continued to pull at the leech but had no luck dislodging it.

"It has suckers on both ends. Here, let me try. Sometimes with the smaller ones you can pick them off with your fingers, but these bigger ones need a little coaxing." When he couldn't remove it, he turned to his niece. "Go inside and bring me a saltshaker."

"Salt?"

"Yes, salt." He watched her waddle toward Wilbur's house.

"They really are harmless," he told Dani.

"Easy for you to say when it's on *my* foot," she quipped.

And a lovely foot it was. Beautifully shaped, with smooth skin and toenails painted a reddish brown. Brendan fought the urge to run his fingers across her ankle and up those sexy, slender legs. Everything about Dani Taylor appeared to be lovely, much to his dismay. He kept his eyes on her foot, however. Considering her present attire, it was probably the safest part of her anatomy.

"I suppose this means the swimming's done," he said wryly.

"You could have warned us," she chastised him. "We could have bought water shoes."

"You certainly could afford them." The minute he uttered the wisecrack, he wished he hadn't said it. After all, look how generous she'd been toward Jodie.

He was relieved to see his niece return with the saltshaker. He unscrewed the cap and poured a liberal amount into his hand. Then he dumped it on the leech. Within seconds, the black, jellylike body curled, enabling Dani to pull it from her foot.

She held it up for his inspection. "Now what do I do with it?"

"Here, I'll toss it back into the lake." Brendan held out his hand.

"Gross!" Jodie protested. "You can't put it back in the water!"

"He's dinner for one of those big walleyes swimming around out there." His glance encompassed Dani as he said, "You're not going to let the thought of leeches keep you from swimming, are you?"

"We won't, will we, Jodie?" Dani looked at the girl for confirmation.

It was slow to come. Finally she said, "I guess not if it stays as hot as it is today. Oooh, even more gross—he was sucking your blood. Look." Jodie pointed to a speck of red on Dani's foot.

Dani dabbed at it with her towel. "There. Gone."

"Can you walk okay?" Jodie asked solicitously.

"Of course she can walk," Brendan said.

"It doesn't hurt," Dani concurred.

"It's a good thing Uncle Bren was here."

Dani looked up at him. "Yes, it was. Thanks for the tip about the salt."

"You're welcome," he said, meeting her gaze.

"Now you're going to have to let me cook you dinner. I won't take no for an answer."

"Besides, we need your help to start the grill," Jodie added impishly.

Brendan knew he had no choice. And the truth was, he didn't want to say no. "All right. I'll change my clothes and be right over."

"YOU DON'T ACT like a schoolteacher," Jodie told Dani as they sat inside eating grilled chicken and potato salad.

"I teach French and English and I also coach the soccer team."

"Really? You don't seem like a coach, either," Jodie said.

Brendan had thought the same thing at first, but now he could visualize her with a whistle around her neck, barking out commands. She was much more athletic than she'd initially appeared.

"We took first place in our conference," Dani said proudly. "Do you like to play soccer?"

"I've never done it." Jodie looked down at her protruding stomach and said, "I don't suppose now would be a good time to learn."

Dani smiled. "No, you might want to wait."

"I've never been very good at sports anyway," Jodie said. "What's it like at the school where you teach?"

"It's a boarding school, so the students live there."

"They must separate the boys and the girls."

"Actually it's all girls, no boys."

"Really? I didn't think they had those kinds of schools anymore. I wouldn't want to go there." She made a face.

"Well, there are good reasons for keeping the boys and girls separate when it comes to education."

"Yeah, so girls don't get pregnant," Jodie said, stating the obvious.

"Even though they're separated during the week, they can see each other on the weekends," Dani explained. "What I was going to say is that studies have shown that young women do better academically when they're not in the same classroom with boys."

"Well, yeah, guys can be distracting," Jodie allowed.

Dani hid her smile. "Well, they can be that, but more importantly, it's a perception problem. Oftentimes girls don't want to appear to be smarter than boys for fear boys won't ask them out on a date. I guess it all goes back to the misconception that guys are supposed to be smarter than girls."

Jodie nodded in agreement. "I know what you mean. Girls attract guys because of how they look, not what they know."

"And do you think that's true?"

"Of course it is. The smartest girls in school are not the ones the guys ask to the prom. They ask out the cheerleaders and the dance-line members 'cause they're all cute.'' Jodie's voice held a note of envy.

Brendan remained silent, his ears tuned to the conversation between the two women.

"So you really wouldn't go to an all-girls school if you had the chance?" Dani asked Jodie.

"No way."

"Why not?"

"Because even if I was smart enough to go to one of those fancy private schools, I'd want to stay in public school. It'd be so cool to be number one in the class and know you'd beaten the smartest guy. I wouldn't care if they thought I was a geek."

Brendan finally spoke. "You are smart enough to go to a private school," he said. "Don't forget, I've seen your report cards."

She rolled her eyes. "That was when I was in elementary school. Everyone gets good grades then."

"Not necessarily," Dani refuted. "What makes you think you aren't smart?"

She lowered her eyes. "Well, just look at me."

"If they took points off your IQ for every mistake you made in life, we'd all be in big trouble." Brendan's comment brought a smile to her face. "Even the brightest and smartest people in this world make mistakes."

"He's right," Dani concurred. "Your environment really does play a big role in how well you learn. Given the right opportunities, many students who are often overlooked as just average turn out to be the brightest of the group."

"Well, school and I didn't get along, so it really doesn't matter to me." Again the tough veneer had surfaced. Jodie acted as if she didn't care at all about the subject at hand, but Brendan knew differently.

"You're not planning on going back?" He refused to let the issue die.

"No, and if you're going to give me a lecture on it, you can save your breath," she said sullenly.

Dani pushed back her chair and said, "How about if I get dessert?"

Neither Jodie nor Brendan responded.

"I don't know about the two of you, but I have a sweet tooth that refuses to be deprived of sugar for even one day." She went to the kitchen cupboard and pulled out a package of cookies. "Look. Fudge fluffs."

She brought them back to the table, ripping open the package before setting it down. "Since we're doing dishes the old-fashioned way, we'll forgo the serving plate. Help yourselves."

After a few awkward moments of silence, conversation resumed, this time centered around the delights of chocolate cookies until Jodie began, "Can I ask you something really personal, Dani?"

Brendan held his breath as Dani nodded.

"How old are you?"

"I'm twenty-six."

"And you've never been married?"

She shook her head. "Is that so unusual?"

"Most people I know are either married or living with somebody by the time they're twenty." She paused, then added, "You must have a boyfriend."

"No, not at the moment."

"That's good. At least you don't have to worry about getting pregnant and making all sorts of decisions."

"Jodie, no woman today has to worry about getting pregnant," Dani said. "She can take birth control pills or use any number of methods of contraception."

"Some of it doesn't work," Jodie replied quietly.

"Then you didn't plan to have this baby?" Brendan asked.

"No!" She looked at him as if he'd insulted her. "I didn't want to have sex. Yuck, I don't even like it, but I was worried that if I didn't do it, Dusty wouldn't love me anymore," she confessed sadly.

And now the very reason for her to have sex had created a baby, which more than likely had produced the very results she was trying to avoid. It was a story Brendan had heard repeatedly in his counseling work at the hospital, yet never had it affected him so deeply.

"You haven't heard any news about him, have you?" Jodie asked in a hopeful voice.

Brendan shook his head. "Not yet."

Jodie shoved back her chair and sighed. "I have to go to the bathroom again."

Brendan grabbed his flashlight and accompanied her to the half-moon. Later, when all the dishes had been washed and dried, he walked Jodie back to her cabin. Long after he put out the lantern in his place, he kept thinking about the conversation at dinner. Always his thoughts came back to the men in Dani's life. Who were they and why was she alone this summer?

Then he reprimanded himself. The less he thought about Dani Taylor the better. But as he fell asleep, he kept seeing her figure in that black-and-pink bikini.

When Dani finally answered, she looked sleep-tousled
and so attractive that his insides felt odd.

"Your real estate agent's here," Brendan told her.
"He's out back waiting for you."

"My what?" She looked startled and clutched the sash
on her robe more tightly in a futile effort to emphasize
her outrage.

CHAPTER SEVEN

BRENDAN WAS UP EARLY the following morning. He
needed to make several phone calls—all involving
Jodie. His primary focus was on finding the errant
Dusty, although he was pretty much convinced that
even should the boy be found, he would offer Jodie little
support.

Just as he was about to get into his Geo, a white
pickup pulled into the driveway. Brendan watched as a
tall, thin man wearing a white shirt and black pants
climbed out. He carried a clipboard in one hand, a tape
measure in the other.

"Can I help you?" Brendan asked, wondering if the
stranger was lost.

The man smoothly whipped out a business card from
under the clip and handed it to him. "I'm Ken Patton
from Lakeside Realty. I'm here to do an appraisal on
the property."

Brendan shouldn't have been surprised. Just because
Wilbur had left Dani a letter asking her not to sell the
resort didn't mean she was going to respect his wish.
He glanced at the big house. The curtains were still
closed, which meant Dani was more than likely still
asleep.

"If you wait just a minute, I'll get the owner," he
told the visitor, then marched up the back steps of the
house. He pounded his fist on the door and waited.

When Dani finally answered, she looked sleep-tousled and so attractive that his insides lurched.

"Your real-estate agent's here," Brendan told her. "He's out back waiting for you."

"My what?" She squinted and tightened the sash around her short robe, which only served to emphasize her curves.

"Real-estate agent," he repeated. "You know, the person who's going to help you sell this place." He looked over his shoulder and saw that the man had already started his job. He was busy measuring the outbuildings, jotting notes on his clipboard. "He's doing the outside first, but it won't be long before he's going to want to come inside."

"I don't want him here," she said irritably. "I'm not even dressed yet."

"Then you should have told him to come later in the day."

"You think I called him out here?"

"Didn't you?"

"No! It must have been my father." She shoved a wisp of hair from her eyes. "He's the one who wants me to sell this place."

"It's not about what he wants, Dani. Your grandfather left this land to you."

"I know," she snapped. "And I haven't had a moment's peace since."

It annoyed him that she could sound so ungrateful. Didn't she realize how hard Wilbur had worked to make Sacred Lake so beautiful? His sweat and toil had made the resort what it was today, and all she could think about was the trouble it had brought into her life.

"You read his letter. He didn't leave you this place

so you could turn around and sell it to the highest bidder.''

"I know that," she snapped again. "But what am I supposed to do with it?"

Brendan didn't respond. He couldn't answer that question for fear he might say something he'd regret.

"I'm going into town in case Jodie wonders where I've gone," he said. And with that he departed, leaving Dani to deal with Mr. Patton.

DANI NEEDED TO SPEAK to Louella Hortense, but she didn't want to leave Jodie alone at the resort. When Brendan hadn't returned by noon, she decided she'd show the teenager how to use the CB radio, then drive over to see the executor of Wilbur's estate. She left Jodie sitting in the shade of a white ash tree, listening to a Smashing Pumpkins CD.

Louella welcomed Dani with open arms. "Care for a beer?" she asked, leading the way to her kitchen.

"No, thanks. I just had lunch. So, have you got a few minutes to spare right now? I've got questions...."

Lou pulled out a chair at the kitchen table. "Sure, if you don't mind me working while we talk. I was just about to start my lutefisk. Some folks only serve it at Christmas, but I like it year-round."

"No, go ahead," Dani answered, although she really wasn't sure what lutefisk was.

Lou smiled broadly and patted Dani's hand. "Your grandfather had a real fondness for lutefisk. It was funny. He refused to taste it when I first tried to offer it to him, but once he met your grandmother..." She grinned at Dani with a twinkle in her eye.

"Then you knew my grandfather well?" Dani asked

as Lou pulled a large white package from the refrigerator.

"Oh, yes. We were very good friends." She chuckled. "He was my first boyfriend." She set the package on the counter next to a pot.

"Really?"

"Mmm-hmm. He taught me how to drive. I remember my first lesson. I drove into a tree and he was quite upset. Not because I damaged the car, but because I hurt the tree. He was always concerned with preserving nature."

"And you remained friends even after you broke up?"

"Oh, heavens, yes. Of course, it helped that I liked your grandmother. Everyone did. She came from the city to spend the summer at one of the lakes. Once he met her, it wasn't long before she'd won your grandfather's heart. But that was okay, because if I hadn't broken up with your grandfather, I'd never have met my husband, George." She sighed. "He and Wilbur were good men. I miss them."

She unwrapped the butcher's paper from the package, and Dani saw what looked to be fish fillets. Lou transferred them from the paper to the pot.

"Just what is lutefisk?" Dani asked as the older woman covered the fish with water.

"It's made from *torsk*—which you probably know as cod. It's dried in the sun, then soaked in water for two weeks. I'm going to soak it again in this lye water until it's soft." Lou gestured to the pot. Dani could hardly believe anyone would soak food in lye; she'd thought lye was used in making soap. Her face must have registered her surprise, for Lou said, "The lye water is actually peeled maple wood in water."

Dani nodded. "Do you cook it after that?"

"Not until it's soaked again in clear water overnight. Then it's placed in a cloth and dropped into boiling water. It's served with lots of melted butter."

"And you said Wilbur liked it?"

"Oh, yes." She rinsed her hands and wiped them on a towel dangling from a drawer handle. "It'll take awhile for that to soak, so maybe now's a good time to go over the business papers I have. Let me get them," she said, then disappeared into another room. When she returned, she carried a legal-size brown envelope in one hand and a photo album in the other. "There's all sorts of information in here," she told Dani as she sat down across from her. "He wanted to make sure you understood how he felt about the resort."

"I know he doesn't want me to sell it to developers, and he doesn't think I should modernize."

"All his life he was determined the place should stay a wilderness. I told him and the rest of the folks in that area that they should get electricity out there, but he and the others are a bunch of stubborn old coots. Wouldn't do it."

"Why was that?"

Lou sighed. "Wilbur wanted everything to be as close to nature as possible. He was also a bit of a hermit, and I think maybe he was a little afraid of the changes electric power and the telephone would bring. I can understand about the telephone—I don't have one myself—but power..." She shook her head.

"It *is* difficult to understand," Dani agreed.

"Well, he wasn't alone in his thinking. Must be at least forty or fifty cabins without power on that chain of lakes."

Dani smiled weakly. "I never thought I'd say this,

but I can see why they might be reluctant to do it. You actually feel closer to nature with fewer of the modern conveniences. A walk through the wetlands showed me that. When I saw the beaver dams and wood-duck nests, I almost felt as if I belonged in their world because I wasn't running power lines and cable TV through their habitat. Does that sound strange?''

''No, I think it's probably exactly how your grandfather felt,'' Lou said. ''Some folks like the rustic way of life and others worry that modernization will bring more people to the area. Then the lakes would soon become crowded with motor boats and snowmobiles.''

''Having just said I understand why my grandfather wanted it that way, you're probably going to wonder why I've decided to check with the local power company to see what would need to be done to bring in lines.''

''I'd say you're just being practical.'' Lou smiled. ''If you could get the others on those lakes to chip in, it wouldn't be so costly. But that's the trick—convincing them they need the power.'' She opened the accordion folder and pulled out a stack of papers. ''Now here's all the information you'll need to run the place. You've probably seen this because I photocopied it and sent it to your attorney.''

Dani hadn't seen it, but she didn't tell Lou that. ''Could I?'' she asked, holding out her hand.

Lou handed her the papers and Dani read them with interest.

''Have you seen any of the paperwork from the probate of your grandfather's will?''

Dani shook her head. ''Until recently, my father handled everything.''

''Here's what's left after all the legal expenses have

been paid.'' She handed Dani a balance sheet. ''I paid
the taxes for this year and there were a few other mis-
cellaneous expenses and, of course, Brendan's salary.''

Dani examined the figures Lou gave her. Seeing the
amount of money Brendan was paid nearly had her
gasping. ''Is this all he gets for the whole summer?''

''Yup. It's all he wanted. I told him your attorney
agreed to a much higher figure, but he turned it down.
Said staying at the resort was a fair trade-off for the
work he'd be doing.''

Until she had seen it all written down, Dani hadn't
thought of herself as Brendan's employer. But it was
clear that she was.

For the next half hour, they went over the financial
status of the resort. ''Now that you're officially taking
over the place, I guess I can turn this stuff over to you.''
Lou slid everything back into the folder and tied it.

Then she directed her attention to the photo album.
''Now on to the fun stuff. I should have some pictures
of your grandfather in here. Most of them were taken
when we were teenagers, but I think there are a few
recent ones, too.'' She flipped through several pages,
then shoved the album closer to Dani, her finger pointing to a black-and-white snapshot. ''See. That's your
granddad as a teenager. Wasn't he handsome?''

Dani looked at the young man with his foot up on
the running board of an old car. He was handsome all
right, and familiar in a way she couldn't describe.

Lou pointed out several other photos, including one
in which he was playing a saxophone. ''He played the
sax?''

''Oh, yes, in the school band. It's probably still in a
closet somewhere.''

Dani smiled wistfully. "I played the sax in high school, too."

"You did?"

She nodded. "My father thought I should play the flute, but I insisted on the sax."

"See? There was a reason, wasn't there?" Lou didn't wait for an answer but flipped several pages ahead to a color snapshot of a man with gray hair and a white beard, who was wearing a red flannel shirt and dark slacks. "This was taken last winter. He came over for supper and I made him sit in front of the fire."

"He looks kind," Dani said.

"He was. Look. Here he is with Pete and Vera at Christmas." She fingered a picture of him wearing a white shirt, red suspenders and a bow tie. "You'll have to excuse me just a minute. I need to check my fish."

Dani looked at the photographs for a second time. There was so much character in his face.

She glanced at Lou and saw her lift the lid on the pot, poke at its contents with a large fork, then replace the cover. Next she watched her go to the refrigerator and pull out a second package wrapped in butcher's paper, only this one was smaller. Dani didn't ask what Lou was putting into the second pot on the stove.

She focused her attention on the photo album and noticed several pictures of Brendan, including one in which he and Wilbur were feeding baby ducks off Lou's dock. They looked so content with their feet dangling in the water, the baby ducks huddling around their toes.

"There. In fifteen minutes I'll be ready to mix it up," Lou announced, once more sitting down at the table. "Now, where were we?"

"Brendan and Wilbur were good friends, weren't

they?'' Dani remarked, staring at another picture of the two of them.

"Yes, they were," Lou replied. "That's why I was so pleased when your lawyer said it would be all right for Brendan to take care of the place this summer. Your grandfather would have let him have the cabin for however long he needed it."

"Then I've done something right," Dani said.

Again Lou patted her hand. "You've done lots of things right. Don't let Brendan or anyone else tell you something different. It's not easy being a stranger in Hidden Falls. Tell me something. Why do you call your grandfather Wilbur?"

"Because I had two grandfathers who were a part of my life ever since I can remember. But my birth family…" She hesitated, wanting to find the right words to describe how she felt. "Because I never knew them, they don't feel like family to me. Somehow, if I were to call Wilbur my grandfather, it wouldn't seem right. That probably doesn't make any sense to you." She smiled awkwardly.

"It sounds like a very honest response to me," Lou said with admiration in her tone.

"I guess I should call him my birth grandfather, because that's what he was." Dani flipped through several more pages of photographs, then asked, "What about my birth mother—Bridget? Do you have any pictures of her?"

Before she could answer, a car door slammed and the dogs started barking and Lou jumped up. "Now who do you suppose is here?" She walked out onto the deck and Dani heard her call out, "Well, ain't this a surprise. Come on in."

A few minutes later, Brendan walked through the

door. "Smells like you're making lutefisk," he said to
Lou, wrinkling his nose.

She pointed a finger at him and said to Dani, "He
won't touch the stuff."

"No way," Brendan confirmed, raising both palms
defensively.

To Brendan, Lou said, "I've got to tend the fish.
Keep Dani company while I finish."

"No, it's all right." Dani closed the photo album. "I
should go. I've taken up enough of your time."

"Then I'll have to move my car. I parked behind
you," Brendan told her.

"Both of you sit down and stay awhile," Lou urged.
"Besides, Brendan can't leave without having a beer."
She opened the refrigerator, pulled out a bottle and
twisted off the cap. "How's that generator working for
you?" she asked, setting the beer in front of him.

Brendan took a long sip. "So far so good. It's noisy,
though. That's why Wilbur hated to use it. It drowns
out the sound of the loons."

"If I can get the electric company to bring in power
to the resort, that won't happen," Dani pointed out.

"Getting tired of hauling water to the shower?"
There was a sly grin on his face.

"It's an inconvenience, yes, but that isn't the only
reason I want power. That gas refrigerator isn't safe,"
she answered.

He gave her a puzzled look. "What makes you say
that?"

"Vera told me that there was an accident over on
Little Eagle Lake. She said a couple and their dog died
of poisoning from a malfunctioning gas refrigerator."

"There's no danger as long as you keep it serviced.
Lou, didn't you say you had one for years up there in

the Boundary Waters?'' He turned his head and Dani noticed for the first time a small scar on his neck as well as the one on his jaw.

''Yes, but we kept it outside on the porch for that very reason,'' Lou answered, getting up to check on her pots cooking on the stove. ''I think Dani's right. She should get that place hooked up.''

''I suppose you're going to bring in telephone wires, too.''

She didn't miss the disapproval in his tone. ''I'm thinking about it.''

''We have the CB.''

''Yes, and as long as there's someone within range of another CB, we're all right, but what if there isn't?'' she asked with a lift of her chin.

''She has a good point,'' Lou said.

Dani gave the older woman a grateful glance.

''Does this mean you're selling the place?'' Brendan asked.

''I haven't decided that, either.''

Lou wiped her hands on her apron and said, ''You two are going to have to excuse me. I need to go outside for a few minutes.'' She disappeared out the back door, leaving Dani and Brendan alone.

''Have you been able to find Jodie a place to stay?''

''She wants to go back to Minneapolis, so I'm hoping to get her into a group home there. The good news is that she's on the waiting list, and it looks as if there'll be an opening in the next couple of weeks.''

''So she should be able to move in before the baby comes?''

He nodded, then rubbed the back of his neck. ''She'll probably need to stay at the resort for at least two more weeks—if that's all right.''

"Of course. I enjoy having her around. She's a nice young woman."

"Yes, she is."

"And remarkably mature for her age."

"She's had to be. Poverty's robbed her of her childhood."

"I'd like to help her in any way that I can," Dani said, meaning it.

"Like buying her CDs, water toys and new clothes?"

"If that's what it takes to ease some of the stress she's going through, yes." She refused to be intimidated by the man. "What would you rather I do? Let her sit in the cabin and stare out at the lake? She didn't come to the resort to meditate."

"No, and she's not there to relieve you of your boredom."

"You think I'm amusing myself at her expense?"

"Aren't you?"

"No! Maybe it's time you tell me just what it is I've done to cause you to have such a terrible opinion of me. Is it because I have more money than you think I'm entitled to have? Is it because I inherited a property you don't think I deserve? I don't know how you can say I'm insincere about wanting to help Jodie. You hardly know me, and ever since I got here, you've done nothing but look for reasons not to like me."

He frowned. "You're wrong."

"What's she wrong about?" Lou asked, stepping back inside and catching the tail end of their conversation.

Brendan didn't answer but raised one eyebrow in Dani's direction. She was tempted to say something to Lou Hortense, but had second thoughts. What good would it do to involve the older woman in her trouble with Brendan? And would it be fair to put her in the middle?

"Brendan and I disagree about a few issues, that's all," she answered vaguely.

Lou looked at Brendan. "Is Jodie more of a handful than either of you expected?" she asked, taking a chair at the table.

Dani shrugged. "I enjoy her company."

"I'm not complaining," Brendan acknowledged.

"Then what's the problem?" Lou asked.

"There isn't one," Brendan assured her.

Lou looked at Dani, then back at him. "The resort certainly is big enough for three people," Lou remarked.

"It is," Brendan agreed while Dani nodded.

As if she suddenly remembered the photograph album, Lou said, "Oh, I almost forgot. We were looking for those pictures, weren't we?" Noticing Brendan's curiosity, she added, "Dani wanted to see pictures of Bridget Latvanen." Lou pulled the photo album toward her and flipped through it. "I'm quite certain I don't have any. You see, shortly after I married George, we moved to Duluth. I worked there as a nurse until George got a job as a park ranger in the Boundary Waters, so I was gone when your birth mother was born."

"Then you never knew her?" Dani asked.

"Well, sure, I knew her. When we came to visit, she was here." Lou's face softened. "You're wondering what she was like, aren't you?"

Dani nodded.

"She was a tiny thing with blond hair, blue eyes, and fair-skinned, just like you. Except she wore her hair long—kind of like the pictures you often see of Alice in Wonderland." She studied Dani's face, then said, "I think you look more like your grandmother than your mother.''

Dani blushed under the scrutiny, for she could feel Brendan's eyes on her, as well. She didn't really want to be discussing her birth family while he sat critically appraising her.

''I imagine you're interested in learning more about all of them,'' Lou said.

''The lawyer gave me some information, but yes, I would like to find out more.''

''I'm sorry I don't have more photographs. Have you looked through your grandfather's things? I'm sure he has some in a box somewhere,'' Lou said.

Dani shook her head. How could she tell this woman it didn't feel right to go through a man's personal belongings when she'd never known him? Although he was her biological grandfather, he was a stranger to her.

''Get Brendan to help you,'' Lou suggested.

That was easy for the older woman to say. She didn't realize the tension that existed between her and Brendan. And Brendan didn't look as if he wanted to help her with anything—least of all looking for family photographs. She doubted he regarded her as a member of Wilbur's family.

Which was why she was surprised later that evening when he knocked on the door.

''We should probably talk.''

Dani ushered him inside and gestured toward the leather recliner. ''Can I get you something to drink?'' she asked politely, then sat across from him when he shook his head.

Brendan was amazed at how, in a few short days, Dani had put her mark on the place. A battery-operated boom box sat on the coffee table with several CDs scattered beside it—Shawn Colvin, Fiona Apple and Alanis Morissette. A pair of strappy sandals lay next to the rocker, a flimsy orange shirt dangling across its back. Fresh-cut flowers graced the wooden coffee table. Then there were the books—a stack of them on the end table. One was a travel guide to northern Minnesota, another a *New York Times* bestseller, along with several paperbacks, including one on pregnancy and childbirth.

He rubbed a hand across the back of his neck. "Knowing Wilbur the way I did, I believe he would have wanted me to be the one to answer your questions."

"Did you know my mother?"

"No, but Wilbur often spoke to me about her. How much do you know about her?"

"Very little, other than what the lawyers told me when Wilbur's estate was settled. I know she died in a boating accident several years before he did."

Brendan nodded solemnly.

"She was all he had in life, so when she became pregnant at sixteen, he had difficulty dealing with the situation."

"Are you saying they were estranged?"

"For a while. When she ran away to New York, he went after her." He shook his head in disbelief. "Your grandfather, who'd never been on a plane or driven on a city freeway."

"He told you this?"

Brendan nodded. "He wanted her to come home with him. He told her she could live here at the resort, that he'd help her take care of the baby."

"But she didn't go home."

"No. Your birth father convinced her to stay."

"Do you know who he was?"

"Wilbur told me he was an actor. A man by the name of Kevin Connoy. He and Bridget had met that summer. He had a part in a touring theater production but went back to New York in the fall."

"An actor?" Dani repeated.

Brendan nodded. "He wasn't the kind of man your grandfather wanted dating his daughter for a variety of reasons, but mainly because he worried that she'd quit school and follow him to New York. His fears materialized when she became pregnant. Wilbur confronted her, they had words, and then she left for New York with him. That's when your grandfather hired a private investigator to find them."

"And did he find them?"

"Yes. He went out to see her, but she refused to come home. Told him she was going to get married and live happily ever after in New York. She harbored hopes of making it as an actress on Broadway."

"Did they marry?"

Brendan shook his head. "He was killed in a freak accident backstage at one of the theaters where he was performing. A heavy prop suspended from the ceiling fell on him. After that happened, your grandfather paid her a second visit."

"He went back to New York?"

Brendan nodded. "He told her to come home, but she refused. She liked New York and she was determined to work as an actress. Wilbur sent her money every month. He told her to call him when the baby came. She never did."

"But she must have come back because the adoption agency she used is located in Minnesota," Dani deduced.

"Apparently she returned to Minneapolis right before

the baby was born. She decided the Minneapolis theater community would be a better place than New York for her to get a start."

"Yet she never told her father?"

"Not until after she'd placed you with the adoption agency. At that time, there weren't open adoptions. She had to accept the agency's word that you were with a loving couple."

"I was. They've been very good parents to me," she said emphatically.

"That was where Wilbur found comfort—in the fact that you were happy and living with good people."

"But he didn't approve of the adoption."

"He did, but he had to deal with losing a grandchild. He wanted to get to know you. That's why when Bridget told him she was trying to trace your whereabouts, he gave her the money to do so," he said simply.

"Then they must have reconciled at some point before she died."

He could see the hope in her eyes and he didn't want to disappoint her. "They talked over the phone, but she lived the remainder of her life in Minneapolis. There had to have been a strong love between the two of them or she wouldn't have named you after him."

She gave him a puzzled look. "I don't understand."

"Didn't you know? Wilbur's middle name was Daniel. One of the requests Bridget made when she went to the adoption agency was that your adoptive parents keep the name she'd chosen—Danielle."

Dani picked up a wood carving of a duck. She fingered it carefully, tracing the lines her birth grandfather had whittled with his knife. "You said he sent me letters."

"He told me he did."

"I never received any."

"Would you have answered them if you had?"

She didn't respond right away, but continued to finger the duck. Finally she said, "I'd like to think that I would have. At any rate, it doesn't matter now, does it?"

She met his eyes and he could see the sheen of tears. Brendan wanted to believe that, had Dani come to visit Wilbur, neither one would have been disappointed. He wanted to think she was a caring and compassionate woman who'd never had the opportunity to meet the lonely man who longed for his granddaughter.

"He knew you taught French and English. It made him feel proud to think of you spreading knowledge. He believed in education. Did you know his wife—your grandmother—was a schoolteacher?"

"No." Dani set the wooden duck back down.

"Wilbur was a wise man who saw the beauty of nature and did whatever he could to preserve it."

"I'm sorry I'll never know him," she said sadly.

"Oh, I think you will. All you have to do is look around you."

CHAPTER EIGHT

"WHAT ARE YOU READING?" Dani looked at the young woman sprawled on the blanket in the shade of an oak tree. Except for her protruding belly, she could have been any one of the students at the Marchand Academy for Young Women—freckled face scrubbed clean of makeup, listening to music through earphones.

Jodie pulled them off her head and let them rest around her neck. "It's one of the booklets the doctor gave me. He said it would answer some of my questions about what's going to happen when the baby comes."

"You mean the delivery?" Dani knelt beside her, sitting back on her heels.

Jodie nodded. "Now that it's getting closer, I'm feeling a little scared."

"I guess it is a little scary when you've never done it before."

"I know it's going to hurt. My friend, Shawna, told me she thought she was going to die, the pain was so bad. And did you know that if the baby's head is too big, they sometimes have to cut you down there?" She grimaced.

Dani didn't comment.

"One time, I went with Shawna to her prenatal classes at the hospital and they showed this movie of a woman having a baby. I mean, they showed *everything.*

It was so gross.'' She shuddered. ''There was so much blood I had to close my eyes.''

Dani, too, had seen films on childbirth when she'd taken a college biology class so could understand why the teenager had had such a reaction. Still, she didn't want Jodie to worry about what lay ahead of her. ''Well, you know, it's different for everyone,'' she said optimistically. ''And I think it looks worse on film than it really is.''

''You can get drugs if you want, but it's not supposed to be that good for the baby. I'm going to try to do it without any.''

''I understand there are breathing techniques you can use during labor to help you cope with the pain.''

''You think they really work?''

''I've heard women say they do. And I don't think they would have classes on them if they were useless, do you?''

''Probably not.'' Jodie flipped through the pages of the book. ''It tells how to do them in this booklet. I was thinking about trying them, but you can't do it without a partner.''

''I can help you practice,'' Dani offered.

''It's really nice of you to say that, but it says here you should have the person who's going to be with you in the delivery room. I'm going to have my baby in Minneapolis so Dusty can be there with me.''

Dani's heart contracted. ''I'll tell you what. Why don't we practice anyway? That way, at least, you'll know what to do and you can always tell Dusty what he needs to do when the time comes.''

''You really want to?''

''Sure.'' Dani took the book from her hands and read the section on breathing. ''This doesn't sound too complicated. The key is to focus on your breathing so that you're distracted from the pain and the anxiety. When you relax and conserve your energy, then you'll feel more in control. Want to give it a try?''

Jodie's smile was a bit shaky. "Sure, if you think it'll work."

"Wait here and I'll get you some pillows." Dani scooted into the house, grabbed a couple of pillows from the bed and returned to Jodie. "Why don't you roll over onto your side? You can use these as cushions." Dani knelt beside her, holding the booklet out in front of her. "Now I want you to breathe in and out, concentrating on what I'm saying. Okay, inhale through your nose, imagining cool, pure air, then exhale through your mouth and imagine all your tension blowing away."

"Like this?" Jodie took in slow, deep breaths and let them out.

They'd reached the instruction on "pattern-pace" breathing and Jodie was in the middle of a "ha-ha-ha-hoo" and a "hee-hee-hee-hoo" when Brendan arrived.

"Do I dare speak or will I break your concentration?" he asked.

Jodie rolled over onto her back with a sigh. "Dani's helping me practice breathing so it won't hurt as bad when I go into labor."

"I'm coaching," Dani said, giving a smile that did funny things to Brendan's insides. "Looks like you stopped at Vera and Pete's." She eyed the huge watermelon in his hands.

"Yeah. I had to make some phone calls. I hope you two like watermelon," he returned.

"I love it," Jodie said, still flat on her back.

"Me, too," Dani said.

"Oh, good!" Jodie declared. "We can have a seed-spittin' contest." She rolled to her side so she could get to her feet.

"A seed-spitting contest?" Brendan raised an eyebrow.

She nodded eagerly. "Get a knife and we'll cut it up right now."

"I'll get some plates, too," Dani offered, then disappeared into the house while Brendan set the watermelon in the center of the wooden picnic table.

"Dani's cool, isn't she, Uncle Bren?" Jodie said, straddling the picnic bench.

"Cool how?" Brendan asked innocently.

"You know what I mean," she said with a sly grin.

"Are you asking me if I think she's attractive?"

"Do you?"

"Well, sure. All of God's children are beautiful," he said, tongue in cheek.

She slapped him playfully on the arm. "Come *on*. You *know* what I mean."

He chose not to respond but instead changed the subject. "It'll be a week tomorrow since you went to see the doctor. I believe he said you need to be checked again."

"Why? I feel fine and the baby's not due for another three weeks," she protested.

"Doesn't hurt to take precautions."

"Precautions about what?" Dani asked when she returned carrying a long knife, three plates and a stack of napkins.

"Her health," Brendan replied. "She needs to see Dr. Sellers again."

"I know you're in the middle of painting the shed,

so why don't I take her?'' Dani offered, handing the knife to Brendan.

"You don't mind?"

"Uh-uh. What do you say, Jodie?"

"I don't want to go," the teen grumbled.

"It's important for your baby," Dani reminded her gently.

Brendan glanced up and saw that the top button on Dani's blouse had come undone. He needed to concentrate on the job at hand or he could very well risk cutting off a finger, especially considering the effect Dani had on his nerves. When they each had a slice, he asked, "So where do we spit these seeds?"

"Maybe we should spit them into the woods," Dani suggested.

Both Jodie and Brendan seconded the idea. The three of them walked over to the area behind the first cabin and spaced themselves about two feet apart in a line facing the trees.

"Okay, we'll see who hits the most trees," Dani stated.

They ate the watermelon, pausing frequently to spit the seeds. Brendan could see that it took several bites for Dani to lose her inhibitions about spitting anything from her mouth in front of other people. Not so Jodie, who not only ate fast, but spit far and accurately.

When they were finished, Jodie was declared the winner. She proudly raised her hands in triumph, then asked for a second slice of watermelon.

"But save it till I get back, Uncle Bren. I need to go to the bathroom." With that, she headed for the half-moon.

"That was...interesting," Dani said, wiping watermelon juice from her chin.

"I thought maybe I was going to have to get you a fork," Brendan teased as they headed back to the picnic table.

"It was my first time."

"Really? You never spit seeds as a kid?"

She shook her head. "Although now I can see that I'll have to feature this at my next party. It's a way to loosen people up, isn't it?"

"You don't strike me as the type who needs any help in that direction," he said. "You make people feel at ease."

"You think so?"

"Yeah. And you're a good sport. I bet you're popular with your students."

"I like kids, especially adolescents. They have so much energy. They're on the brink of discovery—trying to figure out who they are, where they're going, how they're going to get there, yet still maintaining an innocence most adults long ago traded in for cynicism."

They were seated at the picnic table across from each other and Brendan noticed, not for the first time, how beautiful her eyes were. At first he'd thought they were blue, but now he saw they were actually blue-green and fringed with long brown lashes. Her blond hair had not a trace of dark roots, so he knew it must be natural. She had the Nordic coloring so many Minnesotans had.

"What about you? Do you like kids?"

Her question brought an unwanted flash of memory. Caroline had asked him that same thing the first time he'd asked her out on a date. And with good reason. She was the eldest of six, and they were seldom alone whenever they were at her house. That was the reason she had wanted to delay starting a family when they had married. There would be plenty of time for children, she'd told him. Only there hadn't been.

"Yeah, I like kids," he admitted, trying not to think about what might have been with Caroline. It was too painful, even after all this time.

"Judging by the way you relate to Jodie, I'd say you'd probably make a good teacher."

The smile on Dani's face was friendly, not flirtatious, yet Brendan found his body reacting as if she was making a pass at him. He hadn't been very nice to her, yet she resiliently made an effort to be cheerful around him.

"I have a degree in education," he admitted with a grin that *was* flirtatious.

"Really?"

"Mmm-hmm."

Her attention was distracted by a movement in the woods. "Oh, look! There's a deer over there."

Brendan followed the direction of her gaze. "That's because I put corn out for them. They're getting bolder about coming when people are around."

"Ooh, I wish I had my camera. I suppose by the time I get it, it'll be gone."

Brendan liked the way her eyes lit up at the sight of the deer. Liked the way she appreciated nature.

"I've found that photographs can't capture the magic of actually being close to such an incredibly beautiful animal," he said almost reverently.

"Mmm. I know what you mean. There really is something about the peace and tranquillity of nature that's very soothing to the soul. It's almost therapeutic being here."

"Well, it hasn't exactly been tranquil, has it? Not with Jodie's sudden appearance. Those phone calls I made today when I was in town..." He sounded uneasy.

"Did you find Dusty?" she asked.

"Father Dorian located him. It was as I suspected. He's in Minneapolis, not on the road, and he claims he's not the father."

"Certainly a blood test can prove that," she said.

"I doubt he'll be around to take one. Father Joe said he heard from the other kids on the street that Dusty was planning to disappear since he was already in trouble with the law. He's the kind of kid who's always on the move. When he gets in trouble in one place, he takes off for another."

Dani sighed. "Jodie's counting on him being there for her."

"He wouldn't be much help if he was," Brendan said soberly.

"No, but now she'll have to go through this alone." Dani's brow furrowed.

"She needs to make some decisions."

"You want her to give the baby up for adoption, don't you?"

It was said in an accusatory tone. Brendan didn't want to argue with Dani about Jodie's options, yet he didn't understand why she would think a sixteen-year-old in Jodie's position should keep her baby.

"Yes, I do. Considering her circumstances, I think it's the best thing for both mother and child."

"I see." Dani didn't disagree with him but simply tugged on her lip with her teeth.

Brendan wondered if her view of the situation was obscured by her own history. Her birth mother had given her up for adoption, and she'd never had the opportunity to know her. Was that why she'd taken a defensive posture whenever the subject of Jodie's baby arose?

Of one thing he was certain. The decision Jodie had to make about her child was an emotional issue for Dani. It had changed the whole tone of their conversation. He wanted to recapture the easy camaraderie that had existed between them before the discussion of Jodie's predicament had come up. From the set of her shoulders, he could see it wasn't possible.

Later, when he was alone, he tried to concentrate on reading, but it was useless. All he could think about was Dani. The sparkle in her eyes when she'd spotted the deer. The glimpse of flesh he'd caught when her button had come undone on her shirt.

It was going to be a long summer.

INSTEAD OF A SHOWER the following morning, Dani opted for a swim. The water was surprisingly warm. She wasn't sure if it was because the air was cool, which made the water feel warm, or if after so many cold showers, the lake was beginning to feel warm in comparison.

Brendan was nowhere in sight. She'd hoped he might see her swimming and join her. He didn't.

Since Jodie was sleeping in, Dani ate breakfast alone on the deck. Still there was no sign of Brendan. She suspected he had either gone for a morning walk or taken a bike ride. To her surprise, he'd done neither. As she gazed out at the water, she saw a boat come round the bend. In it was Brendan, rowing toward the shore.

When he pulled the boat up onto the sandy beach, she walked down to meet him. He reached inside and pulled out a wire-mesh basket. "Dinner," he told her, holding up his catch for her perusal.

"What are they?"

"Sunfish. Very tasty when panfried." He motioned

for her to follow him behind cabin number three where the fish-cleaning shed was located. "This building has but one purpose," he told her as he stepped into the partially screened wood frame. Dani watched as he pulled a leather-encased knife from a nail on the wall. "We need newspaper and a bucket of water."

"What do you mean *we?*"

"I thought you'd want to help," he said, a hint of challenge in his dark eyes.

She looked down at the basket of fish. Some of them were flipping and flopping against the wire mesh. "You mean you're going to clean them while they're still alive?"

"They won't be breathing once we cut into them."

She had the suspicion that he expected her to flee. Well, she was about to prove him wrong. "I'll get the newspaper. You get the bucket of water," she told him. A short while later, she had a bowl of sunfish fillets chilling in the refrigerator. "Aren't you going to ask me if I know how to cook them?" she asked as they washed up at the kitchen sink.

Amusement sparked in his eyes. "Do you know how to cook them?"

"No, but I bet Lou could tell me." She got on the CB radio and contacted the ex-park ranger, who was all too happy to explain the ritual involved in panfrying the fish. By the time Dani had signed off the airwaves, she had the instructions written on the back of an envelope.

"Those fish are my peace offering," Brendan said. "I think I may have misjudged you and I'm sorry."

The apology was so unexpected she was speechless for a moment. Then she said, "Apology accepted."

He was standing close—so close she could smell the scent of his aftershave. It was easier not to be aware of him as a man when he was being cool toward her. Then she could ignore the fact that he was one of the most attractive men she'd ever met. But now that he was treating her nicely...

"A man who apologizes...it's a rarity these days," she added lightly.

"You sound as if you've run into your share of the wrong kind of men." He cast a curious eye in her direction.

"More than a few. I think I must send out radar that attracts the losers of this world."

"I'm sure you attract all sorts of men."

She couldn't tell if he was flirting with her or not. "Are you asking me about the men in my life?"

"*Is* there a particular man in your life?"

"Not at the moment." She decided to be a bit bold. "I suppose you wish there was."

"Why do you say that?"

"Because I bet you're thinking that if I had a guy in California, at least I wouldn't be here invading your solitude. I know you only came to the resort because you thought you were going to be alone. Instead, it's been one distraction after another."

He shrugged and grinned. "Maybe I need the distraction."

This time, she could see that he was flirting with her and she liked it. A lot.

"Am I a distraction?"

"Yes. A nice one."

He was looking at her the way a man looks at a woman he desires, and it was enough to make her tingly all over. Her eyes moved to the vee opening of his shirt collar and caught sight of a gold cross. It reminded her that he wasn't just an ordinary single guy.

"Why did you decide to become a priest?" The question slipped from her lips almost automatically.

She could see it caught him off guard. "That's not an easy thing to answer."

"I'm sorry. I shouldn't have asked it." She felt a little embarrassed.

"No, it's all right. The problem is, I'm not sure I know why I entered the seminary. I thought it was because I had a calling."

"But now you're not so sure?" she prodded gently.

He sighed and turned away from her, taking a seat on one of the stools at the kitchen counter. "It's funny how fast things can change. Until a few weeks ago, it was an open-and-shut case. One more year and then I'd be ordained. Now..." He gave an expressive shrug.

"You still might go back?" She didn't realize how she was holding her breath while she waited for his reply.

"I might."

It wasn't the reply she wanted to hear.

He rubbed a hand over the back of his neck. "In the neighborhood where I grew up, there was a man named Joseph Dorian. He was our parish priest and he was also the reason I spent more time at the youth center in the basement of the church than I did in school."

"He's the one you called when you were looking for Dusty?"

He nodded. "He's not only been a mentor for me, but a good friend. If it hadn't been for him, I could very easily have ended up in jail. Put any kid in a neighborhood where drug lords rule the streets and there's gunfire every night, and there's no telling what will happen. But the point is, I did survive, thanks to Father Joe, and

I thought I could make the same kind of difference in another neighborhood that had kids like me.''

''You don't think you can do it without being a priest?''

''That's one of the things I'm asking myself.''

Before they could say any more, Jodie was at the door, expecting to be taken to her doctor appointment. Brendan slid off the stool and went in search of a paintbrush and paint. Dani climbed into the Explorer and headed for the clinic.

While she drove, her thoughts were on Brendan. He was attracted to her just as much as she was to him. She'd seen it in his eyes. Was she a fool to even think about acting on that attraction? Come September, he could return to the seminary. That alone should have been enough of a deterrent to keep her from thinking such thoughts.

It wasn't.

JODIE WAS QUIET on the way to her appointment. Dani figured it probably had something to do with the fact that Brendan had told her Dusty was planning on leaving town and probably wouldn't return. On the way home from the clinic, however, Jodie was eager to talk.

''Do you think you could speak to my uncle for me?'' she asked.

''About what?'' Dani asked cautiously.

''Well, I've been thinking about the baby. I've decided I want to keep it even though he says Dusty won't be here to help take care of us.''

''And you don't think your uncle will approve?''

Jodie made a negative sound. ''He thinks I should give the baby up for adoption.''

''And that isn't what you want?''

The girl chewed on her lower lip. "I don't know. Every time I think I've made up my mind, something happens and I change it. I mean, there are good reasons for me to keep this baby."

Dani could see she was trying to convince as much herself as Dani.

"I could be a good mother."

"I believe you could," Dani agreed, keeping her eyes on the road in front of her.

Jodie pushed her bangs off her forehead. "Dusty did promise he'd always take care of me. I think Uncle Bren is wrong. As soon as Dusty saves up enough money, he's going to come back for me."

Dani could see how desperately Jodie was trying to build a case in favor of keeping the baby. She wasn't sure what she should say to this confused young woman, especially now that Brendan had told her about her own birth mother. Bridget Latvanen had probably had the same fears and hopes that Jodie had.

"Being a parent is a huge responsibility," Dani reflected, the words surprising her as much as Jodie.

"I thought you wanted me to keep the baby," she said sulkily. "You're just as bad as my uncle." She shrank away, huddling close to the door.

"I'm not saying you shouldn't keep your baby, Jodie." So what *was* she trying to say? It wasn't a black-and-white issue, as Brendan wanted it to be, and she tried to explain that to the teen. "I just want you to be able to make a decision you're going to be able to live with. I'm not sure there's a right and a wrong here."

"That's why I'm so confused," Jodie moaned, dropping her head into her hands. "I swear, Dani, sometimes it's just like running around in a circle. One day I decide

I should go through with the adoption and the next day I feel like the meanest person alive to even think about giving up my baby.''

"It's not mean to want what's best for your baby. And that's what you really want, isn't it?"

"Yeah. I'm trying to be unselfish. I know I don't have enough money to buy all the stuff a baby needs."

"A child *is* expensive."

"And one thing I don't want is for my baby to have to know what it's like to be poor. But then there's another part of me that says no one's going to love this baby the way I would." Unconsciously her hand moved to her stomach. "I know it's not going to be easy giving this baby everything it needs, but giving it to strangers is so scary."

"They don't have to be strangers. Didn't Brendan say you could meet with the adoptive parents?"

"Yeah, but they're still going to be strangers."

"Who will give your baby a loving home."

"You think so?"

"I know so. You see, I'm adopted."

"You are?"

Dani nodded. "And I had a wonderful childhood. I loved my parents and I wouldn't have changed a thing."

"It didn't bother you that you were adopted?"

"No," Dani answered honestly. "I never looked at my mother and father as my adoptive parents. They were just my parents."

"Do you know what happened to your real mother?"

"I do now, but because of the way adoption laws worked twenty-six years ago, she didn't know where I was and I didn't know who she was. A few years ago, she made a search and found out where I was living, which is why I inherited this place. It belonged to my grandfather.''

"So did you get to meet her?"

"No. She and my grandfather both died before that happened.''

"Oh, that's sad.''

"In a way it is, but I'm learning quite a lot about them now," Dani answered. ''That wouldn't necessarily be the case with you because you can choose the adoptive parents.''

"All my friends think a baby is better off with its real mother even if she *is* poor.'' Jodie's voice reflected her uncertainty.

"And do you agree?''

The teenager shrugged. ''Well, yeah, but I've been in homeless shelters and seen women there with babies, and one thing I promised myself is that I would never take my baby to one of those places.''

"I can understand that.''

"Uncle Bren thinks I should move into a group home for teens.''

"Would that be so bad?''

"You've never lived in one, have you?''

Dani shook her head.

"It's not that it's bad exactly, but I want a place of my own. That's why I want my uncle to lend me the money to get into an apartment.''

Dani felt her heart swell with sympathy. It would have been so simple for her to offer the girl the money herself, yet she knew it wouldn't be a solution to Jodie's problems. ''And after the first two months' rent was gone, what would you do? You'd have to get a job, find day care—''

"Oh, just forget it. I don't want to talk about it right now." She leaned her head back and closed her eyes.

Dani felt pulled in two different directions. Logically she knew adoption was the better choice for Jodie, yet she understood why it was such a difficult decision to make. She wondered how her own birth mother had ever found the courage to do it alone.

BRENDAN SHOULD have been happy. He had the entire resort to himself. True to her word, Dani had taken Jodie to the clinic in Hibbing.

Still, he wasn't happy. From the moment he'd opened his eyes, he'd been restless. He attributed it to the uncomfortable humidity, which had risen to an almost tropical level. Very seldom did one need air-conditioning at the resort, but if the temperature continued to climb...

Besides the weather, something else was starting to bother him. Although the spartan surroundings had always seemed fitting for meditation and prayer, for a guy who no longer was at the resort strictly as a seminarian, they now seemed primitive. He didn't consider himself a materialistic guy, but he wanted running hot water and electricity. Discontented. That was a good word to describe his state of mind and he knew there was more than one reason for it.

By noon, the air was sultry and he was even more restless. He decided to take a quick run into town for one of Vera's hamburgers and a chat with Pete. While there he learned that the weather center had issued a severe thunderstorm watch for the Hidden Falls area.

It didn't surprise Brendan. With the heat and humidity, one could almost smell a storm brewing. As soon as he got back to the cabin, he pulled on his swim trunks and went for a dip in the lake. As he floated on his back, he recalled what it had been like playing in the water with Dani and Jodie. Fun. It had been a long time since he'd had such fun.

He liked being with Dani. But he realized that something was happening between them that shouldn't be happening. Emotions were flowing, trust was building, and attraction was growing. For the first time since Caroline had died, he had feelings for a woman. Out of habit, he tried to stifle them but realized he couldn't.

Instead of getting dressed, he stayed in his trunks and stretched out on the rope hammock suspended between two trees. Not a breeze ruffled the heavy air as he tried to concentrate on the book in his hand.

The sound of tires crunching on gravel alerted him to Dani's return. As tempting as it was to meet her, he resisted the urge and stayed in the hammock. It wasn't long before Jodie appeared.

"Hey, Uncle Bren, we're back."

"And what did the doctor have to say?"

She shrugged. "Nothing much. He doesn't think the baby's going to come for a while."

"You want to go for a swim, or did the leeches scare you away?" he asked with a grin.

"I don't know. I feel kinda funny."

He swung his legs over the side of the hammock and sat upright. "Funny how?"

Again she shrugged. "I've got a backache, for one thing. Dani thought it was from riding in the car."

"Maybe the water would feel good, then."

"Uh-uh. I think I'd rather take a nap."

"All right. I'll call you when dinner's ready." It had become a regular occurrence for the three of them to eat dinner together. At first Brendan hadn't liked it, but now he found himself looking forward to it.

Since it was so hot, Dani suggested they have a light supper—the fish Brendan had caught earlier that day, salad, watermelon and the sourdough bread she'd picked up in town. Although Jodie did get up to eat, she only picked at her food, telling Brendan and Dani that she still felt funny.

"You don't have any pains anywhere, do you?" Dani asked, concerned.

"Uh-uh, just my back aches. But that happens a lot. Shawna said she had a backache the whole time she was pregnant."

Both Brendan and Dani dismissed the complaint as a typical symptom of pregnancy. While they were eating, Lou called over the CB radio to tell them the weather service had confirmed that a severe thunderstorm was headed their way.

It wasn't long before the dark clouds rolled in. "Why is the sky that ugly green color?" Jodie asked as she and Dani did the dishes.

Brendan, who'd been watching the changes in the sky, said, "That a storm's coming any minute now. I'm going to run back and close the windows in the other cabins."

In the short time it took him to accomplish that task, the sky had darkened so much they needed indoor light. He grabbed a kerosene lantern and hurried back to Wilbur's place.

No sooner had he gotten inside than the wind blew the door shut, producing a shriek from Jodie. "This is spooky," she said as trees whistled in the wind, bending at almost ninety-degree angles.

"I think we should go into the storm cellar," Brendan said, waving for them to follow him.

"Where is it?" Dani asked on a note of panic.

"Outside. Grab one of the lanterns and follow me."

They filed outside, clinging to each other's hands as the wind howled around them. The entrance to the storm cellar was a metal trapdoor at the back of the house. Brendan held it open and motioned for Dani and Jodie to go ahead of him. He could see the fear on both their faces when he joined them inside the small shelter. It wasn't even as big as the sauna, though there were benches that allowed six people to sit comfortably.

"Are there bugs in here?" Jodie asked, huddling fearfully in a corner.

Before Brendan could answer, thunder boomed overhead and rain began to pelt the metal door. "It sounds worse than it is," he assured them, noting their wide eyes. "Rain always sounds worse on metal."

There were no windows so they couldn't see what was happening outside. All they could do was listen to the roar of the wind and the pounding of the rain.

"Does this happen often?" Dani asked.

Brendan considered saying yes. It might have been a way to get Dani Taylor to pack up and go home to California. Only problem was, he didn't want her to go. And he hated to see the apprehension in her eyes.

"No. I only know about this place because your grandfather showed it to me once, just in case there was a bad storm and he wasn't here," Brendan answered. "It's not uncommon to have a thunderstorm in the summer, but they're usually not severe."

"I hope it's not a tornado," Jodie whined.

"They're pretty rare this far north," Brendan said confidently.

"Are you sure?" Dani's face grew white. "It sounds so loud."

He wasn't sure, but he didn't need two hysterical females on his hands. He tried to distract them by telling stories of his work as a pinsetter, comparing their small space to the area he and a friend had to work in at a bowling alley when he was only fourteen. They didn't find his tales amusing. Finally he said, "The storm sounds as if it's letting up."

They sat for a little while longer, then Brendan decided to brave a peek outside. As he opened the door, a bolt of lightning lit the sky, but the rain had diminished and was no longer a heavy downpour.

"The worst is over," Brendan announced, then closed the door again. "We'll give it a few more minutes, then we'll go back to the house."

"I don't feel very good," Jodie said. Her face was pale.

Brendan looked at Dani as if she should have an explanation. "I wonder if she ate something that didn't agree with her," Dani said in an aside to him. "I hope it wasn't the fish."

"You probably need some rest, Jodie," Brendan said soothingly, putting his arm around his niece's shoulders. "It's been a long day."

"I feel funny," she said for the third time.

"What does funny mean?" Dani asked. "You're sure you're not having any pains?"

"I told you—just a backache."

Brendan stood. "Come on. I'll walk with you to the cabin and you can go to bed."

"But Dani was going to show me how to play canasta," she protested.

"We'll do it tomorrow, Jodie," Dani said reassuringly, following the two of them up the steps.

As they stepped outside, Brendan could see that it had been a powerful storm. Now that it was over, it was light once again, although the sun was sinking fast. Leaves and branches littered the ground. Several lawn chairs had been blown over. A large silver maple in front of cabin number two had split in two.

"One thing about not having any power—you don't have to worry about losing it when a storm hits," Brendan said in an attempt at humor.

"Thank goodness the house wasn't damaged." Dani scrutinized the log home. "Hopefully none of the cabins was, either."

"I'll have to check all the roofs to make sure they didn't lose any shingles," Brendan told them. "It's still raining, and we don't want any leaks."

"Look at how calm everything is now," Jodie said. "If it wasn't for the fallen branches and stuff, you wouldn't even know we'd had a storm." As she climbed the steps to her cabin, she rubbed her lower back. "Ouch!"

"I'll let you help her," Brendan said to Dani, relinquishing the hold on his niece. "While you put her to bed, I'll get the ladder and check the roofs."

By the time he'd checked all the buildings, he was wet to the skin and dusk was only minutes away. As he carried the ladder back to the shed, he saw Dani standing in the doorway of the house waiting for him. "Stop in when you're finished, would you?" she asked when he passed.

As he grabbed a dry shirt from his cabin, Brendan assumed she wanted to talk about Jodie. He was wrong. When he stepped into the house, she handed him a beer and said, "Sit down." He took a seat on the sofa. Instead of sitting across from him, she dropped down beside him. "I think after what we went through today, we both deserve something stronger than lemonade." He saw that she, too, had a beer in her hand.

That wasn't all he saw. Her top was skinny—almost too skinny for the size of her. And her shorts exposed a long length of leg. There was a smudge of dirt on one thigh—from being in the storm cellar, no doubt.

"Oh! You're cut!" she exclaimed, picking up his hand.

He hadn't noticed. It must have happened when he was using the metal ladder. It was just a small scrape with a little dried blood, but she acted as if it needed stitches. She jumped up and disappeared only to return with a first-aid kit and a wet cloth.

She dabbed at the abrasion with the cloth, then sprayed it with some disinfectant. "Does that hurt?" she asked.

There was only one part of him aching and it wasn't his hand. Her nearness, her touch on his hand, were enough to send his blood rushing and his heart pounding. She was one beautiful woman and she was fussing over him as if he were mortally wounded.

He wanted to kiss her. And when his eyes met hers, he could see she wanted to kiss him. It was there in the air. In what they didn't say. In what they didn't do. It had been a long time since Brendan had kissed a woman. But it was one of those things a person never forgot. What he did forget was why he shouldn't be kissing Dani Taylor.

His mouth brushed hers. Gently. Sweetly. Moved over hers in a sensuous exploration that was exquisitely tender. She shifted closer to him, her lips parting beneath his in an invitation to intimacy. He didn't hesitate to deepen the kiss, and a small sound of pure pleasure came from her throat. His whole body trembled as he felt himself being swept into an incredible flood of sensations. Just as his body ached for more, she pulled back.

It only took him a second to realize why. There was a pounding on the door. Brendan glanced over and saw Jodie in her nightgown.

"Something's wrong—I'm leaking."

CHAPTER NINE

DANI USHERED the trembling girl inside. "What do you mean, you're leaking?"

"Look." She turned around and the entire lower half of her nightgown was wet. "I was lying there on the bed and suddenly all this stuff just gushed out!"

"Your water broke."

"What does that mean?"

"Didn't you read those pamphlets the doctor gave you?"

"Not all of them..." Jodie looked at her anxiously. "Is this bad?"

"No, it happens to women before they go into labor."

"You mean the baby's coming?" she asked.

Brendan's eyes widened. "I thought you said the doctor told you it wasn't going to happen for another three weeks."

"He did!" Jodie exclaimed, her voice rising an octave. "Maybe something else is wrong!"

Dani put an arm around her and gave her a reassuring squeeze. "Calm down. Everything's fine. We're going to take you to the hospital and let the doctor check you out. First you need to get dressed and pack a few things—like your toothbrush."

"Omigod! You think I'm going to have the baby tonight, don't you?"

Dani could hear the hysteria in her voice. "We don't know that. I'm going to try contacting Lou." She walked over to the CB, but there was static blocking the transmission. "I can't get through, so we'd better take you to the hospital." She urged Jodie toward the door. "Do you need me to help you get your things together?"

The girl nodded, her lower lip quivering.

"We should probably take my car," Dani told Brendan. "That way, she can stretch out on the back seat." He nodded, and she followed Jodie out the door into the darkness where lightning still flickered in the distance.

There was little in Jodie's gym bag besides a small stuffed bear, a CD player and several CDs. Dani grabbed a change of clothing, a nightgown, the few toiletries on the dresser and a pillow and blanket from the bed, then carried the canvas bag to the car while Jodie waddled along beside her.

Brendan was waiting for them, the back door on the vehicle flung open. "Oh, I'm getting a really bad pain," Jodie cried, doubling over. "I think it's a contraction."

Dani helped her into the car. "Try to relax. It'll pass."

"But it *hurts*," the girl moaned.

When Dani was about to climb in on the driver's side, Brendan stopped her. "Maybe I should drive."

"I'm capable of getting us there safely," she told him as raindrops splattered on the roof of the Explorer.

"I know you are. I was thinking that if I drove, you could help Jodie do those breathing exercises."

"Good idea." Dani hurried around to the passenger side. Instead of taking the front seat, she slid in back with Jodie, who was moaning in pain. She knelt on the floor beside her.

"It really hurts, Dani!"

"All right, then we need to get you to focus on something other than the pain." She looked around the interior of the car and finally said, "Now remember, you have to try to relax—especially your jaw. Let me know when a contraction starts."

"It hurts," Jodie wailed again.

"Listen to me, Jodie. Breathe. In one-two, out one-two, in one-two, out one-two—"

"It's not working," Jodie cried. "The pain's getting worse."

Dani could see perspiration beading on the girl's forehead. "Don't worry. Everything's fine. We just have to work harder."

"Son of a gun," she heard Brendan exclaim as he slammed on the brakes.

"Why are we stopping?" Dani asked.

Brendan didn't answer, but put the car in park and climbed out. Dani looked out the windshield and saw the reason. An enormous tree had fallen across the road. Brendan was trying to shove it aside, but Dani could see it was futile. There was no way the car was going to get through.

Brendan returned to the car, winded, his hair and clothes peppered with rain. "We're going to have to go back and try the CB again. Maybe Lou can get Earl to come move the tree." He turned the vehicle around and started back toward the cabin.

"What's going to happen to me?" Jodie wailed.

"Shh. Everything will be fine," Dani said calmly, although she herself was fighting rising panic. "We'll get a message to Lou somehow and she'll get Earl to bring his tow truck and then Brendan will be able to get through."

"I don't think we have enough time," Jodie agonized.

"Sure we do." Dani patted her hand reassuringly. "Here. I'll time your contractions. That way, Lou can call the doctor with the information. and find out what we should do." It was silent in the vehicle except for Jodie's moans and groans. Finally Dani looked up from her watch and announced, "They're five minutes apart."

"Omigod. That means the baby's coming, doesn't it?" Jodie shouted. "Am I going to have it here in the car?"

"You're not going to have it in the car," Dani said calmly. "Even when contractions are five minutes apart, you usually have plenty of time to get to the hospital."

Of course, the question was, were they going to be able to get through to the road that would take them there? Once they were back at the resort, Brendan ran inside to get an umbrella before helping Jodie into the house. Dani insisted she lie on the double bed while Brendan worked the CB radio.

Again, static jammed the lines. Frustrated, Brendan ended the transmission. "It's no use. I can't understand a word she's saying and I doubt she can understand me."

"What are we going to do? Jodie needs to get to the hospital," Dani said in a low voice.

"I'm going to ride my bike over to Lou's." Brendan strode over to the closet with Dani following behind. "I should be able to lift it over the downed tree and continue on the road."

"You can't ride a bike in weather like this!" Dani protested.

"It's just a little rain. It's the only chance we have of getting her out of here tonight." Dani watched him sift through the clothes in her grandfather's closet to find some rainwear. He pulled out a green rain jacket and matching pants, then yanked them on, drawing the hood up over his wet hair. "Do you think you'll be all right until I get back?"

Dani nodded weakly, wanting nothing more at that moment than for him to stay and comfort the both of them. But she knew she couldn't ask him to do that. He needed to get help for Jodie.

"We're stuck here, aren't we?" Jodie asked when Dani went to check on her.

"For now we are, but your uncle's riding his bike over to Lou's."

"How long will that take?"

"Not very long," Dani said vaguely. As she thought about all the obstacles Brendan could face, sudden fear gripped her heart. "Now let's work on your breathing to see if we can make you more comfortable during these early stages of labor."

However, it soon became apparent to Dani that Jodie wasn't in early labor. She was well advanced, and the contractions came closer and closer together until finally she quit timing them.

"Where are your books, Jodie?" she asked urgently.

"You mean the baby books?"

"The ones the doctor gave you. I want to go over them so I know what to do," she answered.

"They're in the top dresser drawer in the cabin," Jodie answered breathlessly.

Dani grabbed a flashlight and the umbrella, then flew

out the door, running all the way to Jodie's cabin. Once inside, she quickly located the information she needed. She flipped through the pages until she got to the section on delivery. Then she took a deep breath. "Okay, I can do this if I have to."

She ran all the way back. One look at Jodie told her there was a good possibility that she was going to have to deliver the baby. The teen's face was contorted in pain, and her fingers clung to the bed linens in desperation.

"Dani, I'm scared. What if the baby comes before Brendan gets back?"

Dani sat beside her and brushed the damp hair from her forehead. "It'll be all right. I'm going to go to the kitchen and put a kettle of water on the stove."

"Why?"

"Just as a precaution," she answered, then quickly left the room. She pumped two potfuls of water, set them to heat on the stove, then unwrapped a bar of soap and pulled several towels and a washcloth from the cupboard. When she returned to the bedroom, she said, "Why don't you change into a nightshirt and I'll put some clean sheets on the bed?"

"You think I'm going to have the baby here, don't you?" Jodie said as she rolled off the bed.

"Just in case you do, we need to be ready," Dani answered, spreading two clean blankets and another sheet over the bed. "I'm sure Lou will come back with Brendan, and even if we can't get the road cleared, you'll be okay. Don't forget she's a midwife."

"She knows what to do?"

"You heard her say she's delivered over seventy babies." She plumped the pillows and, as soon as Jodie had changed, helped her back into bed. "Now I'm going to check on the water and get you some ice cubes to suck on.''

''Can't I have something to drink?''

''Better not. It says ice chips or ice cubes in the manual.''

''What about the pain? It hurts so bad I can't stand it,'' the teen wailed.

''I'll see what I can do.''

As confident as Dani sounded, she was actually a bundle of nerves. The thought of having to deliver Jodie's baby terrified her. While she was in the kitchen, she tried again to use the CB, but there was still too much static to connect with anyone.

So she prepared as best she could for a home delivery. By the time she was done, there was a basin of warm water, a washcloth, towels, a bar of soap, a syringe and a cup of ice cubes on the nightstand beside the bed. Across Jodie's forehead she draped a cold cloth and under her back she slid a hot water bottle.

When Jodie started grunting with the contractions, Dani tried to get her to stall. ''Jodie, you're pushing. You're supposed to be breathing.''

''I can't. I have to push. I can't stop it,'' Jodie said, her face growing redder.

''Then we're going to have to get ready for the baby to come. Scoot your back up against the headboard and spread your legs,'' Dani instructed, propping the pillows behind the girl. ''Now sit upright and push down with your contractions.'' She slipped a towel underneath her.

Seeing how exhausted the teenager was, Dani frantically flipped through the pages of the book until she came to the breathing techniques. ''Okay, it says here, Jodie, that you have to take a couple of deep breaths at the start of the contraction, then put your chin down on your chest and push down for as long as you can. If you need to take another breath, that's okay."

"But I can't tell when the contraction's starting," she grumbled. "It's just one continual pain."

"Try hard," Dani urged, with one eye on the door, hoping Lou would arrive before the baby did push its way into the world.

But Jodie's baby was not waiting for anyone. With a gigantic push on Jodie's part, the top of the head became visible.

"Owie-owie-owie!" Jodie cried.

"Pant, Jodie! Don't push, just pant!" she ordered, and to her credit, the teenager did as she was told. Suddenly the head popped out and Jodie screamed. "It's coming, Jodie!" Dani cried. "I can see all of it, the arms, the legs... It's a girl! Jodie, you have a little girl!" Dani held the infant in her hands, and it was such an overwhelming emotional moment she started to cry. Tears streamed down her face as well as down Jodie's.

"A girl? Let me see her."

Dani tipped the little body to give her mother a better look.

"She's all bloody," Jodie said on a note of alarm. "Is she breathing? Dani, I don't think she's breathing!"

How could she when she was covered with blood? Dani reached for the syringe and cleared her mouth and nose. Suddenly the baby cried and Dani and Jodie heaved sighs of relief.

"We need to clean her up." Dani dipped the washcloth into the basin of water and wiped the baby's eyes, nose and mouth. Again the newborn let out a tiny cry. "Listen to that. She speaks!"

"Can I hold her?" Jodie asked.

"Sure. I need to find something to cut the cord,

though," Dani answered. That something was a pair of scissors in Wilbur's desk, along with two large clamps that normally held a stack of papers but today squeezed the umbilical cord tight.

"Omigod, I feel good!" Jodie gushed. "I can't believe the pain is gone."

"The miracle of childbirth," Dani said with a smile.

At that moment, Lou and Brendan burst through the back door.

Hearing him calling her name, Dani yelled, "We're in here."

Brendan could hardly believe the sight that greeted him. Dani quickly pulled a sheet over the lower half of Jodie's body.

"Looks like you did all right without me," Lou said. She put a black medical bag on the floor.

"We did the best we could," Dani answered. "Brendan and I should probably step out of the room and you can check to make sure. Do you need anything?"

"Maybe another basin of warm water," Lou replied.

Dani nodded and left the room. Brendan followed her into the kitchen. It was there she realized how she looked.

"Oh, my. I'm a mess, aren't I?" she said, glancing down at the bloodstained clothes.

"I'm sorry it took so long."

"The baby wasn't going to wait," Dani answered, pumping water into the pot and setting it on the stove. Then she took a bar of soap and scrubbed her hands under the water that came directly out of the pump.

"You did a good job."

She scrubbed harder. "Lou needs some more warm water."

He carried the pot into the bedroom. When he returned, Dani was still at the sink, scrubbing away.

"It must have been quite an ordeal," he sympathized.

"It was," she said in a tight little voice. When she finally turned around, her eyes were filled with tears.

He lifted her chin with his fingers. "Dani, are you okay?"

She bit her lip and nodded, then began to shake. Brendan pulled her into his arms and let her cry, whispering words of comfort.

"I didn't know what else to do...the baby was coming...Jodie was frantic...and I..." She choked on a sob and cried some more. After a while, she pushed herself away from him. "I'm sorry. I didn't mean to fall apart like that. It's just that...it was such a traumatic experience. And I wasn't sure the baby was alive at first." She shuddered, and tears filled her eyes once more.

"The baby is alive, thanks to you," Brendan said tenderly. Again he pulled her into his arms. "You're one special lady, Danielle Taylor."

She stood there in his arms, drawing strength and comfort from him until Lou came into the kitchen.

"How's the baby? And Jodie?" Dani asked anxiously, stepping out of Brendan's grasp.

"They're both fine. Other than a few soiled linens, everything looks pretty damn good in there," she said heartily. "Congratulations, Dani. You deserve a pat on the back."

"They're really going to be all right—both of them?"

"You betcha. The baby's small. My guess is she'll have to be kept in the hospital a few days, but Jodie should be able to come home in a day or two. Right now, she's awfully tired and needs to rest."

Outside the kitchen window, Dani saw red lights flashing through the trees. "I think the ambulance is here," she told them.

"Earl must have been able to clear the road," Brendan said, grabbing a flashlight.

"How did you get through?" Dani asked.

"We drove Lou's truck till we got to the tree, then we walked the rest of the way."

She realized for the first time that Lou and Brendan were soaking wet. "You need to dry off." She reached into a cabinet and pulled out a couple of towels.

Lou accepted one, saying, "This is nothing compared to what I've been through before. In my ranger days, I used to dive into ice-cold water and rescue capsized hypothermic canoeists. At least this rain is warm."

Brendan didn't bother with the towel. "I'll get the paramedics," he said, and hurried out the door.

"Jodie wants you to come along to the hospital," Lou told Dani.

"I will. I can follow in my car."

"Brendan will probably want to go, too." At Dani's nod, Lou asked, "Are you going to be all right? You're shaking."

Dani looked down at her hands and realized she was trembling. "I'm fine. It's just that everything happened so fast." She noticed that her T-shirt, damp from contact with Brendan's wet clothing, was also splattered with blood. Until now it hadn't bothered her, but suddenly it made her feel queasy.

Lou must have noticed for she said, "What you could use is a good stiff drink. You got any booze in the house?"

"Just some wine. It's in the refrigerator."

"You need something stiffer than that. I bet Wilbur

has a bottle stashed somewhere. You go sit on the sofa in the living room and I'll take a look.''

Dani complied, and moments later, Brendan led a team of paramedics into the house. While they were in with Jodie and Lou was in the kitchen rummaging through the cupboards, Brendan sat down beside her on the sofa.

"Are you sure you're okay? You look a little pale.''

"She won't be for long,'' Lou shouted from the kitchen. "I found a bottle of Wilbur's brandy.'' She returned carrying a glass half-full of the dark liquid. She handed it to Dani. "Here. Drink this. It'll do you good.''

Dani took a sip and grimaced. "It burns.''

"Yeah, but it'll do the trick.''

As the paramedics wheeled Jodie out of the bedroom, the baby bundled in her arms, she called out to Dani, who hurried to her side. "I'm sorry I messed up the bed.''

"Don't worry about it. It can all be cleaned.''

"Thanks for helping me with the breathing stuff, too, although it didn't work very well.''

"We gave it our best shot.'' Dani grinned.

"You're gonna come to the hospital, aren't you?''

"Yes. I'll be there as soon as I've changed my clothes and cleaned up a bit.''

"Me, too,'' Brendan said.

As soon as they were gone, Brendan gave Lou a ride back to her truck. Dani changed out of her bloodstained clothes and rolled up the soiled sheets and blankets which was what she was doing when Brendan returned.

"Here. Let me help you.'' He took a corner of the bedding and rolled it back.

"I'm going to have to wash everything. At least the

mattress is okay,'' she said as the last of the linens were piled on the floor. She placed her hands on her hips. "Now what do I do? No washing machine, no running water." She shook her head. "I should have modernized this place the day I arrived."

"You haven't been here long enough to get power hooked up," he said logically.

She hated logic when she was tired, and she was very tired right now. "What about all the years you came here? Why didn't you encourage my grandfather to put in electricity and plumbing?"

"Why? So that if a baby happened to be born at the resort, it would facilitate the process?" he asked sarcastically.

"Oh, you're no help at all!" She shoved the dirty linens into a big plastic trash bag.

"You're really stressed out, Dani. Maybe you should stay here and visit Jodie tomorrow. I'm sure she'd understand if I told her you're exhausted."

His suggestion only added to her irritation. "I'm not exhausted," she said. "And we should get going. It's getting late."

With annoying calmness, he said, "I'll drive. I think you've done enough for one night."

She was about to protest but knew he was right. "I'll let you drive, but I'm not riding in the toy you call a car."

"That toy gets more than fifty miles to the gallon." He held up his hands. "Oh, but I forget. You don't need to concern yourself with something as trivial as gas mileage."

She grabbed her windbreaker, shot him a nasty look and headed for the door. She didn't bother to look back, assuming he would follow. He did.

She climbed into the passenger side of the Ford Explorer and sat there. He looked as if he might simply jump into the Geo and drive off without her, but then he opened the driver's side of the Explorer and asked, "Do you have the keys?"

"Yes," she answered primly.

It was well over an hour's drive to the hospital, an hour that passed in silence except for the slap of the windshield wipers. Dani didn't care. She was too tired for conversation, certainly too tired for an argument. Once they reached the hospital, she went in search of Jodie's room while Brendan stopped at the nurses' station.

Dani was surprised to see Jodie so wide awake. "Did you see Chryssa?" the teen asked, her face bright with animation. "She's in an incubator because she's only five pounds."

"You've named her?"

"She needed a name. I mean, I didn't want the nurse to keep calling her Baby Fisher," Jodie explained.

"Chryssa's a nice name," Dani said. "How are you feeling?"

"I'm a little sore. But the nurse gave me a painkiller to help me sleep," she answered. "Chryssa has to stay in the hospital until she gains some weight and they make sure she's okay. They said that's normal with premature babies."

"Lou said she looked good for a preemie," Dani commented.

"She's bald." Jodie grinned. "You probably noticed that right away, but I didn't realize it because she had all that gunk over her head."

"I thought I saw a little tuft of hair on the back of her head down near her neck," Dani remarked. Jodie yawned and Dani said, "You should probably get some sleep. How about if I come back in the morning?"

The girl carefully shifted lower beneath the covers. "I am tired. Where's Uncle Bren?"

"I left him at the nurses' station."

"Is he deciding what's going to happen to my baby?" Jodie asked anxiously.

"No, he can't make that decision," Dani answered calmly. "It looked to me like he was just visiting with the staff. He used to work here, you know."

"They asked me if I wanted someone from the adoption agency to come visit me."

"And what did you say?"

"I said it was okay," Jodie said tentatively, her eyes full of uncertainty.

Just then Brendan entered the room with a handful of papers. "We need to fill out these medical forms," he told Jodie, pushing a chair close to her bed so he could help her.

While they filled them out, Dani walked down to the nursery to take a look at Chryssa. She was in an incubator, naked except for the tiny pink knit hat on her head and the disposable diaper on her bottom. Dani felt a rush of emotion at the sight of her. Only a few hours ago, she had helped the baby breathe its first breath.

She looked so innocent, so small, so defenseless lying there. Dani wondered what the future held for the infant. There was a whole world out there waiting for her, yet she had no say in choosing the part she would play. Would she live in poverty or would she have a family who would provide her with food, clothing, a warm bed—and love?

Dani didn't know how long she stood outside the

glass wall at the nursery before she realized she was not alone. Brendan was at her side.

"I said good-night to Jodie for you."

"Thanks. Did you see your grand-niece?"

As if against his will, he looked at the premature infant. "She's so tiny. How will she ever survive?"

Dani frowned. "There's nothing wrong, is there?"

"No. She should be all right as soon as she gains some weight and grows a bit."

"Was it only medical forms you were getting at the nurses' station?" Dani asked, suspicion wrinkling her forehead.

"There was some confusion as to where to put Jodie. Normally with women who give up their babies, they're separated from the other new mothers."

"But she hasn't made that decision."

"No. She's seeing a counselor from the adoption agency tomorrow."

"Are you sure that's what she wants?"

He sighed. "Look, I really don't want to get into this right now. Why don't we just go home and wait and see how Jodie's feeling tomorrow?"

Dani nodded. "All right."

As he had on the way to the hospital, Brendan drove home. This trip was done in silence, too, but Dani was content with that. She felt emotionally drained. The kiss they'd shared now seemed as if it happened days ago, not only a few hours ago.

Brendan hadn't mentioned it even though there'd been ample opportunity. Several times on the way home, she dozed off. When they turned onto the road leading to Sacred Lake, Dani said, "I should have had you drop me at a hotel. After what I've been through, I'd love a soak in a hot bath."

"If you want a soothing experience, you could use the sauna," he suggested. "There's nothing like it to relax a person."

"Are you suggesting I use my grandfather's?"

"You might find it a very satisfying experience. Have you ever been in a true Finnish sauna?" She shook her head. "It's a different experience from what you get at a health club or hotel."

"Different how?"

"For one thing, if you're going to do it the Finnish way, you have to leave your clothes in the changing room so *all* your skin is cleansed."

"You're serious."

"Yes. You wouldn't take a bath with your swimsuit on, would you?"

"Well, no, but—"

"There's no problem with privacy. We're the only ones on the lake."

"What about light? Isn't it awfully dark at night?"

"You can't visit the sauna tonight. Besides the darkness, it takes some time to get it heated."

"What about tomorrow? Could I use it around nine?"

Brendan knew that Dani had no idea how early he'd need to get up to have the sauna heated by nine. It didn't matter. He said, "Sure."

So while Dani slept, he crawled out of bed before sunrise—glad to see the rain had completely stopped—tended the woodstove, making sure the stones were hot. He wiped the soot off the benches and walls, then pumped water into a bucket, which he set outside the door to the sauna, and filled the cisterns to the shower. When the preparations were completed, he watched the big house for a sign that she was awake.

Shortly before nine, she opened the patio door and stepped out onto the deck. She wore only a T-shirt that came down to the midthigh. He could only imagine that underneath she wore nothing—a thought that caused a reaction in a certain part of his body.

"The sauna's ready," he called from the doorway of his cabin.

She waved. "Great."

"I'll be right over to help you." He went inside, grabbed a towel, then headed for her place. He'd already pulled on his swim trunks so he could take a swim while she used the sauna. When he got to her deck, he asked, "All set?"

She nodded. Over one shoulder was a towel and in her hand was a bar of soap. "I take the shower after the sauna, right?"

"Yup." He glanced at the emerald on her right hand. "You should take off any jewelry you have. Otherwise the metal will get hot and burn you."

"I'll put the ring in the house." She disappeared inside, only to stick her head back out and ask, "Do I need anything else?"

"No. Follow me." He led her through the woods to the small building made from rough-hewn logs. Then he held the door open for her and handed her a piece of paper.

"What's this?" she asked.

"Directions. It's pretty self-explanatory, but just in case you have questions, I'll be in the lake."

"Aren't you going to join me in the sauna?"

Her question took him by surprise. "Are you sure you're comfortable with my being in there with you?"

"I don't mind. If it's as refreshing and relaxing as

you say it is, you could probably benefit from using it, too.''

Brendan shrugged. These California women were obviously bolder than any women he'd ever met. She knew they would both be naked because he'd explained that last night. Still, he asked again, ''Are you sure about this?''

She nodded. ''If you want to use the changing room first, go ahead.''

He did go first, removing his trunks and T-shirt, draping a towel around his waist. Then he stepped out and gestured for Dani to go inside. Within a few minutes, she was back with a towel tied saronglike around her, too.

''Ready?'' he asked.

When she nodded, he held the door to the sauna open for her. ''Omigosh, it's hot,'' she gasped as she stepped inside.

Brendan had carried the bucket of water inside and set it next to the stove. ''You need to wet down the bench so you can sit on it.''

He demonstrated by tossing a ladle full of water onto the lowest tier of benches next to the stove. He passed the ladle to her and she did likewise to a spot on the bench seat about a foot away.

In the dimly lit room whose only light came through several narrow slits near the ceiling, he said, ''Time to remove the towels.'' He removed the white terry cloth from around his waist and sat down, averting his eyes from her naked form.

Only it wasn't naked. She wore a teeny-weeny strapless bikini, something he discovered when she shrieked, ''Omigosh, you're naked!''

CHAPTER TEN

BRENDAN GRABBED a *vihta,* a broomlike bunch of soft, leafy birch twigs and covered himself. "I thought you understood that in a true Finnish sauna, you bathed *naked.*"

She sat with her back to him, her face to the wall. "You had on your swim trunks."

"Because I was going to take a swim before you asked me to join you. Why do you think I asked if you'd be comfortable with me? I went into the *changing* room."

"I thought it was to take off your T-shirt and your sandals. I never thought... You're practically a priest!"

"I am *not* a priest," he said, replacing the birch *vihta* with his towel, which he fastened securely around his waist.

"Well, you're almost a priest."

"Not anymore—I'm not even close," he said dryly. "And you can look at me. I've covered up."

Gingerly she turned around. He didn't know if her cheeks were flushed from the heat or from embarrassment.

"Have you forgotten you ran naked into the lake the day the bat got into the shower?" he asked her pointedly.

"That was different." She avoided his eyes.

"Okay, I apologize for the miscommunication. Now

let's forget it and enjoy the sauna.'' He climbed to the highest level, putting as much distance between them as possible so she could relax. ''You should stay on the lowest bench since you're not accustomed to the heat.''

''How long should I stay in here?''

''Ten minutes the first time.''

She noticed the birch twigs bunched together at his feet and asked, ''What's that for?''

He handed her a bunch and said, ''It's called a *vihta* and it's used to stimulate your blood circulation.'' Softly he added, ''Or to hide certain things.''

She picked up the *vihta,* eyeing it suspiciously. ''Are you saying I'm supposed to hit myself with this?''

''The correct term is to whisk it against your skin. It works best when the air's really steamy.'' He ladled a scoop of water over the hot stones, then worked the birch twigs over his skin. ''It's a bit like a massage. Most people start at the top and work down until they get to their feet.''

She followed his directions, gently whisking her skin with the *vihta.* ''It's aromatic, isn't it?''

He agreed. ''Birch has a rather sweet fragrance that permeates the room. That's one of the benefits.''

When she'd finished, she set the *vihta* aside. ''Now what? Am I supposed to wash in this room?'' she asked, eyeing the wooden bucket not far from her feet.

''You can if you like. That's why there's an extra bucket of water. The bucket, by the way, was made by your grandfather. You'll notice there are no nails, just wooden hoops holding it together.''

''Did he carve the ladle, too?''

''Yes. He crafted everything in here. It was amazing what he could do with wood.''

"I realized that when I saw all the carvings in the house."

When she shifted on the bench seat, he said, "Everyone has a different tolerance for heat. If you find it becoming uncomfortable, it's time to leave. Do you want to move onto stage two?"

"You mean take a shower?"

"No, cool off in the lake."

"You're saying my grandfather would actually go jump in the lake after sitting in here?"

He nodded. "It's an incredible sensation. You have to experience it yourself before you can understand why people do it."

"Is that what you and my grandfather would do?" She looked at him inquisitively.

"Normally we'd sit in here for ten minutes, cool off in the lake, then relax for a while on the beach before returning to the sauna for a second sitting. Then we'd shower."

She stood, wobbling slightly. "I think it's time for me to cool off. I'm feeling a little weak." He reached for her arm to steady her, his other hand holding fast to the towel.

"What's it going to be? The lake or the shower?" he asked as he held the sauna door open for her.

"I'll try the lake."

He liked her answer. Liked that she was adventurous.

"You can't dip a toe and slowly walk in," he warned. "You need to dive right in. If you wait a minute, I'll put on my swim trunks and we'll do it together."

"That's okay. You don't have to put them on. Just let me run a couple of feet ahead of you," she told him, then made a dash toward the lake, dropping her towel on the shore before diving into the clear water. When she came up for air, she screamed. She turned around and saw that Brendan was about six feet away from her. He'd surfaced with the same invigorated look on his face that she knew must be on hers.

"It's quite a shock, isn't it?" he said, moving toward her.

"Yes, but it feels good." She dove under once more, then popped back up, smoothing her wet hair away from her face.

"If you turn your back, I'll get out first," he told her, squinting as the sun glared off the water. Dani did as he suggested. Then when he called out, "All right, you can come out now," she waded toward the shore. He'd pulled two lounges from the shade into the sun and motioned for her to sit. Once more, the towel was wrapped around his waist. "The time spent outside the sauna is just as important in the relaxation process," he told her, stretching out on the chair. "This is when we enjoy the natural beauty around us."

Dani reclined on the chair next to his. "I love the view from this spot. I can see why my grandfather didn't want any developer to come in and commercialize the lake."

"Shh. No talking about anything that might interfere with our relaxation. Look." He raised an arm and pointed to their left. "There's a pair of loons."

"They're lovely," she said quietly. "I heard them the first morning I was here. They have such a unique call."

He agreed. "It's haunting, yet it's strangely soothing." When one disappeared beneath the surface of the water, Brendan said, "That one must be looking for breakfast."

"I can appreciate that."

"When we're done at the sauna, we'll eat. That's part of the custom, too." They sat for a few more minutes, then he said, "Ready for round two?"

She followed him back into the sauna and this time he kept the towel firmly in place. He stayed in the room longer than she did so she could use the shower first. Unlike other mornings when Dani had boiled water to heat it for the makeshift shower, Brendan had filled the tanks with cold water. After the heat of the sauna, it felt as invigorating as the lake.

While Brendan showered and dressed, she put together a light breakfast of cantaloupe, bagels and juice. By the time he walked out across the front yard, she had the picnic table set for two.

"Would you like some breakfast?" she offered.

"Sure." He climbed the steps of the porch and sat down across from her. "Well, how do you feel now that you've been to a sauna?"

"Wonderful. You were right. It was a very relaxing experience."

"That's why your grandfather used it regularly."

"Even in the winter?"

"Especially then—at least that's what he told me. He used to say it was the best place to be when the ice covered the lake and snow hid the ground. Gave him a feeling of warmth and security."

She stared into her coffee cup, pondering his words. "He wasn't one of those people who would chop a hole in the ice and jump into the lake, was he?"

Brendan smiled affectionately. "No. He told me he did it once when he was a young man and that was enough for him. That and the practice of rolling around in the snow after being in the hot room were more stimulation than he needed.''

"The cold water is enough of a shock. I can only imagine what ice and snow must feel like.'' She shivered at the thought.

"You really do look relaxed now,'' he said. "Last night was quite an experience for all of us, wasn't it?''

She nodded. "I still can't believe I delivered that baby.''

"The proof's at the hospital.'' He speared a chunk of cantaloupe with his fork. "Lou was right. You deserve a pat on the back. Jodie was lucky you were here for her.''

His compliment warmed her. "I still get a little shaky when I think about it. I mean, the baby wasn't breathing right away. I don't know. Maybe babies don't breathe when they first come out, but...'' She choked back the emotion that crept into her throat.

"I'm not sure, either, but it probably didn't help that she was premature.''

Dani set down her coffee cup and leaned on her forearms. "Now what happens?''

He sighed and pushed away his plate. "Jodie needs to make a decision. She's meeting with someone from the adoption agency this morning. It sounds as if she'll be released in a couple of days, but the baby might have to spend more time there. It's too soon to tell.''

"She's welcome to stay here until she knows what's going to happen with the baby.''

"I'll tell her you offered.'' They left it at that. No arguing over what was best for Jodie. And Dani was relieved. She didn't want to argue with Brendan. She just wanted to be with him—which was a revelation in itself.

When they arrived at the hospital, they learned that Jodie had spoken to a counselor from the adoption agency but as yet had made no decision. Dani wondered if it was because the teenager had held little Chryssa and a bond had already been formed.

However, when Dani visited the nursery with Jodie, she saw that the only contact the young mother had with her baby was through portholes in an incubator. Although the nurses encouraged her to put on special gloves and touch her daughter, Jodie was reluctant to do so for fear of spreading germs or hurting the tiny newborn.

When Dani returned to the resort that evening, she still didn't know what Jodie's decision would be regarding the baby. Nor was it a subject she wanted to discuss with Brendan. She didn't want to talk about her grandfather's estate or what she was going to do with her inheritance, either. She wanted to have a pleasant evening with Brendan.

Now that Jodie wasn't around, though, she couldn't be sure he had any intention of spending the evening with her. So when he told her he'd be in his cabin if she needed him for anything, she didn't say, "But aren't we going to have dinner?"

Little did Dani know that Brendan was having similar thoughts. From his spot in the kitchen of cabin number two, he could see her outside on the deck, sweeping away the cobwebs and bugs at the front of the house. He couldn't believe how he'd changed his opinion of her so dramatically in only a couple of weeks.

She really was nothing at all as he'd expected. He'd tried to find fault with her but couldn't. For one thing, she was a hard worker. Since the day she arrived, she'd kept busy at the resort. She'd even cranked up the old lawn mower and cut the grass despite his protests that he'd been hired to take care of the yard. And there was certainly no cause for complaint when it came to her spirit. He'd expected her to be as plastic and artificial as the images of Hollywood, but she wasn't. She was genuine.

While he was watching her at work, a chipmunk scrambled across the deck. Startled, she jumped back, automatically raising the broom like a weapon. Then she lowered the broom and smiled at her foolishness.

The longer he watched her, the more he wished they were spending the evening together. He glanced at the can of beef stew sitting next to the stove. There was enough for two. He could invite her to eat with him— after all, she'd done nearly all the cooking for the three of them ever since Jodie had arrived.

Only one thing stopped him. Being with Dani wouldn't help him resolve the uncertainty regarding his future. It would only complicate it.

He paced the tiny kitchen floor for several minutes before finally walking over to the screen door. "Dani! You feel like a little hobo stew?"

She paused in her sweeping. "Are you cooking?" she hollered back.

"Yeah. Want to join me?"

"Sure. Can I bring something?"

"You bring the beverages, I'll bring the food. Meet me at the fire pit at sunset and wear plenty of insect repellent."

She waved her acknowledgment and he turned his attention to the kitchen. He had a can of stew, two peaches and half a loaf of bread. He opened the cupboard and pulled out a bag of marshmallows. It wasn't much, but it would have to do.

An hour later, he carried his supplies out to the fire pit, a round sunken area rimmed with stones. Small individual benches handcrafted by Wilbur allowed them to sit close to the fire.

Brendan crumpled paper over twigs, then added wood Wilbur had chopped and stacked behind the house last fall. Within minutes, he had a blazing campfire that crackled and snapped in the still evening air. He set the food on one of the benches, the plates on another. When Dani arrived, she carried a pitcher of lemonade, which she set on a third bench. That left two remaining—one for each of them to sit side by side.

"Where did you learn to cook on a campfire?" she asked as he propped the opened can of stew between two burning logs.

"At camp. A bunch of us from school were able to go the summer between sixth and seventh grade. We slept in tents, learned how to cook over a fire, paddle a canoe, how not to attract bears in the wilderness—that sort of stuff."

He noticed she slid closer to him at the mention of bears.

"Didn't you go to camp when you were a kid?"

She shook her head.

"Camping, yes, but not camp. There was never any question of my going. I guess my parents didn't see any need for it." She watched as he spooned the stew onto two paper plates. "Was your camping experience a good one?"

"I liked it," he said. "I'm not sure if it was the actual camp experience I enjoyed so much as the chance to get out of the neighborhood for a week. It probably wouldn't have mattered *what* they had us doing."

She poured him a glass of lemonade. "Did you hate your neighborhood that much?"

"It was no Beverly Hills." He traded her a plate for the glass of lemonade.

"Tell me about it."

"It doesn't make for good dinner conversation, trust me."

"Maybe you should let me be the judge of that."

He really didn't feel like talking about his life in the city. "Why don't you tell me about where *you* grew up instead?"

"All right." She took a mouthful of stew and savored it. "Mmm. This tastes good. Not at all like it came out of a can."

"It's because it was cooked over the fire."

"I'll have to remember that." She took another mouthful, then said, "I grew up in a part of California where iron gates separate the neighborhoods from the public streets, and most houses have separate living quarters for domestic help. We didn't have daily help, but we did have a gardener who kept our lawns beautifully manicured and our gardens filled with flowers. I went to private schools and swam in a pool in my backyard."

"Sounds like a pretty nice childhood to me."

She shrugged. "I'm not complaining. My parents were good to me, and my mother…"

He could see her eyes glisten at the mention of her mother.

"She was a very special woman—compassionate, truly beautiful inside and out."

"You still miss her."

"Yes." There was a sadness in her eyes Brendan

understood all too well. "Do you still have both your parents?" she asked him.

"My mother died last winter," he answered quietly. "My father I haven't seen since I was seven. He got up one morning and said the pressure of having a family was too much for him and he took off."

"And you haven't heard from him since?"

"No. For twenty-three years, my mother waited for him to return. Even though the neighborhood grew more dangerous, I think she was afraid to leave for fear that he would come back and we wouldn't be there."

"Was she still living there when she died?" Dani asked gently.

"Yeah. I have a sister who lives in Ohio who begged her to come stay with her, but she wouldn't do it. She refused to believe she was in any danger even though her place had been broken into half a dozen times."

"It was that bad?"

He chuckled sardonically. "Bad is an understatement. On one corner was a crack house, on the other a free clinic for drug users. In between were the houses where people lived—or tried to live. I say 'tried' because the turnover rate was pretty high in those houses—between drug overdoses, shootings, beatings and arrests, the population changed constantly."

"I'm sorry. It must have been an awful place to be a child."

He shook his head. "It was an awful place to be any human being. It might have been worse for the adults because they knew there was no way out. The kids...well, some of them were able to fight their way out, but the adults were stuck there. Trapped by poverty." He stared into the fire and saw memories of the past in the flames. "My mother died from a heart attack, but she could have easily been murdered. Just a couple of months before her death, gang members put bullets through her living-room window. Fortunately she was in the kitchen at the time and wasn't hurt, but that's the kind of stuff that happened on a regular basis. So you see, it was definitely not the kind of neighborhood anyone would choose to live in.''

"So is it just you and your sister now?"

"No, there are four of us. I have three sisters—two older, one younger. Besides the one in Ohio, there's one in Nebraska and a third who's still in Minnesota.'' He washed the stew down with a drink of lemonade.

"Then you must have other nieces and nephews."

"Six."

"And do you see them very often?"

"Unfortunately, no."

The sun had disappeared below the horizon now, and dusk settled around them. "That was good," Dani said as she ate the last of her stew.

"Now it's time for dessert." He reached into a paper sack and withdrew a package of marshmallows. "You roast these things in California?" he asked as he handed her a stick with its end whittled to a point.

"Mmm—I love roasted marshmallows." She eagerly reached for one and pierced it with her stick. She held it in the flames until it caught fire. Then she quickly brought it out and extinguished the flame by puffing on it. "I love how gooey they get," she told him, licking her fingertips.

"Want another one?" he asked.

"I'd better not," she said. He put one on a stick and dangled it in front of her nose. "Brendan Millar, you do know how to tempt a woman."

With those words the atmosphere changed. Tension

crackled like the burning logs. Suddenly the kiss they'd shared last night leaped up between them like a tongue of fire, kindling the memory of a moment they'd both avoided talking about.

"I could say the same thing about you," Brendan said. "I came here looking for solitude, yet now when I'm alone, I find myself glancing out the window in hopes of catching a glimpse of you."

"You shouldn't say that."

"Why not?"

She didn't answer, but Brendan suspected she felt awkward with him because he'd recently left the seminary.

"I'm not a priest, Dani. I haven't been ordained."

"But..." She fell silent.

"I didn't come here thinking I was going to meet a woman who could make me feel giddy with one single look."

"Is that the way you feel when I look at you?"

He nodded. "As if someone is filling my body with helium and I'm about to float away."

She held up both hands. "Not guilty. Look, no helium tanks anywhere on me." Her smile was flirtatious. "Maybe it's all this fresh air that's causing your giddiness."

"I've never known fresh air to make me want to kiss a woman before."

She met his gaze. "Do you want to kiss me?"

"You need to ask?" The only sound was the crackling of the fire. Brendan extended his hand to Dani. "Come here."

As if it was the most natural thing in the world, he pulled her onto his lap so that she faced him with her legs spread on either side of his. She locked her hands behind his head and gazed into his face. "You have sexy eyes."

Her compliment went straight to his heart. "What is it that makes my eyes so sexy?"

She shrugged. "They just are. You have a way of looking at me that makes me go all tingly."

"I can do that with just a look?"

"Mmm-hmm."

"What would happen if I were to do this?" He placed a butterfly kiss on her lips. "Or this?" He placed several kisses on her lips, each one lasting a little longer than the one before.

"My heart's racing. Feel." She reached for his hand and pressed it on her breast.

It had been a long, long time since Brendan had touched a woman's soft breast. Feelings that had long ago been stifled burst back to life. Hormones he'd successfully kept under control now escaped with a vengeance. Desire he'd never imagined feeling again threatened to overcome his self-control.

Once more he placed his lips on Dani's, but this time there was no hesitancy, no teasing. His mouth captured hers in a kiss that matched the urgency coursing through his veins. When her lips parted, he gave in to the temptation to explore the sweetness of her mouth.

As his tongue entwined with hers, a small sound of wonder escaped her throat. She clung to him with a hunger that only increased his desire. When his hand caressed the fullness of her breast through the knit shirt, sighs of pleasure encouraged him to slide those fingers under the fabric until they found the scantily clad flesh beneath.

Brendan fumbled like a teenage boy to slip his hand inside the satiny covering of her bra. As his fingers found the hardened nipple, he began to shake. It had been so long since he'd been intimate with a woman. He was afraid if she touched him, he'd explode.

She did touch him. Without lifting her mouth from his, she unbuttoned his shirt, sliding a hand inside to curl her fingers in the smattering of his chest hair. Brendan wondered why she didn't get scorched, his body was so hot.

When the hand slid lower and tried to find its way into his pants, Brendan had to pull his lips from hers to catch his breath. "Maybe this bench isn't the best place to be doing this." He could see his passion reflected in her eyes.

"My place or yours?"

"Yours is closer." When she started to stand, he pulled her back down. "First I need to look at you."

"You've been looking at me all night."

He unbuttoned her shirt and exposed her bra. "Do you know I nearly drowned when I saw you in that piece of material you call a swimsuit?" He gazed at the shapely bosom tucked inside the pink satin bra. Then he reached around the back to unhook the fastener. Only there wasn't one.

"It's a front closure," Dani told him, her voice husky. "Just press the button."

With a movement of his thumb, the bra came undone. Brendan saw all of her, not just the tantalizing rounded flesh that had spilled over the cups of her bra. She was so beautiful his breath caught in his throat made him ache in places he'd tried to forget ever existed.

He pulled her closer so he could taste her. With one hand cupping a breast, he placed featherlike kisses on the other before finally capturing the hardened nipple. For a man who'd always prided himself on his self-control, he found himself dangerously close to losing it. Her moans of pleasure only contributed to his lack of restraint. For one brief moment, he wondered what it would be like to make love to her right there in front of the fire.

Reality, however, intruded. The honking of a car horn alerted them to the fact that, although they were at The Last Place on Earth, they were not alone.

Startled, Dani said, ''Someone's here!''

They fumbled with the buttons on their shirts. He reached for hers, she reached for his, then both realized they should be doing their own.

''I hope nothing's wrong,'' she fretted as she finished buttoning. She ran a hand over her hair and straightened her clothes one more time before heading toward the entrance to the resort.

Brendan had to take long strides to keep up with her. The area behind the big house was in total darkness. Neither Dani nor Brendan had stopped to get a flashlight, but it didn't matter, for the car parked in the driveway had the engine running and the headlights turned on.

As they approached, a man climbed out of the driver's side. ''Dani? Is that you?''

''Matt?''

The man rounded the front of the vehicle and pulled Dani into his arms, giving her a proprietorial hug. ''Thank God, you're all right. I've been worried sick about you.''

In the headlights of the car, Brendan could see the guy was in his twenties, tall, well dressed. He looked like Mr. Hollywood. Brendan had only one question. Who *was* this guy?

''Matt, why are you here?'' Dani asked.

"I came to spend the summer with you. I couldn't bear to think of you here all alone," he said, still clinging to her.

"I'm not alone," Dani told him, trying to pry his fingers loose.

It was then that Matt noticed Brendan. He stepped forward, hand outstretched and said, "Hi. You must be the priest. I'm Matthew Wellington, Dani's fiancé.

CHAPTER ELEVEN

"WE ARE NOT getting married!" Dani removed Matt's hands from around her waist and took a step away.

"Aw, come on, Dani. You're not still mad at me, are you?"

Dani could hardly believe this was happening. What was wrong with Matt? Had he not heard a single word she'd said before she left?

"I don't understand why you're here." She wished she could see Brendan's face. But it was too dark and he was out of range of the headlights.

"I wanted to see your place. Hey—look what I brought along." Matt grabbed her hand and tugged her around behind the vehicle—a Ford Explorer, just like she had rented. Brendan followed. Sitting on a trailer were two Jet Skis.

"Where did you get those?" she asked, aware of the disapproval radiating from Brendan.

"Steve Cannady's dad knows a dealer here in Minnesota. I rented them from him. I figure we might as well have some fun while I'm here."

At that point, Brendan spoke up. "If you'll excuse me, I'll say good-night."

Dani wanted to urge him to stay, then decided that wasn't a good idea. For the more Brendan saw of Matt, the more awkward the situation was going to become.

She would just have to explain everything in the morning.

But as he walked away, her heart sank. The man she wanted by her side was leaving, and the man she wanted to leave was camped on her doorstep.

"I can't believe you're here," she said irritably, shooing away a moth that had flown into the light. "Did my father send you?"

"He's worried about you, and so am I. And judging by the amount of time it took me to find this place, I'd say he has good reason to be. I thought I was driving off the face of the earth. There's nothing around here for miles!"

"That's what makes it special," she said. "It's dark now, but in the daylight, this place is beautiful."

"Your dad says it has great potential. I'll shut off the engine and you can show me around." He climbed into the Explorer and switched off the engine and headlights. Then he reached into the back and pulled out a suitcase and a florist's box. He gave the box to Dani. "These are for you."

She didn't want flowers. She didn't want Matt, yet she had little choice but to give him a bed for the night. "You shouldn't have brought me anything. You shouldn't even be here."

"How can you say that after all we've been through together?"

"Oh, what's the use?" she grumbled, then motioned for him to follow her up the steps to the house. Inside, she turned the switch on a battery-operated lamp.

"So this is it, eh?" He set his suitcase down on the floor in the living room and looked around with a critical eye.

"This was my grandfather's house." She set the box of flowers on the table and gave him a quick tour.

When he saw the refrigerator, he said, "I don't suppose you have any leftovers from dinner you want to get rid of."

The mention of dinner reminded Dani of the supper Brendan had cooked for her at the campfire. Her body warmed at the thought of how that meal had ended. "I can make you a sandwich if you're hungry."

He sat down at the kitchen table. "I'm starving. You know what airplane food is like, and then all I had on the way up here was a couple of hot dogs at some fast-food place along the way."

Dani made him a ham-and-cheese sandwich, which he washed down with a bottle of mineral water. While he ate, she retrieved the last set of clean sheets from the linen closet and put new batteries into a flashlight. As soon as he'd finished, she reached for the ring of keys hanging over the kitchen sink.

"The cabins are outside to our right. I'll put you in number three, which is at the far end." She handed him the flashlight. "Here. You're going to need this."

"Wouldn't it be easier if I just slept in here on your sofa?" He gave her his lost-puppy look.

"No."

Her tone dared him to disagree. He didn't.

They headed outdoors. "The outhouse is over there." She waved her flashlight in the direction of the half-moon while Matt groaned. "There's also a makeshift shower in the sauna building, though you'll need to pump water and fill the tanks first." She deliberately made her voice sound impersonal, like an innkeeper explaining the rules to a new guest.

"So it really is primitive," Matt said petulantly as he followed her to the cabin.

As they passed the second cabin, Dani noticed the lights were out. Brendan had already gone to bed. She glanced back to where they'd had their campfire. Only a few dying embers still glowed and her heart ached.

"Why can't I use the cabin closest to you?" Matt asked as she led him up the steps to the third cabin.

"Because I'm putting you in here."

"It smells damp," Matt said as she fumbled with the door.

She sighed. "That *is* a lake out there. Plus, we had a lot of rain last night." She pushed open the door and reached for the matches in her pocket. "This is a kerosene lamp. You can use it as long as you're awake, but extinguish it before you go to bed." She lit the lamp in the center of the round table, which gave the room a warm glow.

"That's it for light?" he croaked in disbelief.

"Plus the one in your hand." She went into the bedroom and propped her flashlight on the nightstand so she could make up the bed. She could hear Matt opening closets and drawers in the other room.

"Where do I wash up?" he asked, standing in the doorway.

"At the sink. You'll have to go outside and pump water at the well. If you're in desperate need of hot water, you're out of luck at this time of night."

He stood watching her make the bed, his mouth open.

When she was finished and he still hadn't moved, she asked, "Is something wrong?"

"I can't believe you're living like this. Are you that angry at your father?"

She planted her hands on her hips. "What is it with

you and my dad? He thinks I'm only staying here because I'm angry at you, and you think I'm here because I'm angry at him. Is it so difficult for either of you to understand that I might *want* to be here?''

''The Dani I know would have taken one look at this place and beat it back to her whirlpool bath without ever looking back,'' he answered.

''I've changed.''

He studied her for several moments. ''I noticed you're not wearing any makeup.''

She shook her head. ''I mean, I've changed inside.''

''Yeah, I believe you have,'' he said thoughtfully. ''You really don't want me here.'' It was said with such amazement, Dani almost felt sorry for him. Until this moment, he honestly hadn't considered the possibility that she wouldn't want him in her life. It was a discovery that hurt him. She could see by the expression on his face.

When he slumped onto the couch, she sat down beside him, reaching for his hands. ''I'm sorry, Matt. You've been one of my best friends ever since I can remember, but I don't love you the way a woman should love the man she's going to marry.''

He winced. ''Dani, how can you say that?''

''Because it's the truth, and if you're honest with yourself, you'll admit you don't love me that way, either. If you had, you wouldn't have been interested in Zoe Starbuck.'' She held up her hands when he was about to protest. ''I know you claim it didn't mean anything, but you were attracted to her, weren't you?''

His sheepish look was her answer.

''I've been doing a lot of thinking since I've been here. At first I was hurt because you were seeing Zoe, but then I realized what was hurt was my pride.''

"Gee, thanks," he drawled. "That's just what I came all the way from California to hear. That you never loved me."

"I do love you and I always will, but as a *friend*."

He groaned. "Sheesh, Dani, take it easy on me. Don't you know what it does to a man to hear those words?" He clutched his chest as if his heart were breaking.

He'd always had a flair for the dramatic. "Think about it, Matt. Did we really make the decision to get engaged because we were in love, or did we do it for our parents?"

"That's ridiculous, Dani," he protested. "I've loved you since the third grade and you know it."

"That's because when we were eight years old, our parents starting telling us how perfect we were for each other. It was just assumed that one day we'd get married. I mean, why did you finally buy the ring after all those years we dated? Did your father suggest it?"

He sighed and rubbed the stubble along his jaw. "We did have a father-son discussion on the subject," he admitted.

"Would you have proposed if he hadn't encouraged you?"

"Of course I would have!"

"Then how come it took you so long?"

"There never seemed to be any need to rush into marriage."

"That's my point. When I marry, I want it to be because I can't bear to spend another minute apart from the man I love—not because my father thinks it's a good idea."

Matt sat silently, staring at her with an odd expression on his face. Finally he said, "I'll always care about you, Dani."

"And I'll always care about you."

"But I guess it's really over."

She nodded solemnly. "I'm just sorry you made this long journey for nothing."

"Does that mean I can't stay for a while?"

She chuckled. "One day without running water and you'll be out of here. Besides, you'd get bored. You can't use a Jet Ski on the lake."

"Why not?"

"Because this is a wildlife preserve. My grandfather didn't want motorized boats and such here."

"I don't get it. Why are you so worried about what this guy wanted? You never even met him."

"It doesn't matter. The longer I stay here, the more I realize the need to respect what he's given me. He spent a lifetime trying to preserve a way of life. I feel I owe it to him to try to manage this place as best I can."

"What does that mean? You're not selling it?"

"I'd rather not sell it. What I want to do is figure out a way to put it to good use, yet still have it retain its charm. I want to put it to a use that Wilbur Latvanen would have approved if he were here."

"Maybe you should talk to the conservation department," Matt suggested.

"I have an idea in mind that might work. When I find out if it's possible, I'll let you know."

He motioned with his thumb toward the outdoors. "So I suppose you're going to tell me I hauled those things 250 miles for nothing?"

The petulant look on his face was very familiar to her. Ever since they'd been children, he'd used it when he didn't get his own way. She reached out and ruffled his hair as she'd always done. "It wouldn't be the first time you had an idea that didn't pan out."

"Ouch."

She shook her head in regret. "Coming here was not a good idea."

He sighed. "What about tomorrow? Can we at least spend the day together?"

If she was going to spend the day with anyone, she wanted it to be Brendan. "There's really not much to do here."

"All right. I get the message. You want me to leave."

Again he looked hurt and Dani felt a twinge of guilt. "I'll tell you what. I'll fix you breakfast in the morning, then show you around the place. We can take a nice long walk and look at the wood ducks and the beaver dams, maybe even swim a little—but I have to warn you. There are leeches in the lake."

He grimaced. "I'll pass on the swimming." He leaned back and stared at her. "You have changed. I used to be able to guilt you into doing the things you didn't want to do."

"Then it's a positive change, isn't it? I told you before. It's important that I make my own decisions."

He grinned. "All right. You've made your point. You said there's a makeshift shower. Are you sure I can't use it tonight?"

"You're going to have to wait until morning if you want to see what you're doing."

He nodded and opened his arms. "Give me a hug and then I'll say good-night."

THE FOLLOWING MORNING Dani showed him how to heat water to fill the tanks, then take a quick shower.

As she expected, he had little patience for the inconveniences of the resort. He hated insects, especially when there was the possibility they could climb on certain parts of his anatomy during a private moment. When he whined about not being able to dry his hair, she took pity on him and invited him into her house so he could plug his hair dryer into the power strip connected to the generator.

That was how Brendan found him—standing in Dani's kitchen in a pair of shorts with his chest and feet bare, drying his hair. With all his toiletries spread out on the counter and his suitcase open on the living-room floor, it looked to Brendan as if Matt had spent the night in Dani's place.

"I'd like to speak to Dani." Brendan tried to keep his voice calm and fought the urge to smash this tanned beach bum's surgically altered nose.

"She's in the shower, Father," Matt replied almost reverently, which really disturbed Brendan. Hadn't Dani told him that he wasn't a priest? She'd had ample time. They'd stayed up late last night—he'd seen her lights on long after he had gone to bed.

Not that he had fallen asleep right away. He hadn't. Couldn't. He kept thinking about Dani and this guy who looked like he'd walked off the set of *Baywatch*. It had clawed at his insides to see him with his arm around Dani and behaving as if they'd been lovers.

Brendan wanted to know just who this Matt really was in Dani's life. Not that he had any right to know. It wasn't as if he and Dani had a relationship. Or did they? Last night, they'd nearly made love. Would have if Mr. Hollywood hadn't shown up.

"Is there anything I can get you?" Matt asked.

Brendan felt like saying, *Yeah, you can get out of*

Dani's house and out of her life. But there was the possibility that this man meant something to her. Dani had told Jodie there were no men in her life, yet this guy had introduced himself as her fiancé and had obviously spent the night in her place.

Jealousy like he'd never known before burned his insides. *He* was the one who'd wanted to spend the night with Dani, yet this...

"Would you tell her I drove to Hibbing to visit my niece?" he grumbled, then started for the door.

"I sure will. You have a good day now, Father," Matt said amiably.

"You, too," Brendan automatically responded.

"Oh, we will," he assured him with a grin.

Brendan didn't miss the fact that Matt had said "we," which meant he was planning on spending the day with Dani. Maybe he was planning even more. Maybe they were lovers who'd patched up their differences, and this golden boy would be at the resort the rest of the summer. It was a possibility Brendan didn't want to consider.

And here he'd been thinking he might get something going with Dani. Was this what being out of circulation did to a person? Was he trying to move in on a woman who was already involved with someone else? Feeling like a first-class fool, he got in his tiny little car—which truly did look minuscule next to the two other vehicles—and drove off.

BRENDAN'S ABRUPT departure worried Dani. She wondered if there'd been some word from the hospital that would cause him to leave so early to visit Jodie, yet Matt assured her nothing had come over the CB radio while she'd been in the shower.

She'd assumed she would go to Hibbing with Brendan, which would have been possible since Matt left shortly after noon. As soon as he was gone, Dani climbed in her rented Explorer and headed for the hospital.

To her relief, there was no emergency with either Jodie or the baby. When she walked into Jodie's room, Chryssa was at the foot of her bed in a bassinet.

"She doesn't need the incubator anymore?" Dani said with a smile.

"Nope. She's doing just fine, the nurse told me. If she eats all right, I get to take her home tomorrow. Do you want to hold her? You can if you want to."

Dani didn't miss what the teenager had said. She was taking her baby home. She wondered where home was. Did she mean back to Minneapolis or back to the resort?

Dani picked up the tiny bundle as if it were a bomb about to detonate. "She's so small," she whispered, carefully easing herself onto the chair beside Jodie's bed.

"I know. She doesn't drink very much when I feed her. She falls asleep about halfway through her bottle."

Dani noted the deep blue eyes staring at the ceiling. "She's awake now."

"That's because I just gave her a bath. They have classes here to show you how to do everything."

"That's good." Dani studied the little face peeking out of the pink blanket. A miniature fist emerged from the folds. She slipped her little finger into its grasp.

"Where's Uncle Bren? Didn't he come with you?"

"No. We came in separate cars because I had a visitor stay overnight—a friend of mine from California," Dani explained.

"Did she leave already?" Jodie asked, automatically assuming the friend was a woman.

Dani didn't correct her but simply nodded.

"Then maybe you'd like to stay here for dinner. I can get you an extra meal."

Dani shrugged. "Sure."

Gingerly Jodie lowered her feet to the floor and stood. "I'll go tell them at the nurses' station."

"Maybe I should be the one to tell them."

"Uh-uh. You stay here with Chryssa. Besides, I'm supposed to get exercise." She winced as she walked, her pace like that of an old woman.

While she was gone, Dani talked to the newborn. "You are so special," she cooed. "You are going to grow up to be a smart and beautiful young lady."

"Do you think she understands what you're saying?"

Startled, Dani turned to see Brendan standing in the doorway. At the sight of him, her heart raced and her skin tingled. She could have stared at him for hours.

"When did you get here?" she asked.

"A few minutes ago."

"But you left this morning."

"I had things to do." He glanced around the room. "Where's Jodie?"

"She went to the nurses' station. I'm surprised you didn't see her in the hallway."

He walked over to the window to look outside. Dani had the distinct impression he was angry with her. Gone was all the warmth he'd shown her last night before Matt's arrival.

"Jodie says she might be able to bring Chryssa home tomorrow," she told him, wanting to break the silence.

That brought a frown to his face. "So soon?"

"That's what she says."

"I'd better check with Social Services and see what the plans are for the baby." He was on his way out of the room when he bumped into Jodie.

"Hi." Dani could see that the teenager was nervous around her uncle. "I just asked the nurse if Dani could stay for supper and she said it would be all right. Do you want to stay, too?"

"I have some business to take care of," he answered. "Dani tells me you and the baby are going to be released tomorrow. Is that right?"

Jodie took small steps as she walked over to where Dani sat with the baby. "Uh-huh. I'm going back to Minneapolis if I can scrape together some money."

Dani noticed she didn't come right out and ask her uncle for a loan.

"Are you taking the baby with you?" Brendan asked the question that was on both their minds.

"I think I want to keep her, Uncle Bren," she said quietly, gradually easing herself onto the bed.

"Where will you stay when you get there?" he asked calmly.

"My friend, Shawna, said she'll let me stay with her," she answered.

"And what about formula and diapers and all the other things Chryssa's going to need? How will you buy them?"

Jodie turned to Dani and said, "Would you lend me some money?"

Brendan's eyes met Dani's. Nothing like feeling caught between a rock and a hard place. She did want to help the girl, but she also knew that Brendan disapproved of such a short-term solution.

"I might be able to help you," she answered, and immediately felt the wrath of Brendan's gaze.

"So that'll take care of the problem for a couple of weeks," Brendan said, "but what about next month, next year? When you were thirteen, you ran away from the neighborhood you want to return to now. Is that where you want to raise your child?"

"I know it's going to be hard, but once Dusty comes back, he'll make sure we're taken care of," she said defensively.

There was silence in the room. No one said a word, not Brendan, not Jodie. Finally Brendan said, "I told you, Jodie—Dusty's not coming back."

"I know that's what you think, but that's just what other people have told you. I know that when I see him again, everything will work out."

"It sounds as if you've already made up your mind," Brendan stated evenly.

"I have. I told the counselor this morning." This time she spoke more confidently.

To Dani's surprise, Brendan didn't argue with her. "All right. The decision is yours to make. I respect that."

"Thank you, Uncle Brendan."

There was another awkward silence, then Dani said, "If Jodie's being discharged tomorrow, she'll need someone to pick her up."

"Would you like me to come for you tomorrow?" he asked his niece.

"Would you?"

He nodded. "Are you planning to go directly to the bus station?"

"Chryssa needs to be checked by the doctor in a week. Do you think I could stay at the resort for a few days?" she asked Dani. "I'll help out with the cooking and stuff."

"Of course you can stay with us," Dani answered, unwilling to look at Brendan.

He stayed for just a couple of minutes longer, then told Jodie he was leaving. Dani would have gone with him, but she knew that Jodie had ordered dinner for her. The rest of their visit was spent talking about the baby, but just before Dani was going to leave, Jodie brought up the subject of Brendan. Dani almost felt as if she was taking a test the way the teenager asked so many questions.

"Is Uncle Brendan going back to the seminary?"

Dani wished she had the answer to that one. "I don't think so, but I honestly can't say for sure," she replied.

"Then has he told you what he's going to do when he leaves Hidden Falls?"

"No. Is there some reason he would tell me?"

Jodie looked down at the sheet, which she was pleating between her fingers. "I thought the two of you were getting close." She glanced up shyly. "I saw you kissing the night Chryssa was born."

"Oh." Dani felt her cheeks grow warm.

"I know you like him."

Dani figured there was no point in lying. "Yes."

"He likes you, too," Jodie said. "I bet you're glad he's changed his mind about becoming a priest, aren't you?"

"If he truly *has* changed his mind."

"He has. The priests I know don't look at women the way he looks at you."

That caused Dani to blush as she remembered the way Brendan's eyes had devoured her naked chest. No, he definitely had not behaved as if he intended to return to the seminary.

"You're embarrassing me, Jodie," Dani said lightly.

"It's true. Uncle Brendan looks at you the same way he used to look at my aunt Caroline. When the two of you were in this room today, his eyes were on you practically the whole time."

Again Dani could feel her face flush. "That was probably because he was angry at me and wanted to tell me so."

"Why? Did you two have a fight?"

"Not exactly," she answered evasively, not wanting to add that Jodie and her baby were also a source of conflict between them.

That evening when Dani got back to the resort, Brendan's car was in the driveway. Automatically she swung her gaze to his cabin, hoping to see him sitting inside, but it was in darkness. She assumed he had gone to bed early.

Which was why she screamed when she climbed the steps to her porch and found him sitting there. "You scared me half to death! What are you doing?"

"Waiting for you." When she fumbled for her keys, he took them from her trembling hands and unlocked the door. "Wilbur never locked the door when he lived here," he said as he held it open for her.

"I don't care if this is The Last Place on Earth, it's too risky to leave it unlocked." She dropped her purse on the table and switched on a battery-operated lamp. "I suppose you're here to yell at me for offering to give Jodie money so she could get home to Minneapolis."

"No."

"Good, because I'm too tired to argue with you." She stretched muscles tense from sitting behind the wheel of her car.

"What happened to your boyfriend?"

"Matt is not my boyfriend."

"He seemed to think he was."

"Well, he's not, and by the time he left today, he had the same opinion as me. Is this what you wanted to talk to me about? My relationship with Matt?"

"No, I want to talk about your relationship with me, but it's kind of hard to do that when this morning I come over and find pretty-boy Matt half-naked in your kitchen, after we nearly made love last night."

Dani stared at him in disbelief. "You think he spent the night with me?"

"Didn't he?"

"No! He slept in cabin three, took a shower first thing this morning, then used my kitchen to dry his hair and shave because he truly cannot get along without electricity."

She could see the skepticism in his eyes.

"I would never go to bed with a man who could make love to one woman while engaged to another."

"Is that what he did?"

"Whether he did or didn't really doesn't matter anymore. He wanted to be with her more than me." At one time, those words would have been spoken with emotion, but now they were simply a statement of fact.

"He's not worth losing sleep over," Brendan told her.

She chuckled sarcastically. "Don't I know it. It was my pride, not my heart, that was wounded. He was my father's choice for a husband, not mine."

"Then it's a good thing you didn't marry him."

"Is that why you were so cold to me today at the hospital? Because you thought I'd slept with Matt?"

"I was so jealous I could have broken every tooth in that condescending smile of his," he admitted with a slow grin.

Dani didn't find it humorous. "Is that the kind of woman you think I am? Someone who could be with one man part of the evening, then switch to another a couple of hours later?"

"No. I don't think that." He raked a hand through his hair. "I'm sorry. I'm not very good at this. You have to remember I've been in a seminary for three years. I'm out of touch with this...this...stuff."

"What stuff?"

"The fact that I'm very attracted to you. And that every time I'm alone with you, I have to fight the urge to pull you into my arms and tear every piece of clothing from your body, then make wild, passionate love to you."

"Why fight the urge?" she asked in a husky voice. When she extended her hand to him, he clasped it and allowed her to lead him into the bedroom. Instead of turning on the battery-operated lamp, she lit candles until the room was bathed in a romantic glow. Then she stood before him and said, "Let the ripping begin."

Brendan knew it would have been easy to tear off her clothes in the blink of an eye, but he didn't want to rush one minute of the pleasure he knew lay ahead. Using every ounce of self-control he could summon, he undid her blouse one button at a time until the front fell open. Lacy wisps of lingerie veiled the soft fullness of her breasts. As he pulled the blouse from her shoulders, he trailed kisses across her neck and shoulders.

Next he knelt before her and unsnapped her jean shorts. With trembling fingers, he eased them down her legs. As she stepped out of them, she used his shoulder to steady herself. "Do you ache as badly as I do?" she asked in a near whisper.

His answer was a kiss that told her in no uncertain

terms that his body was about to demand nothing less than a full surrender. They tumbled onto the bed, their arms around each other. While his fingers found the clasp on her bra, hers worked the buttons free on his shirt until her breasts pressed against his naked chest.

Although he wanted to love her slowly, to savor every caress, every discovery he was about to make, years of celibacy fueled a hunger that refused to allow the luxury of relishing each moment. Her skin was hot to his touch and he felt her tremble as his hand slid inside the lace-trimmed bikini briefs.

When they'd finally freed themselves of their clothes, he buried himself in her softness, tasting the sweetness of her as their bodies came together. With the rhythm of passion at one with the tempo of their heartbeats, they gave themselves to each other until the tremors of ecstasy left them sighing in satisfaction.

As they lay in the afterglow of their lovemaking, Brendan had a stunning realization. Until tonight, he'd never known the true meaning of passion.

CHAPTER TWELVE

WHEN DANI AWOKE the following morning, she was disappointed to find Brendan no longer beside her. The memory of their lovemaking tickled every nerve in her body. It had been so good being with him, so very good. She wondered why he wasn't still here.

She pulled on a robe and headed into the kitchen, hoping to find him at the table. No luck. Nor was he in the living room or out on the deck. A quick peek out back revealed that his car was gone.

She frowned. Surely he hadn't gone to get Jodie without waking her? Not after last night. They hadn't even had a chance to talk about what had happened between them. Again her insides trembled at the memory. Never had she expected to have such an intense physical reaction to a man, let alone someone she'd known such a short time. Love was the last thing she'd expected to find at The Last Place on Earth.

Love. Was it possible she'd fallen in love with Brendan? Until a few weeks ago, she'd thought she was in love with Matt. But that relationship paled in significance compared to what she had found with Brendan.

How did one fall in love so quickly? She'd read stories about great romances where it was reported that the minute the couple set eyes on each other, they knew that their lives would never be the same again.

Looking back, Dani could see she'd fallen a little in

love with Brendan the first night she'd arrived at the resort. It was only because she'd thought he was a priest that she hadn't allowed herself to recognize the power of the emotions he stirred in her.

When she went to heat water for her shower, she found a note next to the stove. It was from Brendan. "I filled both of the tanks for you. Enjoy." While water cascaded over her soapy skin, her mind was occupied with thoughts of him. Once Jodie and the baby were gone, they'd be able to swim naked and make love on the beach with the sounds of nature all around them. It would be the best summer of her life, and all because she'd finally met a man she truly loved.

Although she was sure of her feelings for him, she wasn't as confident of his. Later, when she saw him sitting on the wooden swing that overlooked the lake, she found herself feeling a bit shy. She wished she knew what he was thinking about as he stared out at the water. Her? Jodie and the baby? The seminary?

That last possibility bothered her more than she cared to admit. She didn't want to think the sober look on his face had anything to do with regret over what had happened between them last night. But she knew it might be the reason. She didn't doubt he was attracted to her. Still, maybe he didn't *want* that attraction. She realized he'd come to the resort this summer to be alone to sort through his feelings and make sure that leaving the seminary was what he wanted to do.

Dani didn't want to believe he could return to a life of celibacy after they'd shared such a night of passionate lovemaking. She took a deep breath and approached him. "Good morning."

He turned his head at the sound of her voice and all her uncertainty disappeared. Because he smiled—the kind of smile that told her he was happy about what had happened. Then he pulled her onto his lap and kissed her until she was breathless. One hand slid beneath her shirt to cup a breast, and Dani sighed.

"When I woke up and saw you weren't there, I thought last night might have been a dream," she said huskily.

"It was no dream," he said, his fingertips caressing the nipple beneath the satin of her bra.

"Where did you go?"

"I wanted to talk to Lou."

"This early?"

"She's a morning person." He undid her bra and caressed both her breasts. "See the advantages to having a private resort?"

"Is this your way of trying to convince me not to develop the lakeshore?"

He continued tracing patterns on her flesh, and Dani sighed with pleasure.

"You keep that up and I'm going to get all hot and sweaty and have to take another shower," she warned him with a seductive smile.

"Did you enjoy the warm water?"

"Mmm. It felt almost as good as what you're doing to me now."

He chuckled. "I'd rather be doing this than hauling buckets of water."

"Another reason for me to put in plumbing and electricity," Dani said dreamily.

His hand stopped moving. "You sound as if you've made a decision."

"Well...yes. It isn't just based on the fact that Jodie had her baby here, although that was a deciding factor. I know Wilbur wanted it to remain as rustic as possible,

but there are times when power is not just a convenience, but a necessity. What if someone was sick and
needed a vaporizer, for example."

"You have a point."

She tugged on her ear. "Am I hearing correctly?
You're agreeing with me?"

He nodded. "This summer's convinced me it might
be time to modernize."

"Even if it's not what Wilbur wanted?"

He nodded. "I think what was more important to him
was to keep developers from coming in and putting condominiums all around the lake." He gazed at her pen-
sively. "You're not going to do that, are you?"

"No. I want it to look just like this," she said,
spreading her arm in an encompassing gesture. "Except
with power. I'm going to contact someone next week
to give me estimates on the cost," she said. "I wish I
could get it done sooner. It's not going to be easy to
have a newborn here with no running water."

"It's only temporary. Speaking of which—" he
glanced at his watch "—we should probably get going.
We need to check Jodie out of the hospital by eleven."

His attitude changed at the mention of Jodie and the
baby. Gone was the playful, sexy man who'd been caressing her breast. Dani wanted to talk to him about
Jodie's decision to keep the baby, but she didn't want
any tension between them, so she deliberately avoided
the subject on the way to Hibbing.

At the hospital, Dani saw the professional Brendan
at work. He smoothly took charge of getting Jodie and
the baby discharged with the ease of someone who'd
spent many hours working in a health-care environment.
It was obvious from the way the staff treated him that
he'd earned their respect.

The doubts Dani had managed to dismiss surfaced again, however, when several of the patients referred to Brendan as Father. He must have sensed her uneasiness, for the minute they were outside he said to her, "They only call me Father because my work here was through the church. But I've left the seminary, Dani."

Despite his assertion, her mind was still not put at rest. As much as she wanted to believe he wouldn't return, she wondered how easy it could be to turn his back on years of studying.

Although grins came easily for Brendan on the way home, it was not so for Jodie. Dani wondered if the teenager was suffering from postpartum depression. Gone was the euphoria that only yesterday had her talking nonstop and making plans for her future. In its place was a quietness, a look of confusion and weariness. And maybe it was apprehension that made her stare out the car window.

Once they were back at the resort with no nurses to assist in Chryssa's care and provide answers to Jodie's questions, the teenager was faced with the reality of just how much of a responsibility it was to take care of a newborn. To Dani's surprise, Brendan had borrowed a portable crib, which he'd set up in Jodie's cabin. Dani could see, however, that Jodie wasn't thrilled at being alone with the baby.

"Gee, it seems so quiet in here compared to the hospital. Someone was always around there," she said as Brendan carried a shopping bag full of baby items into the cabin. "I kinda got used to having people around me."

Dani was about to suggest that she bring the baby and sleep in the house when Brendan said, "Once you made the decision to take the baby home from the hospital, you chose to accept responsibility for Chryssa.''

Dani knew he had a point. If Jodie wanted to be the mother to this child, it meant she would do it alone, since it was unlikely Dusty would be back—no matter what Jodie believed. Still, she could empathize with the teen who was obviously intimidated by the problems she now faced.

"I know that," Jodie said sounding awfully close to tears.

"That doesn't mean you have to eat dinner alone," Dani pointed out. "I'll bring you supper. We can all eat together—just like we did before. Would you like that?''

The teen nodded, but continued to look as if she would burst into tears at any moment. Brendan's expression seemed to say he wasn't quite sure whether he approved or disapproved of the arrangement. Dani was relieved that he didn't insist Jodie take care of herself.

Most of the afternoon centered around the baby's activities. Getting fed, getting diapered and getting cuddled was how Brendan described it.

In the hospital, Jodie had been eager to take care of the infant. Now that she was on her own, she seemed hesitant around her daughter. She turned to Dani every time the baby needed attention, as if she didn't trust her own instincts.

The three of them ate dinner in Jodie's cabin as Dani had suggested, although it was not exactly like meals they'd shared previously. Jodie ate little, poking at her food rather than eating it. She looked as if she'd rather be anywhere else but at the dinner table. Nor did she have any interest in their conversation. Shortly after the dishes had been cleared, she burst into tears for no apparent reason. Dani, who had her hands in soapy dish-water, reached for a towel, but Brendan was already comforting his niece.

"Tell me what's wrong," he said soothingly as he held her in his arms.

"I...I'm afraid I'm going to screw up and do something wrong with Chryssa," she said in between hiccups.

"It's a scary thing, having a baby," Brendan said softly. "I think every mother has those feelings when she brings her infant home from the hospital. Being a parent is a big responsibility, and unfortunately there's no training required. People just have babies and expect to know what to do with them."

"What if I make a mistake and she gets hurt or sick or something?"

"That's one of the reasons I wanted you to live in the group home for teenage mothers. The counselors there can help you with any problems you might have," Brendan said reasonably.

Dani could see Jodie stiffen and pull away from her uncle. "I don't want to go to a group home. I want to go back to Minneapolis."

"Father Dorian could find you a place to stay there," Brendan suggested.

"Uh-uh. I'll make it on my own. I have for the past three years," she said toughly.

"But you only had yourself to worry about then. Now you have a daughter, too."

She shrugged. "We'll be okay." She got up and went over to the crib and lifted Chryssa, cuddling her close.

"I wish you'd reconsider the group home," Brendan said, his voice full of concern.

"And what happens when Dusty gets back? He won't be able to stay there with me."

Dani's heart ached for the young mother. She simply refused to believe that her baby's father wouldn't be coming back for them.

There was compassion yet firmness in Brendan's voice as he said, "You can't count on his being there, Jodie."

"Yes, I can!" she insisted. "I don't care what Father Joe told you. Dusty will be there for us!"

Dani had finished doing the dishes and was wiping her hands on a towel. "Brendan, you and I should let this new mom and her daughter get some rest." To Jodie she said, "I've put clean bottles and the formula on the counter. All you have to do is open the can and pour it in."

Jodie nodded in understanding.

Dani really didn't want to leave the girl alone, and again she started to suggest Jodie stay at her place. She was preempted by Brendan saying, "How about if I sleep on the couch so you don't have to be alone on your first night?"

His offer took Dani by surprise. Initially, he'd said it was good that Jodie was on her own in the cabin and had actually been a bit gruff when he'd told her about accepting responsibility for the baby. Now he'd offered to spend the night with her. So he *did* have a compassionate soul after all, she thought.

"That couch isn't very big," Jodie said weakly.

"I've slept on worse. Won't it be easier if I'm with you out here?"

She nodded, her eyes glazed with tears.

"I'll get my stuff and be right back."

As soon as her uncle had stepped out the door, she

turned to Dani and said, "Thanks for giving me the money. Uncle Brendan wouldn't do it because he thinks I'm making a mistake keeping the baby."

Jodie had obviously interpreted her loan as approval that she'd done the right thing. Dani was uncomfortable with that thought. "What's important is that you believe you've made the right decision." The girl's face was pale, prompting Dani to ask, "*Are* you having second thoughts about keeping Chryssa?"

"No." The answer was a long time coming, which told Dani she was having doubts.

"You're sure."

"Yes. I told you. I want to raise her. I just wish I knew what Dusty wanted."

Dani, like Brendan, didn't think Father Dorian was wrong about Jodie's boyfriend. She had the feeling the teenager was pinning her hopes on an irresponsible young man who was not only going to break her heart, but abandon their daughter.

"What if Dusty doesn't want the baby? What will do you do then?" Dani asked gently.

"He does want her," the girl insisted. "He's a good guy. Really. I thought you of all people would understand."

"I'm trying to, Jodie, but..." Brendan chose that moment to return with his things.

As soon as he stepped inside, Jodie confronted him. "What have you been telling Dani? She was on my side until you got her to listen to you," she said heatedly.

Calmly Brendan took her by the hands and eased her down beside him on the couch. "There are no sides in this, Jodie. All three of us want the same thing—what's best for you and Chryssa."

"Then why are you making me feel so bad about taking her home?" she asked, close to tears once more.

"I don't want you to feel bad. What I want to do is ask you some questions. You don't have to tell me the answers, but you think about them, all right?"

She nodded.

"First of all, what are your goals? Are those goals possible with a baby? Can you get a decent job without finishing school? Do you like caring for a baby? Are you willing to take on the responsibility of raising a child for the next eighteen years? If Dusty does want to be a father to Chryssa, do the two of you agree on how to raise a child? Can you give Chryssa the future you want for her?"

It was a solemn-faced Jodie who listened to her uncle. When they'd finished their conversation, Dani decided it was time to head back to the house. "If you need anything, just come on over," she announced to no one in particular.

Later that night, as Dani climbed into the big pine bed, she thought about Brendan asleep on the couch in Jodie's cabin. When she caught the faint scent of his aftershave still clinging to the pillow case, waves of longing rushed through her. She hoped that Jodie would send Brendan over to get something, because then she could have one more look at him before she went to sleep.

What she really wanted was to fall asleep in his arms as she had last night. Would there be more nights like that? One thing she knew she had to do was find out what it had meant to him. Was she going to be a summer fling to him, a temporary distraction while he contemplated his future? Or did he feel the same as she

did—that what they had together was something too
good to let slip away?

Dani didn't know how long she'd been asleep before
a loud pounding came at the door. Thinking it had to
be Brendan, she hurried to answer it. As she expected,
he stood on the steps, a pair of pajama bottoms and
wearing a shirt open at the front as if it had been pulled
on in a hurry. Jodie was standing beside him carrying
the baby.

"What's wrong?" Dani asked as she ushered them
inside.

"I think something really bad is happening. Chryssa
won't stop crying," Jodie said frantically, thrusting the
baby at Dani.

Dani unfolded the layers of blanket to find the infant's tiny face red and pinched. "Did you feed her?"

"Yes. She drank nearly all the bottle. See?" She
pulled the almost empty bottle from her pocket and
shoved it in Dani's face for her inspection.

"And you've checked her diaper?"

"She's not wet," Jodie assured her.

The way Jodie had the baby bundled up Dani had to
wonder if the infant wasn't simply too warm. She unwrapped the layers of clothing until only a T-shirt and
diaper remained. The baby continued to cry, pulling her
knees up to her abdomen.

"She's tightening up—like she's in pain," Dani ob-
served anxiously. "Maybe she needs to be burped."

She put the tiny baby to her shoulder and patted her
back gently. The crying continued. Then she got up and
started walking the floor, still rubbing the infant's back.
To her relief, the crying waned, but the minute Dani
stopped moving, it resumed.

One of Dani's co-workers had recently given birth to

a little girl, but except for a brief visit during which she'd rocked the infant, Dani had had little experience with newborns. "Get that baby book we bought at the bookstore and we'll see what it says," she instructed Jodie, who grabbed a flashlight and flew out the door.

"This is exactly why I don't think Jodie should keep the baby," Brendan said. "Who's she going to run to when she needs help? She needs someone mature and experienced."

"There has to be some adult she can turn to. A friend, maybe?"

He raked a hand through his hair. "She's simply too young to be a mother."

"That may be true, but it's what she's decided she wants," Dani reminded him.

"Maybe we should call Lou."

"I'd rather not disturb her if it's something simple we've overlooked."

Just then, Jodie burst through the door, baby book in hand. Dani gave Chryssa to her while she looked up the information they needed.

"Can you find anything?" Jodie asked eagerly after only a couple of minutes.

"From the way Chryssa's behaving, it seems to me she probably just has a stomachache, which is pretty common for babies," Dani answered.

"But she hasn't spit up at all."

"Maybe that's why she has the stomachache," Brendan suggested.

"Whatever the reason, you'll have to help relieve her pain by putting her against your shoulder and rubbing her back. You can try rubbing her abdomen, too."

So, as Dani and Brendan watched, Jodie paced the

floor, gently massaging the tiny infant's back. Finally, after about ten minutes, Chryssa fell asleep.

"Should I try moving her?" Jodie whispered.

Dani nodded. "I'll spread out her blanket and you can set her down."

To everyone's relief, Chryssa did not awaken as Jodie transferred her from her shoulder to the sofa, where Dani bundled her back up in the receiving blanket. Brendan reached for the flashlight and led the way to the door.

"If she wakes up again and has the same problem, try walking with her," Dani said in a soft voice as Jodie followed her uncle to the door. "And make sure you burp her while you're feeding her."

"I will," Jodie whispered.

Dani watched them disappear into the darkness. As she climbed back into bed, her thoughts weren't on Jodie and Chryssa, but her own birth mother. Like Jodie, Bridget had probably wanted to keep her baby, to give her all the love she'd feared no one else would give her.

Like Jodie, she'd gone through labor and given birth without her parents or even her boyfriend around. She'd more than likely experienced the same emotions Dani had witnessed in Jodie—fear, uncertainty, joy and love—and was probably no better equipped than Jodie to raise a child. Dani felt a rush of sympathy for the mother she'd never known.

Thinking about her birth mother had her pondering how different her life might have been if she hadn't been given up for adoption. Would she have been raised by her grandfather in this resort with no running water and no electricity? Curious about her birth mother's family, she climbed out of bed and opened the chest at its foot.

She sifted through the personal items, which included her grandfather's military medals. There was a Purple Heart from World War II, several ribbons and stripes of merit, as well as a picture of him with his regiment. There were some old postcards he'd sent home to his parents while he'd been in the service and his old army uniform. Nowhere in the chest were there any letters.

Dani sighed. She wanted to know more about Bridget Latvanen. What had she been like? Had she hated living at the resort with its primitive facilities? What had she studied in school? Dani searched through the closet in the bedroom and found no clues whatsoever.

She climbed back into bed and lay in the darkness, thinking of how strange it was that now, after twenty-six years, she was unraveling the story of her past. Ever since she could remember, she'd known she was adopted. Her mother had answered all her questions as best she could, never trying to discourage her from seeking information on her birth mother. Although Dani knew some adopted children who went to great lengths to locate their birth families, she'd never felt any urgency to find hers.

Now that information had come to her. Because of Jodie's experience, she was able to understand some of the emotions her birth mother must have experienced when she'd made the decision to give Dani up for adoption. Although Dani still didn't know much about her, she was certain of one thing. Bridget had given another woman a chance to have a daughter. For that, Dani would always be grateful.

LONG AFTER BRENDAN got back to Jodie's cabin, he lay awake on the couch. And it wasn't Chryssa keeping him awake. The infant was sleeping peacefully in Jodie's room. There was no noise except the occasional cry of a loon.

What kept him from falling asleep was the memory of how Dani had looked in her nightshirt. The minute she'd answered the door, he had felt his body respond to her loveliness. He'd almost told her to cover herself up, but with both women's attention focused on the baby, he knew that neither of them thought much about how revealing Dani's nightshirt was.

It was such a sweet torment to see her holding that baby, with that nightshirt creeping up her thigh and giving him an even more tempting view of her flesh. It didn't help that every time she moved past the lamp the sheerness of the cotton provided him a silhouette that made his blood rush.

If he wasn't going to spend the night in his own bed, he sure as hell would have preferred to spend the night in Dani's, not on Jodie's couch. Yet what choice did he have? He could see that his niece needed the reassurance of another person's presence on this her first night without the support of hospital staff. As much as he wanted to teach her a lesson about what a great responsibility a child was, he couldn't leave her alone.

He sighed and got up, crossing to the window. He opened it and let the gentle, cooling breeze wash over him. As he inhaled the summer smells of the woods and water, he thought how different everything had turned out from what he'd expected when he'd first come to The Last Place on Earth. Instead of being alone, he was with two women and a baby. What was really odd was that it didn't seem strange. At the start of summer, the last thing he'd wanted was company, yet now he couldn't wait for tomorrow so he could be with Dani.

He closed the window and returned to the couch. How could he even think such thoughts? During his time in the seminary, he'd never doubted his ability to sacrifice sex in order to become an ordained priest, even though his friends and family had difficulty understanding how a man could choose celibacy after experiencing the intimacy of marriage.

Brendan wasn't just any man, however. Denying himself the pleasure of sex was a sacrifice he'd wanted to make, needed to make. Overrated was how he would have described the sexual act.

Of course, that was before Dani. Again he thought of the pleasure he'd found in her arms, and his body ached. Nothing could have prepared him for such tremendous rush of feelings or the incredible satisfaction. Not even two years of marriage.

At the thought of Caroline, he felt a pang of remorse. She'd been so different from Dani. So insecure, so unsure of herself. They'd waited to have sex until they were wed. Only now could he look back and see what an irony that was. When they couldn't have sex, they wanted it; when they could have it, they didn't want it. He closed his eyes and forced those memories to the back of his mind.

He had come to The Last Place on Earth this summer looking for answers. But he'd only found more questions. How could he have such strong feelings for a woman he hardly knew? And what was he going to do when Jodie went back to Minneapolis and he was left alone with Dani? Right now, he didn't want to think about summer coming to an end and never seeing her again, yet they hadn't talked about any future together.

How could they? They'd barely had a beginning. With thoughts of Dani on his mind, he fell asleep.

He awoke to the sound of Chryssa crying. It sounded as if she was right beside him. He opened his eyes and saw that she was. Her portable crib was pushed close to the couch.

Brendan crawled out of the sleeping bag and sat up-right, pushing the crib away from the couch so he could slide his feet to the floor. "Jodie?" he called out as he stood. No answer. Thinking she must have gone to use the outhouse, Brendan scooped up the crying baby. "Shh. It's okay. Don't cry," he whispered, carefully cuddling her to his chest. "Mommy will be right back."

Only Mommy didn't come right back. Brendan put the baby up against his shoulder as he'd seen Dani do and walked around the tiny cabin, soothing the agitated infant as best he could.

It was while he was walking between kitchenette and living area that he saw the piece of paper on the countertop. It was folded in half with the words "Uncle Brendan" penned across the middle.

He could almost feel the hairs stand up on the back of his neck. He reached for the note.

Dear Uncle,
I'm going back to Minneapolis without Chryssa. I know you wanted me to give her up for adoption, but I can't. At least not yet. I need to talk to Dusty first. I know you and Dani will take care of Chryssa until I get back. Thank you so much. You are the best uncle in the world.

Love, Jodie

CHAPTER THIRTEEN

ONCE AGAIN DANI AWOKE to the sound of someone pounding on her door. This time it was only Brendan and the baby on her step. Dani could see by the look of consternation on his face that something was wrong.

"What is it?" she asked, opening the door.

"Jodie's gone." He stepped inside, the baby in his arms.

"What do you mean, gone?" Automatically Dani reached for Chryssa.

Brendan didn't hesitate giving her the infant. "She went back to Minneapolis...without Chryssa."

"What?"

"When I woke up this morning, Chryssa's crib was beside me and there was a note on the counter." He pulled the piece of paper from his pocket and handed it to her.

"I can't believe it," Dani said when she'd read the childlike handwriting. "Why would she leave without Chryssa?"

"Maybe because she's sixteen and doesn't realize that a baby isn't like a pet."

Dani could hear the anger in his voice. "But how did she get out of here? There's no transportation."

"She took my car."

"Does she have a license?"

"No, but that didn't stop her. She wants to find this

Dusty character.'' He rubbed a hand across the back of his neck. ''For all I know, she might not stop at Minneapolis. If he's left town, maybe she'll go after him.''

Dani looked down at the crying infant in her arms. ''The first thing we need to do is feed Chryssa. She probably has a wet diaper, too. You didn't change her, did you?''

''No. As soon as I realized Jodie was gone, I came here.''

''You better get the baby things and bring them over here,'' Dani suggested, trying to calm the crying infant as best she could by rocking her in her arms.

''Does that mean you'll take care of her until I can find Jodie?''

''*We* will take care of her,'' she corrected.

''One of us has to look for Jodie.''

''If one of us leaves, that means the other one is stuck here at the resort with a newborn and no running water, no electricity, no telephone and no transportation,'' Dani said. ''I'm not going to be that one and I'm certain you don't want to be, either.''

''So in the meantime we just sit here and wait until she decides to come back?'' His expression looked grim.

Dani understood his frustration, but what choice did they have? ''From her note, it sounds as if she's planning to return.''

Brendan sighed in exasperation. ''Just how much money did you give her?''

Dani knew he hadn't been happy with her offer to help Jodie. His anger now proved she was right. ''This isn't my fault.''

''I didn't say it was.''

''Good, because the reason I gave her the money is

that I knew she was going to keep the baby whether I helped her or not. And the thought of her living on the streets with no place to stay, no food to eat..." Dani shuddered. "Well, I just couldn't let that happen."

Brendan looked down at the fussing infant and Dani saw the anger slip from his face. "I know you were only trying to help."

"I was." Dani stared into Brendan's eyes and saw a strength there. "Why don't you get Chryssa's diaper bag so I can get her changed and fed? The poor thing's hungry and wet."

Without another word, Brendan went to retrieve the portable crib and the rest of the baby gear. While he was gone, Dani changed into a pair of shorts and a T-shirt.

He was breathing hard when he returned and set the crib up in the middle of the room. "I can't believe how much stuff you need for one little baby."

Dani didn't respond, but reached for the disposable diapers, wet wipes and powder. She disappeared with the baby into the bedroom and left Brendan with instructions to unload the rest of the baby's things and to heat some water.

After changing the baby, Dani joined Brendan in the kitchen. Chryssa still fussed, but the sounds came in tiny spurts, as if she was too tired to put up much of a protest.

"Will you hold her for a minute while I prepare her bottle?" Dani didn't wait for an answer but placed the infant into his arms.

Dani washed her hands, then carefully divided the eight-ounce can of formula between two bottles, putting four ounces in each. The one she wasn't going to use, she put into the refrigerator. The other she warmed on the stove in a small pan of water.

"Thanks for heating the water in the kettle." She took Chryssa from him.

"You're welcome. Is there anything else I can do?"

"Not at the moment," she replied, turning so that she could watch the bottle on the stove. After shaking a little of the formula onto her wrist and deciding it was sufficiently warmed, she carried Chryssa into the living room. Then she sat down with her in the rocker, a cloth draped over her shoulder.

Brendan noticed that there was none of the awkwardness or uncertainty in her actions that he'd noticed in Jodie's. As if it was the most natural thing in the world, Dani fed the baby, focusing all her attention on the infant. He wondered how he could ever have thought she was a woman of little substance.

The room was silent except for the tiny sucking sounds the baby girl made as she drank. Brendan enjoyed the way Dani looked holding Chryssa, the tenderness that softened her features. He knew she'd make a good mother. Then the CB radio buzzed and he went to answer it.

"What did Lou want?" Dani asked as soon as he returned.

"She said my car's at the end of Sacred Lake Road. Apparently Jodie must have taken it to the highway, gotten out and hitchhiked home."

Dani shuddered. "That makes me nervous. A teenage girl hitchhiking at night."

"Lou suspects she probably got a ride with a trucker. They're about the only ones who come through Hidden Falls during the early hours of the morning."

"I just pray she's all right," Dani said softly. She set

the bottle down and lifted the baby to her shoulder, gently patting her back. It only took a couple of seconds before Chryssa burped. "Good girl," Dani cooed lovingly, recradling the infant in her arms. "Want some more?" she asked, tipping the nipple against the baby's tiny mouth. Pink lips closed greedily around it.

"If you give me your keys, I'll get my car."

"How are you going to do that?"

"Lou offered to help out. She said if I pick her up, she'll drive the Geo back here, then I can give her a ride home after we bring my car back," he explained. "That way, I'll be able to stop and use the phone at Hidden Falls, too."

"You're not going to call the police, are you?"

"No. I'll call Father Joe and have him check out some of the places she might stay in Minneapolis."

"You think she'll go back to her mother's?"

"It's not likely. But you're right about one thing. It's not a good idea to leave you here alone and go chasing after her. For all we know she could be back tomorrow."

Dani looked at Chryssa. "I can't imagine her leaving this little girl for very long."

Brendan didn't share her sentiments, but he kept silent. "Where are the keys?"

"They're hanging over the sink in the kitchen."

He nodded. "Why don't I pick up some fresh fruit and muffins from Pete's as long as I'm going out, and we can have breakfast when I get back."

"All right," Dani said. "By then, Chryssa should be asleep." She looked down at the tiny mouth clinging to the nipple.

Brendan wasted no time getting Lou or stopping at Pete's Place. By the time he returned to the resort,

Chryssa was asleep. Brendan invited Lou to stay for breakfast, but she declined. After she'd taken a peek at the sleeping baby, Brendan drove her home.

Dani didn't look forward to Brendan's return. She knew that decisions had to be made regarding Chryssa, and she could hardly stand even contemplating the options.

She made a fresh pot of coffee and cut up the melon he'd brought from Pete's Place, then set the table. At the sound of his car on the gravel driveway, she felt butterflies in her stomach. She busied herself organizing Chryssa's things so it wouldn't look as if she was waiting for him.

"How's Chryssa?" he said the moment he stepped through the door.

"She's fine."

"Lou said she'd be happy to help out if we need her."

"That's kind of her."

"Yes, it is." When he saw she had the kitchen table set, he sat down on one of the chairs. She poured him a cup of coffee and took a seat across from him. "I hate to tell you this, but I think Chryssa left you a present on your shoulder." He tried to hide a grin but was unsuccessful.

She twisted her neck and yanked her shirt around to see if there was spit-up on it. Actually she didn't need to see it to know Brendan spoke the truth. One whiff and she knew the baby had left her mark. She got up to run cold water over a cloth, then stood in front of the mirror, rubbing at the spot.

When she returned, he teased, "Still happy you came to stay for the summer?"

"Yes, I am." She shot him a cross look.

She doubted if he believed her. He turned his attention to breakfast, spreading a thick layer of butter across one half of a muffin.

"Well?" she asked when the silence between them stretched into awkwardness. "Don't you think we should talk about what we're going to do?"

"Jodie's put me in a difficult position. I'm not quite sure what to do."

"You're not thinking about turning Chryssa over to Social Services, are you?"

He sighed. "Not yet."

"You can't. Jodie wouldn't have left her if she thought you were going to put her in foster care. It's not like you're a stranger. You're her uncle."

He rubbed the back of his neck. "I realize that, but I can only do this for so long before I have to notify the authorities."

"How long?" she asked warily.

"Thirty days is the max, and then we'll need to formalize some sort of guardianship."

"I can't imagine she'll be gone that long," Dani said with more confidence than she felt. "I want you to know I'm willing to help in any way I can. In fact, you can leave Chryssa here with me since I have a refrigerator."

He looked at her over the rim of his coffee cup. "You're willing to take care of her indefinitely?"

"Yes, although I'd be surprised if Jodie isn't back within a couple of days."

He wasn't as convinced. "It's a big responsibility."

Dani looked him squarely in the eye and asked, "Don't you want me to look after her?"

"Yes, I do. Thank you." He set his coffee cup down

and leaned back in his chair. "I called Father Joe. He's agreed to help me find Jodie."

"What about this girlfriend she always talks about—Shawna?"

"Father Joe knows who she is. He's going over to see her."

"And what happens if he doesn't find her?"

He shrugged. "We wait until she returns."

"And if for some unknown reason she doesn't return?"

"I'll have to notify the authorities. Chryssa will probably be placed in foster care." When she frowned, he added, "You can't just abandon a newborn, Dani."

"I realize that," she answered. Even though her heart went out to the teenager, she knew that Brendan was right.

"So, we'll give her some time to get her act together or whatever it is she's doing. If she doesn't, I'll have to report her disappearance to Social Services."

Dani knew he had no other choice. Chryssa needed to be their primary concern. She deserved to have parents, a place she could call home.

Once again an uncomfortable silence stretched between them. Dani knew she had to say something.

"I know you think I wanted Jodie to keep the baby," she said. "But if you'd heard the conversations we had in the past few days, you'd know I tried to convince her that adoption wasn't the evil she seemed to think it was." He looked doubtful. Annoyed, she persisted, "I hope you don't think that because I'm adopted, I would encourage Jodie to keep her baby."

"Seeing Jodie and Chryssa must have triggered some sort of emotional response in you," he said.

"Of course it did, but not in the way you seem to

believe. I've always been comfortable with the fact that I'm adopted.'' Dani paused to find the right words that would make him understand. ''Brendan, some people might think there was something wrong with me for not wanting to know who my birth mother was, but it just wasn't an issue for me. My adoptive parents loved me and wanted me. There was no reason for me to feel different from any other kid. Even though I never knew my birth mother, in my heart I always believed she gave me up for adoption because she wanted what was best for me. This past week with Jodie has shown me how difficult it is for a young mother to even consider making such a decision. I also know giving a child to another woman to raise can be a very unselfish act.''

''Did you tell Jodie that?''

''Yes. You seem to think that just because I wasn't telling her she should give her baby up for adoption, it wasn't what I believed she should do.'' Dani shoved aside her half-empty plate. ''I think if Chryssa hadn't been born prematurely, Jodie might have made the choice to go ahead with the adoption. She just needed more time.''

''Sometimes life doesn't provide us with the luxury of time. This isn't about taking care of a puppy. There's a little girl in that crib who this very minute could be in a nice home with a loving couple who would cherish her and shower her with love and affection. Instead, she's at a place with no running water and two people who don't have a clue what it takes to raise a child.''

''Speak for yourself. I've read this.'' She picked up the book at her fingertips and waved it in the air. ''Everything you need to know about babies from A to Z.''

He didn't smile at her attempt at humor.

''All right,'' Dani said. ''So we're not experienced

with babies, but at least we both care about Chryssa and want what's best for her.''

He eyed her curiously. ''I think you really *do* care about her.''

''Why wouldn't I? She's an innocent child, so precious and fragile. I look at her and think, that could have been me. My birth mother was sixteen when she had me. For all I know, she could have been just like Jodie.''

''There was a big difference between Bridget and Jodie. Bridget had a father who cared what happened to her.''

''Yet like Jodie, she became pregnant and ran away from home.''

''Yes, and her disappearance caused a lot of pain for your grandfather. He never stopped caring about her, nor did he give up the hope she'd come home.'' He shook his head sadly.

''How come there are no pictures of her in the house?'' Dani asked.

''He must have put them all away somewhere. Maybe it was too painful to have them out. I'm not really sure.''

''Where did Bridget sleep when she was here?''

''In the loft. Haven't you been up there?''

''Yes, but I couldn't get the door open. It's locked.''

Brendan frowned. ''Wilbur never locked anything.'' He got up and climbed the stairs to the loft. Dani followed him, watching as he jiggled the doorknob. Then with a press of his shoulder, he pushed it open. ''It was just stuck,'' he said, stepping aside and allowing her to enter.

Dani felt as if she had walked into a time warp. Judging by the pictures and posters on the walls, nothing in the room had been touched in the past twenty-six years. It was the room of a teenage girl, with a pair of pompoms dangling over the headboard of her bed and a poster of a popular film star tacked to one wall.

In the middle of the bed was an autographed pillow in the shape of a dog. Dani glanced at the names scrawled across it in pen. Friends she'd left behind when she went in search of something better than what Hidden Falls had to offer.

Gingerly Dani touched the objects on the desk—the paperweight that was obviously an art project in school, the empty soup can covered with felt that now housed pens and pencils, a stack of magazines. Dani flipped through them and found they were mostly movie and TV magazines with many of the pictures missing. It was easy to see why—every inch of the bulletin board on the wall was covered with photographs of celebrities.

In a small frame on the desk was a certificate that said she was a member of the Creedence Clearwater Revival Fan Club. Dani opened a jewelry box and a tiny ballerina began to turn to the music of "The Skaters Waltz." Inside was an assortment of rings and bracelets, but it was the tiny gold pin that caught Dani's eye. It said she was a member of the National Honor Society.

Seeing her fingering the pin, Brendan said, "She was smart. She skipped the third grade and could have graduated at the age of seventeen if she hadn't quit school."

"Where did she go to school?"

"All the kids around here are bused to Granville—that's about thirty-five miles east of here."

Dani found a high-school yearbook on a shelf beside the bed and opened it. The inside cover was scrawled with autographs and brief messages. She read one aloud. "'Bridget, you are one terrific actress. I expect to see you in the movies someday.'"

"Wilbur said she was in all the high school plays." Brendan lifted a trophy. "Looks like she was also on the debating team."

"My knees still shake whenever I have to give a speech, and the only time I had a part in a school play I forgot my lines," Dani mused aloud.

"Looks like she read a lot." Brendan examined the shelves of books.

Dani noted that many of the books were plays, including the complete works of Shakespeare and Eugene O'Neill. "Some of these are college texts."

"Wilbur said she was advanced for her age." Brendan pointed to the bottom shelf, which housed a collection of Nancy Drew mysteries. "Those must have been from her younger years."

Dani stooped to pull out one of the books. "I remember reading these when I was a kid." She chuckled. "It's funny. She never got rid of her Nancy Drew books, not even when she was a teenager. I didn't, either."

"Want to look in the closet?"

Dani hesitated only a moment, then pulled open the bifold doors and saw clothing—woolen sweaters and corduroy slacks, a dark green parka and a pair of snow boots. She picked up a pair of mittens that had fallen to the floor. On the shelf above were a couple of purses, several hats and a large box. "Could you reach that for me?" Dani asked.

Brendan pulled the box from the shelf and set it on the bed. Dani lifted the lid and found all sorts of memorabilia—greeting cards, programs of plays, school pictures, postcards, a bundle of letters. Dani flipped through them and saw that most of them were from a Finnish pen pal.

"Do you know if my grandfather kept any of the letters she might have written to him from New York?"

"There's a carved wooden writing box that he kept on his desk. I imagine if he has any, that's where they'd be."

When they were back downstairs, Dani crossed to the rolltop desk and opened the wooden box with the carved lid. Inside were letters. Just as Brendan had suspected, there were a few from Bridget, but there was one written to her father that had been returned unopened with Return To Sender: Address Unknown stamped across the top.

"So he did write to me." Her fingers trembled as they ripped open a sealed flap on one of the envelopes. She pulled out the letter and a second envelope fell out. It was addressed to her. She read both letters, then sank onto the leather chair. "He wanted to see me," she said in a small voice.

"Yes, I told you that."

"He said he'd written many times before and wanted to know why I hadn't answered." She looked up at Brendan. "I never received any letters from him." She looked into the bottom of the wooden box and pulled out a cardboard picture folder. She opened it. "That's my college graduation picture." She looked up at Brendan. "My father must have corresponded with him," Dani said in astonishment. "I don't understand why he didn't tell me."

"Maybe he thought there was something wrong with a man willing to live such a rustic life in the middle of nowhere," Brendan suggested.

"But Wilbur was resourceful. I mean, look at the

shower and the sauna...." She was truly bewildered by
the discovery that her father had kept her grandfather's
letters from her. Did he have so little faith in her, in her
decision whether or not to have contact with a member
of her birth family?

Just then, Chryssa began to cry. Dani put everything
back in the box and closed it. "I'll have to look at this
stuff later."

Brendan got up. "Let me get her."

Dani didn't protest. She watched him go into the bedroom. When he didn't return, she went to see what had
happened to him. To her surprise, he was changing
Chryssa's diaper and didn't seem the least intimidated
by the task. He was talking to the infant all the while,
and Dani's love for him soared. She tiptoed back to the
living room and sat down.

"She's dry and happy," he said when he joined Dani
a few minutes later, carrying the baby as if she were a
carton of fresh eggs. He took a seat beside Dani on the
sofa, using his knees as a table for the infant. It was
only a matter of seconds before Chryssa started to fuss.
"I guess she could be happier," he said with a crooked
grin.

Dani glanced at her watch. "It's been three hours.
I'll get another bottle ready."

Leaving Brendan with the baby, she went into the
kitchen. All the while, her thoughts were on her father.
She realized now that he had known of her birth grandfather's existence and chosen not to tell her.

When she took the bottle into the other room, Brendan suggested they take Chryssa outside to feed her.
Dani didn't object. She followed him out to the lawn
swing where they sat side by side, her thigh touching

his. As she fed Chryssa, he leaned close, watching with interest.

"Maybe you should show me how to do that so I can give you a break when you need it," he suggested, his arm resting along the back of the swing.

"You want to give it a try?"

He looked uncertain, but said, "Sure. Tell me what I need to do."

"Just cradle her in your arms and tilt her head back just a little," Dani told him as she placed Chryssa in his large hands. "You want to hold the bottle so there's always milk in the nipple. If she sucks air, she'll get a tummy ache."

"Like this?" he said.

"Perfect," Dani replied, watching as Chryssa sucked happily away.

Seeing Brendan feeding the infant made Dani wonder what kind of parent he would make. It was obvious from the attention he gave Chryssa that he truly liked children. It was hard to believe that someone who could be so gentle and caring with a child wouldn't make a wonderful father.

"Do you see yourself as a father somewhere down the road?" she asked.

"I take it you mean the kind of father who's a parent." When she nodded, he continued, "I pretty much had accepted that it wasn't going to happen. You see, for most of my life I wanted to be a priest."

"Yet you were married."

"Yes, but I shouldn't have been."

"Why do you say that?"

"We were incompatible." He handed her the bottle. "I think she's fallen asleep."

Dani could see he wasn't going to talk about his marriage. She had so many questions she wanted to ask him but was reluctant to probe an area he apparently wasn't ready to let her enter.

"Do you think we should take her inside and put her down in the crib?" he asked in a low voice.

"We can stay here if you don't mind holding her."

"No, she's so light I hardly notice she's in my arms."

They sat there on the swing on the most perfect of summer days. They swayed gently back and forth, the air around them silent except for the occasional cry of a bird or the rustling of a squirrel in the undergrowth.

It was a scene that was repeated often over the next few days. Dani bore most of the responsibility for taking care of Chryssa, but Brendan was never far from her side, always ready to help. And although Brendan and Dani spent nearly every waking moment together, not once did he make any effort to be intimate with her. Dani longed to feel his arms around her, to taste his kiss on her lips. With each passing day, she fell more in love with him, yet he gave her no indication that he looked at her as anything other than Chryssa's baby-sitter.

Dani suspected he was taking the opportunity to get to know her, for he'd told her the night they'd made love that he hadn't meant to rush her. What Brendan didn't understand was that Dani was ready to move their relationship to another level. She wanted more from him than affectionate glances. At last, she decided to take the bull by the horns.

It was one evening after dinner when Brendan noticed her yawning. "Why don't I take Chryssa to my cabin tonight?" he said. "That way you can sleep through the night without getting up for her feeding."

"I have a better idea," Dani said boldly. "Why don't you sleep at my place?"

The silence that ensued knocked the wind out of her sails. Brendan's face was unreadable. For all she knew, he was trying to think of the world's best rejection line. So she quickly added, "You can use the sofa bed."

"Then I'll be over as soon as I get my things together."

CHAPTER FOURTEEN

THE ONLY REASON Brendan had agreed to spend the night at Dani's was that she truly needed to get a good night's sleep. He knew that ever since Jodie's disappearance, Dani had been getting up at least once, sometimes twice, in the middle of the night to feed Chryssa. In the short time they'd been taking care of the baby, he'd also discovered that feeding time could last as long as an hour.

Since Chryssa's things were all in the big house, it didn't make much sense to haul everything down to his cabin. And just because he and Dani had made love on one occasion, he wasn't ready to make any sort of commitment to her. That was why, considering everything that had happened between them, Brendan knew the best place for him was on the sofa bed.

"Yeah, right," he muttered to himself as he packed an overnight bag. No matter how hard he tried to convince himself convenience was the reason for staying at her house, it didn't change the fact that he wanted to be sleeping in Dani's bed.

He had thought from the way she'd looked at him when she'd suggested spending the night that she wanted the same thing, yet when he arrived, she treated him as if he was simply a houseguest. She'd already pulled out the sofa bed and was putting a sheet over the

mattress, giving no indication that she wanted him anywhere but on the sofa.

"Chryssa usually wakes up around two-thirty," Dani
said, tossing two pillows onto the bed. "I've left a bottle
in the refrigerator, so all you have to do is heat it."

The living room was in near darkness except for the
little bit of light coming from the lamp in the kitchen.
Chryssa was asleep in the portable crib, not far from
the sofa bed. Dani kept her voice low as she talked.

"How long will a bottle hold her?" Brendan asked.

"Usually two or three hours." She added a hand-
stitched quilt to the bed. "One night, she didn't wake
up again until almost five. That was a real treat."

He nodded in understanding. "I can take care of the
next two feedings if you want to sleep in tomorrow
morning."

"That's sweet of you, but I'll take the second one."
She finished smoothing the covers on the bed, then
stood. "There." She stretched her arms up over the top
of her head, causing the fabric of her shirt to pull tautly
across her breasts. "I guess you're all set. Gosh, it'll
feel good to sleep through the night without any inter-
ruptions."

"Sleep's important," he said inanely.

"Yes, it sure is." There was a brief, awkward silence,
then she said, "Well, I'll say good-night."

"Good night."

More awkward silence. "You want me to turn off the
kitchen light?"

"If you don't mind."

She padded out to the kitchen. "Good night," she
called again as darkness settled around them.

When he heard the bedroom door close, he undressed
but for his boxers and T-shirt, then slid between the

covers. He lay on his side so he could see the sliver of
light beneath her door. He kept staring at it, wondering
what she was doing behind that closed door. All sorts
of fantasies popped into his head. Then the light disappeared.

He rolled over and willed his mind to go blank. It
didn't work. Again he looked toward the bedroom, but
there was still no light. She was probably sleeping,
which is what he should have been doing since it
wouldn't be long before Chryssa needed his attention.

But the harder he tried not to think about Dani, the
more she haunted his thoughts. He kept remembering
their night together, the way she'd felt in his arms, how
they'd made love as if their bodies had been created for
each other. Heat had him kicking off his covers and
rolling over once more.

A short while later, the bedroom door creaked. He
lifted his head and saw a flashlight beam move from
Dani's room into the kitchen. Then he heard the squeak
of the pump handle. She was getting a glass of water.

Then the beam came toward him. It moved behind
the sofa bed and around the end table until it found its
target—the portable crib.

"She's all right," Brendan said in a low voice.

Dani gasped. "You're awake."

"Yes."

"I needed a drink of water so I thought I might as
well check on her." She aimed the flashlight so it only
indirectly shone on the baby.

"She seems to be the only one who *is* sleeping
soundly," he remarked.

"Yeah. I think I must be too tired to sleep. What's
your excuse?"

"I can't stop thinking about you."

His words had the effect of someone dropping a glass onto a concrete floor. Slowly the flashlight beam traveled across the living room to the sofa bed, then across the rumpled pile of sheets and quilt. When it reached his bare legs, the light went off with a decisive click.

"You're not naked, are you?" she asked.

"No."

She clicked the flashlight back on, but this time kept it aimed toward the floor.

"I don't make a habit of feeding babies in the nude," he said dryly. "And I don't know why you're so prudish about my naked body. You've already seen it," he reminded her.

"Shh. We shouldn't be talking. We'll wake the baby."

"Well, then, maybe we should go someplace where the baby isn't sleeping," he suggested.

She hesitated only a minute before saying, "Follow me."

Brendan needed no second invitation. He was off the sofa in a flash. He tiptoed behind her as quietly as he could, trying his best not to awaken Chryssa. He'd gotten this far; he didn't need a baby's crying to stop his progress.

She led him into the bedroom, quietly closing the door behind them. Instead of turning on the battery-operated lamp, she propped the flashlight on the nightstand so it shone on the ceiling.

"I think we should turn on a lamp. We'll look like a couple of jack-o'-lanterns with the light shining that way," he told her.

She leaned over and flipped on the lamp. In its soft glow, he could see that her bedclothes were rumpled, too. She'd been having just as much trouble sleeping as he had.

She wore another nightshirt—this one white satin. It came to the middle of her thighs and only added more oil to the fire where his fantasies burned. He wanted to tell her how her beauty affected him, how he couldn't look at her without thinking about the night they'd spent together, but there was something magical about the nonverbal communication happening between them.

She climbed onto the bed, then knelt, sitting back on her heels. She gestured for him to join her. "This is where we should be talking."

Only, there was no talking between Dani and Brendan when he lay down beside her. No talking, only lovemaking, as their bodies came together in what seemed more a union of souls. It was every bit as intense and powerful as it had been the first time they'd made love. If Brendan had any thought that what he felt for Dani was purely physical, it was quickly banished.

When it was over, they lay side by side, their arms wrapped around each other, their legs entwined. Brendan had never felt so content in his life. "No wonder I haven't been able to stop thinking about you," he said, placing a kiss on her brow. "This is more than just sex."

She lifted her head. "Is that what you thought it was the first time we were together?"

"I wasn't sure," he admitted honestly. "I knew there was this incredibly strong physical attraction between us, but I wasn't sure if the intensity was simply because I had been celibate for such a long time. I thought maybe it was a case of the dam bursting."

She stiffened and began to pull away from him.

"And you think the dam would have burst with any woman?"

He could see his words had hurt her. He held her close and said, "No. Definitely not." He kissed her breasts, then covered her lips tenderly with his. "What's happening between us goes way beyond physical pleasure. That's why it's so overwhelming. I never expected to feel this way."

"And how do you feel?" she asked, her fingers tracing circles on his chest.

"Like the luckiest man alive. I love you, Dani, and I don't want to think about the summer ending."

She sat forward. "Does it have to end?"

"I haven't known time to stand still for anyone no matter how hard they wished," he said wryly. Suddenly the sound of Chryssa's crying had him grimacing as he draped an arm across his forehead. "I'm needed."

She placed a kiss on his naked chest and said, "By more than one female in this house." As he rolled off the bed and pulled on his boxers, she said, "When two people share what we just shared, they should talk about it, Brendan. We really need to discuss what happens next, or else we're going to end up like we did the last time we made love—avoiding each other."

He planted another quick kiss on her lips. "That will never happen. I won't let it. I agree—we need to talk. If you're not awake when I get back, we'll do it in the morning."

"Maybe I should get up with you," she suggested.

"Uh-uh. This was supposed to be my job. You keep the bed warm and I'll be right back," he promised as he reached for the flashlight. He gave her one last kiss.

Brendan wasn't exactly right back. Chryssa took what he thought seemed to be forever to drink three

ounces of the formula. He had to put on Dani's head-
phones and play some music to keep from nodding off
himself. When at last he had the infant back in her crib,
he went back into Dani's room. As he suspected, she
was asleep. She looked so tantalizing lying there in her
satiny white nightshirt, her cheek buried in the pillow.
He had to fight the urge to wake her and make passionate love.

He knew she was in a deep sleep, for when he
climbed in beside her and pulled her into his arms, she
didn't stir. She simply curled into his chest as if she
belonged there. Brendan had only one prayer. *Please let
Chryssa sleep until after sunrise.*

DURING THE TIME Jodie was gone, Dani had learned
much about Brendan. And the more she learned, the
more she loved him. For she'd determined that it was
indeed love she felt for him. A glorious feeling, it was
the reason she was singing to Chryssa as she fed her
that morning.

Although there hadn't yet been time for the two of
them to finish the talk they'd begun during the night,
Dani felt confident that once Brendan returned from his
quick trip into town to get more formula and diapers,
they would spend the rest of the morning discussing
their future together.

Dani ignored the niggling doubts that made her wonder if they truly did have a future together. After last
night, there should have been no doubts. Brendan had
said he didn't want to see the summer ending. She
would have preferred if he'd asked what they were going to do *after* the summer came to an end. And she'd
have liked to hear that what they had together was not
merely a holiday romance to be fondly looked back

upon. It couldn't be, not after last night, and especially not after his declaration of love.

Nothing remained to come between them now. As soon as Jodie returned for Chryssa, the issue of adoption would be resolved once and for all. And when Brendan came home, she was going to tell him she'd decided not to sell the resort to developers but would maintain it as a wildlife preserve. No obstacles would stand in the way of their happiness.

Dani had just finished feeding Chryssa when she heard a car drive up. When two doors slammed, curiosity got the better of her. She placed Chryssa in the crib and went to the door. To her astonishment, her father and a man she didn't know were walking toward the house. She stepped out onto the porch.

"Dad! What are you doing here?"

"I came to see you." He spread his arms wide. "Give me a hug."

Like a dutiful child, Dani went into her father's arms. "Are you planning on staying?"

"Don't look at me as if that's a punishment," he scolded. "It's not like you don't have the room, is it?" He glanced at the guest cabins.

"Well, yeah, but you're the one who said it's primitive," she reminded him. "How are you going to get by without your telecommunications?"

He waved away her concern with a flap of his hand. "Don't you worry about me. I don't mind roughing it if I can spend some time with my little girl."

Dani noticed he didn't say we, but I. "Dad, who's this man?" she asked in a whisper.

"This is Clark Westin. He's from Country Lakes Real Estate," her father answered in a loud voice. The man extended a hand to Dani, who reluctantly shook it.

She pulled her father aside and said in a voice meant only for him, "I'm not interested in selling this place, Dad."

"He's doing an appraisal," her father whispered back.

"One's already been done."

"We need more than one opinion."

"No, we don't."

Her father ignored her. He turned to the other man, who was looking out at the lake, and said, "Well, what do you think? It's got possibilities, yes?"

"Oh, definitely. With this much shoreline undeveloped, it's quite valuable. Most lakeshore in the state is populated, even as far north as this is."

"Danielle, Mr. Westin and I could use something cold to drink," her father said, dabbing at his brow with a handkerchief. "Out here on the deck would be nice."

While her father and his guest made themselves comfortable on the lounge chairs, Dani went inside to make a fresh pitcher of lemonade. She took her anger out on the lemons, which she squeezed with a vengeance. As she filled the glass pitcher with water, she was tempted to leave out the sugar, but decided that Mr. Westin didn't deserve to share in the anger she felt toward her father.

Just as she carried the tray with pitcher and glasses out onto the deck, another car arrived. This one she didn't recognize, either, although there was no doubt that the man who emerged was not one of her father's associates. He was dressed in black and wore a clerical collar.

"This must be Father Millar," her father said as the man approached the house.

"No, it's not," Dani said, setting the tray down on

the picnic table. She walked over to the steps to greet the middle-aged man. "Good morning."

"You must be Dani. I'm Father Joseph Dorian."

Dani shook his hand. "It's nice to meet you. I'm afraid Brendan's not here. He went into town. We ran out of diapers," she said with a crooked grin.

"Diapers?" Robert Taylor stood. "Why on earth would you need diapers?"

"Oh, Father, I'm sorry. This is my dad and a friend of his." She made the introductions and offered Father Dorian a glass of lemonade.

"Danielle, you haven't answered my question. What's this about diapers?" Robert Taylor demanded.

"I'm taking care of a baby," she said calmly.

"Whose baby?"

"It's a long story, Dad," Dani answered. "I'll tell you later." She tried to steer the conversation toward the general, avoiding talking about the two hot issues—the resort and the baby. It wasn't long before her father grew bored.

He finally stood and announced, "Well, it was a pleasure meeting you, Father, but you'll have to excuse us. We have work to do." He gestured for Clark Westin to follow him. "I'm going to show Mr. Westin around the place," he told Dani.

As soon as they were gone, Dani sighed.

"Sometimes it's not easy being the daughter of a successful businessman, is it?" Father Dorian said perceptively.

She smiled. "No, it's not, but I'm learning."

"I'm really glad to have this opportunity to meet you, Dani. I've heard so much about you I feel as if I already know you," he said with a warm smile.

It gave her a warm feeling to know that Brendan had told his mentor about her.

Then he said, "Jodie has talked practically nonstop about you. I never expected she'd talk so fondly about a schoolteacher."

Dani's heart fell. Here she'd thought it was Brendan singing her praises when it was Jodie. "Jodie and I have shared a very special moment," she said wistfully.

Just then, the Geo pulled into the driveway. Brendan got out, a large plastic sack of diapers in one hand, a case of formula in the other. On seeing his mentor, his face lit up. He set his packages down and embraced the priest. His joy was quickly subdued, however. "This must be something serious if you drove 250 miles to tell me in person."

"It's not bad news," the priest quickly assured him. "I've brought you something." He reached into his jacket pocket and pulled out an envelope, which he gave to Brendan. "Actually there are two things. One is a letter from Jodie for you. The other is…well, you can read it for yourself."

Brendan carefully read the contents of the envelope, then handed the papers to Dani and said, "Jodie's decided to give Chryssa up for adoption."

Dani first read the letter the teenager had written. It was addressed to both of them.

Dear Uncle Brendan and Dani,
Thank you for being there for me. I'm sorry I had to leave Chryssa the way I did, but I needed to find Dusty and I didn't want to drag her all over while I did.

Uncle Bren, you were right. Dusty doesn't want to be a father. And the truth is, I'm not ready to be a mother, either. I want my little girl to have the kind of life I didn't have. That's why I'm giving her up for adoption.

Please find parents who will treat her like a princess, because that's how special she is. She will always be my little princess in my heart. I hope she will love her parents as much as Dani loves hers.

I would have come to do this in person, but I'm afraid if I did, I wouldn't be able to say goodbye to her. So give her a kiss from her mommy and tell her I love her.

Jodie

Dani wiped away the tears that trickled down her cheeks before looking at the other document. It was a release form giving up all legal rights to the baby and was signed by both Jodie and Dusty.

"Now what?" Dani looked to Brendan for an answer.

"We'll let Social Services take it from here. We can take Chryssa to Hibbing this afternoon."

Dani nodded numbly. She looked at the package of disposable diapers and the carton of formula sitting on the picnic table. "I guess you shouldn't have bought the economy size."

"We'll give them to the new parents," Brendan said.

Again Dani nodded.

"Thanks, Joe, for helping her make this decision," Brendan said to the older priest.

"I'm glad I could be a part of this, but to be honest, I think Jodie's mind was made up before I ever spoke to her. You two are the ones who were there for her when she needed you most," he said respectfully. Then he said to Dani, "She could have easily had that baby on the side of the road if you hadn't given her a place to stay."

Dani shrugged self-consciously. "There were plenty of rooms at the inn," she said with a smile.

"And a lovely inn it is," Father Dorian said, giving the resort an appreciative gaze.

"You're going to stay overnight, aren't you?" Brendan asked.

"I'd like that, if Dani doesn't mind..." He looked to her for approval.

"No, of course not. You're welcome to stay," she said sincerely.

It was then that Brendan noticed her two other visitors walking along the shore. "You have company?" he asked Dani.

"My father and someone from a real-estate firm," she answered. When his eyes narrowed, she quickly added, "He surprised me. I wasn't expecting either of them."

"Looks like this is your day for unexpected guests," Father Dorian said cheerfully, unaware of the undercurrents.

Dani didn't like the look on Brendan's face. Surely he didn't think she wanted her father here? There was no time to discuss what either of them was feeling, however. Her father returned—without Mr. Westin, to Dani's relief—which prompted Brendan to suggest he show Father Dorian where he could put his things.

As soon as she was alone with her father, Dani wasted no time telling him in no uncertain terms that he was not in charge of making any decisions regarding The Last Place on Earth.

"Dad, you're going to have to stop this right now," she told him.

"Stop what?" he asked innocently.

"Trying to sell this place without my permission. It's not going to happen," she said firmly.

"Danielle, I don't think you realize how valuable this piece of property is."

"Yes, I do, but I think it's valuable for a different reason than you do." She folded her arms across her chest and faced him squarely. "I know you don't want to hear this, but Wilbur Latvanen left me this resort with the request that it remain a quiet, solitary retreat. I intend to honor his wishes."

Her father rolled his eyes. "Dani, be reasonable."

"I am. You're the one who's behaved unreasonably."

"And what's that supposed to mean?"

"Why didn't you tell me you knew Wilbur Latvanen was alive?" She was unable to keep the quiver from her voice.

He began to deny that he did, but she cut him off.

"Don't lie to me, Dad. Not now." She felt a lump lodge tightly in her throat.

"He was a recluse. He'd lived alone for so long he'd lost his grip on reality."

"No, Dad, you're wrong. He was not some crazy old hermit. He was a man who loved nature and didn't want to see it spoiled. Those beliefs put him at odds with people who wanted him to develop this lake, but they didn't make him crazy."

"You didn't know the man, Danielle," he argued.

"No, I didn't, because you wouldn't allow it." She gestured for him to follow her inside where she unlocked the hand-carved box on the desk. She pulled out the letters and waved them in the air. The guilt on her father's face did little to ease Dani's pain. "All he wanted was a chance to know me, but you wouldn't give him that chance, would you?" she said sadly.

For the first time since her mother had died, Dani saw uncertainty on her father's face. "I was worried he'd hurt you. I thought he was a lonely old man who had already ruined one young woman's life—I didn't want to see him ruin another."

"He didn't ruin Bridget's life," she said in defense of her grandfather. "They had a troubled relationship, yes, but it wasn't the cause of her death."

He sighed. "Well, he did some foolish things. I couldn't take the risk that his foolishness might hurt you. After your mother died, you were all I had. I've always taken care of you, and in my eyes he was just one more person from whom you needed to be protected."

Dani softened. "You should have let me make that decision, Dad."

"I'm sorry, but you must know that I've only wanted what was best for you. It's all I've ever wanted," he said, his shoulders hunched.

Dani put her arm around him. "I know that, Dad, but the time has come for me to take care of myself. I'm still going to need you to be my dad, but I have to be an adult. You can't protect me from everything that's out there."

"What are your plans for this place?"

She hesitated, then plunged in. "I want to turn it into a place for unwed mothers, but I'm not sure if it's possible. I've hired some people to help me find out."

"You can't just leave it sit vacant, and you only have a few weeks before you have to return to school."

"I realize that." She wanted to tell him that her plans hinged on what Brendan decided, but she couldn't. Not yet. "I'll have to get a caretaker until I know for sure."

Just then, Chryssa began to cry. It startled her father.

"You really are taking care of a baby?" His face showed his disbelief.

"After today she'll be with her new family," Dani said, going inside with Robert and picking up the infant. "I guess you could say I've been doing a type of foster care."

"You still haven't told me whose baby this is," he reminded her.

"That's because I'm not sure who her mother and father are going to be," she answered, smiling down at the child cradled in her arms.

"She's being given up for adoption?"

"Mmm-hmm. She has one very unselfish mother who loved her enough to give her to some lucky couple who'll treat her like a princess, just like me," Dani answered.

"They won't be perfect," her father said.

"Nope, they'll make mistakes, but she'll forgive them."

Her father placed his arm around her and gave her a gentle squeeze.

CHAPTER FIFTEEN

ROBERT TAYLOR STAYED five days at the resort in cabin number one. It was four days too many as far as Brendan was concerned. During those days, he and Dani had no time alone, and he was beginning to question whether it even mattered to her. With summer slipping away, he wanted to make the most of every day, yet she seemed content to have the company of her father. Which made Brendan wonder if he was rushing her into a relationship. Uncertainty had him backing away.

Brendan didn't understand her behavior at all. She'd announced she wouldn't be selling the resort, yet there was a continual parade of contractors on Sacred Lake Road. He wondered if maybe her father *had* convinced her to make a deal with a development corporation and she simply hadn't bothered to tell him.

Finally the morning came when Robert Taylor loaded his suitcases into his rental car. Brendan heaved a sigh of relief. While Dani said goodbye, he went back to his favorite spot—the hammock strung between two trees in front of cabin number two.

It wasn't long after he heard the sound of tires on gravel that Dani surprised him with a kiss. He was lying in the hammock reading when she snuck up beside him, kissed him and jumped on top of him, nearly overturning the both of them. ''Alone at last,'' she said, snuggling close.

He gave her a long, passionate kiss that had both of them breathing heavily by the time he pulled away. "I've been wanting to do that for five days."

"You could have done it. I told my father about us," she announced.

"Is that why he was giving me all those dirty looks?"

"He was not," she said indignantly. "I thought maybe you were mad at me. You hardly came around while my father was here."

"In case you didn't notice, I was busy painting. I didn't want my boss to think I was slacking off on the job. Besides, I figured you two could use the time alone," he told her, not wanting to admit to the doubts that had troubled him.

"We did have a lot of legal business to take care of regarding the resort." When he didn't comment, she said, "You can wipe that suspicious look off your face. I'm going to make some improvements, but I'm not putting up condominiums or selling the land to developers. I'm keeping it pretty much the way it is."

Brendan gave her a kiss of approval. "I was worried. I thought maybe he was going to talk you into changing your mind."

"No. Actually I'm glad he came. We needed to talk."

"About why he didn't tell you Wilbur had tried to contact you?"

She nodded. "That was one of the things. He's still having trouble accepting the fact that he doesn't have to take care of me, that I can do that myself."

Admiration sparkled in Brendan's eyes. "Yes, you can. It's one of the many things I love about you."

"So you really do love me?" She lifted her head so their eyes met.

"Yes." The admission came without hesitation.

"Good, because I love you, too," she said with a smile that made Brendan want to make love to her right there in the bright sunshine. When his hand started unbuttoning her blouse, she stopped him. "I don't think that's a good idea. I'm expecting workers to arrive this morning."

Brendan groaned.

"The good news is that the power company should be out next week and then we'll have lights!"

"It's still more romantic making love by candlelight." He kissed her again. "I've missed you."

She sighed. "I've missed you, too. Why is it that we can never spend two nights in a row together?"

"Maybe we can remedy that problem in the next few days," he said huskily. "Isolated as this place is, it's certainly had its share of visitors this summer."

"And now we're going to have construction workers crawling all over it." She grinned apologetically. "The one request of Wilbur's I can't honor is to go without indoor plumbing and electricity."

"I think his main concern was that the area not become commercial."

"And I agree it shouldn't be. I'd like to think that someday, if I have children of my own, they'd be able to come here and appreciate nature as it is."

"Do you want to have any children?" he asked.

"Mmm-hmm, at least two, although if you'd asked me ten years ago, I would've told you I was going to have at least six or seven. Growing up as an only child, I swore I'd have a big family."

"But you said you had a happy childhood."

"Oh, I did, but you know what they say about the grass being greener on the other side of the fence. I envied my friends who had brothers and sisters even though they continually told me how lucky I was to be an only child.'' She smiled wistfully. ''I do like kids, though. I always have.''

''Which is why you became a teacher,'' he said. ''Wilbur would have been proud of you. It's what he wanted for Bridget. Her dream was to be an actress, but his was for her to be a schoolteacher like your grandmother.''

''What did she teach?''

''Elementary school, I think. You can ask Lou. She could tell you for sure.''

''It still seems so strange to me—finding out all this information about people I never expected to know.''

''You don't seem to find it unsettling,'' he noted.

''No, I don't. I suppose it's similar to the feelings people have when they do a genealogical search. You trace back through the generations and discover all this fascinating information about your ancestors, but you never get the opportunity to really know them.''

''You want to know what I think?'' She nodded eagerly. ''I think that if you had received those letters from Wilbur, you would have contacted him.''

''So in the past few weeks I've managed to convince you I'm not quite the narcissistic heiress you thought I was?'' She arched one brow.

He gave her a penitent look. ''I was wrong, but I promise I'll make it up to you.''

''And how do you plan to do that?''

''How about if I spend the remainder of the summer convincing you that I think you are the most wonderful creature on this earth.'' He planted kisses all over her face.

"What if it takes longer than summer?" she asked, giggling.

"You'd be surprised by what I can accomplish in a short time."

When he went to nibble on her ear, she pulled away. "Seriously, Brendan, what is going to happen to us when summer ends?"

"What if I said I don't know the answer to that question?"

She stiffened. "Are you saying that we've just been having a summer fling?" He could see she was hurt by the possibility.

"No. You wanted an honest answer and I gave you one. I wish I knew what was going to happen at the end of summer, but I don't."

In a flash, she was out of the hammock. Her mood had switched from affectionate to confrontational. "You just told me you loved me, and I don't think you're a man who says those words easily."

"I'm not." He, too, got to his feet.

"Then I don't understand how you can say you love me yet not know if you still want to be with me when summer's over."

He looked out at the peaceful waters of the lake, searching for the right words to tell her why he didn't have the answer she expected. There was no easy way to tell her that he wasn't ready to make the kind of commitment she wanted.

He pulled her into his arms, placing her head on his shoulder. "It's not a question of whether or not I love you."

"Then what is it a question of? Whether or not you'll go back to the seminary?"

"No, I'm not going back," he stated resolutely.

"Then I don't understand what the problem is."

She could see he was struggling to explain. "Dani, for as long as I can remember, I've been preparing for a life-style that isn't going to be mine. Surely you can understand why I need to be cautious."

She pulled away from him. "Cautious? As in maybe you rushed into something you're not sure you want to be in?"

He didn't try to pull her back into his arms.

"We did rush in, but that's not the only problem. I came here looking for answers to some serious questions. As much as I'd like to be able to tell you I've resolved those issues, I can't."

Dani didn't like the direction their conversation was taking. "So you're saying you don't know where you want to be in the future."

"I do want it to be the place where you are, but it's not an easy path to follow, Dani. It isn't simply two steps away from the seminary and three steps forward to a new life."

"If you're worried about finding a job, I'm sure my dad could find a position for you."

He stared at her in disbelief. "I don't understand how you can even suggest such a thing. You're the one who's been struggling to be independent of the man, yet you want me to be beholden to him?"

"All right, so it wasn't the greatest idea I've ever had," she snapped.

"I'll find my own job," he stated firmly. "After all, I have degrees in social work and education."

There was an uncomfortable silence, then she said, "You're not sure about us, are you? Despite everything you told me when we made love, you really aren't sure."

"I want to be, but I feel like this young kid who's fallen in love for the first time and doesn't know what to do about it," he admitted candidly.

"But this isn't the first time for you, is it? I mean, Brendan, you were married."

"That was a long time ago," he said quietly. "And when Caroline died, I started to prepare for a life as a priest, even though I was at college first."

Neither spoke for a moment, then Dani said, "So where do we go from here?"

He reached for her hand. "You have a teaching contract this fall."

"I'll get out of it," she said in a rush.

He shook his head. "No, I don't want you to do that. I talked to Father Dorian. There's a church-run youth group in Minneapolis that needs a leader. I'm thinking about taking the job."

Dani's heart sank. He was saying goodbye. She couldn't prevent the tears that stung her eyes. "I'll never see you again."

He brought her hand to his lips. "Yes, you will. The time apart will give us a chance to sort through everything that's happened this summer."

"And we'll be able to see each other when?"

He shrugged. "Whenever it works out."

Which meant he wasn't sure if anything was going to work out. She wrapped her arms around his waist and placed her cheek against his chest, liking the sound of his heart beating. "I don't want to think about not being able to see you every day."

He kissed the top of her head. "Then don't think about it. We still have three weeks of summer to be together."

For Dani it wasn't enough. She was determined to

make it the most glorious three weeks of his life in hopes that he would tell her he couldn't bear to part from her. When it was time for him to leave, she'd make sure there was no doubt in Brendan's mind about what their future would hold.

He gave her no reason to question that his feelings for her weren't as intense as hers for him. He read her poetry, gathered bouquets of wildflowers and cooked her dinner over a campfire. Among his many talents, she also discovered that he was skilled in the art of massage and graced with a baritone voice that could sing her to sleep.

Although Dani tried to get Brendan to discuss the subject of the priesthood, it was a futile effort. She thought that if she could get him to talk about it, she could help him resolve whatever it was that still troubled him. But it was a part of his life he refused to share with her.

The more time they spent together, the more confident Dani became that nothing was going to separate them—not her job back in California or his past life as a seminarian. Then the phone was installed.

The first call that came was from Father Dorian. Brendan was needed for orientation in the new job. "I need to go," he told Dani as soon as he had hung up.

"Now? But we had a week left...." She swallowed the lump in her throat.

He took her in his arms and held her for several moments. "I don't want to, but I promised Joe."

Dani nodded in understanding although she didn't understand at all.

"I don't think you should stay here alone," he said.

"I'll be fine." She nodded toward the telephone. "I can call someone if there's a problem."

He still looked uneasy at the idea of leaving her. "Lou would come and stay if you asked her to."

She shook her head. "I'll be okay. How long will you be gone?"

"Joe said it'll only be a couple of days."

Dani looked at the calendar. She only had eight days before she needed to fly home to California. "Hurry back," she said, unable to check the tears that suddenly welled up in her eyes.

He pulled her into his arms once more and comforted her, much the way he had Jodie. "It's going to be all right. I'm coming back. We have unfinished business."

Dani wondered what the unfinished business was. She never did find out. Three days came and went, then four, then five. He called her on the phone, but they were strangely impersonal conversations that did little to ease the doubts she had regarding their relationship.

By the sixth day, she decided she'd had enough. When her father called with the news that an old school friend was coming to Montecito for a visit, Dani decided to go home a couple of days early rather than risk the heartbreak she'd suffer should Brendan not show up at all.

So she called Lou, packed her things and went home. She left a note that said only, "Call me when you're ready to finish our business." Since she didn't think he was coming back, she didn't know why she left it.

What she didn't anticipate at the time was that an electrician was going to see that note, put it in his pocket and call Louella Hortense.

BRENDAN DIDN'T UNDERSTAND why there was no answer at the resort. It was nearly midnight, his car had broken down on the county road that passed through

Hidden Falls and he couldn't reach Dani. He'd had no choice but to walk the couple of miles to the small town where he'd awakened Pete so he could use the phone.

"Who you trying to call?" the grocer asked as Brendan hung up the receiver.

"Dani. Do you think she's staying at Lou's?"

"Lou's? Haven't you heard? Dani went back to California."

He was too late. Brendan slumped against the wall. "When?"

"Yesterday. Lou said she hired old Shorty Babcock to take care of the place for her. They're still doing the renovations out there, you know—plumbing, electricity...the works."

"I thought she wasn't leaving until Saturday."

The grocer shrugged. "Maybe something came up."

Brendan nodded, although he thought it was more than likely she'd left because he hadn't returned. He'd wanted to come back and he almost had several times, but something stopped him. Fear.

What if he let her down the way he'd let down the other women in his life? His mother. Caroline.

Now he was too late.

"You need a place to sleep tonight?" Pete asked.

"Yeah. I'll have to get my car towed tomorrow."

"If you'd rather borrow my car and take it to the resort, you can do that," the old man offered.

"You wouldn't mind?"

"Naw, go ahead. Just bring it back in the morning." He handed him a set of keys. "You'll probably be more comfortable there."

Not without Dani he wouldn't be. Why hadn't she called to tell him the change in plans? Maybe she'd left him a note....

"DANI, YOU HAVE A MESSAGE." The school secretary handed Dani a pink slip when she stopped in the office on her lunch hour.

Dani shoved the paper into her pocket, grabbed the stack of photocopies she'd ordered and headed for the teachers' lounge. While she ate, she graded the quiz she'd given her students that morning. It was only as she reached into her pocket for a tissue that she remembered the message slip.

As soon as she read it, she jumped up to use the faculty phone.

"Lou? It's me. Dani Taylor," she said when the older woman had answered.

"How are you doing?"

"I'm fine, but I'm ready for the holiday break. What about you? Is everything okay?"

"Oh, I'm good. No problems, but I needed to talk to you because I have someone who wants to use one of the cabins for a couple of weeks over the Christmas holidays."

Dani frowned. "I thought we closed the place for the winter."

"We did, but there's really no reason you can't open up now that you have power out there. It's just a question of whether you want anybody staying there."

"That depends. Is it one of the priests who wants to use it?"

"No, it's Brendan."

Dani's stomach clenched. It was going on four months since she'd seen him. Four months and two days to be exact. She'd spoken to him only once—when he'd called and tried to explain why he hadn't come back to the resort in two days as promised. Now he wanted to spend the Christmas break there? All she could do was wonder why.

"Dani, are you there?"

"Yeah, I'm here, Lou." She rubbed two fingers across her forehead. "I don't think it's a good idea to have anyone there in the winter."

"All right. I'll tell him." She went on to ask Dani about her holiday plans, but Dani only halfheartedly answered her questions.

Just before Lou was about to hang up, Dani asked, "Do you know why Brendan wants to use the cabin?"

"He said to tell you he's ready to take the plunge."

"The plunge?" she repeated, puzzled.

"He must mean in the frozen lake. You know, after the sauna. Wilbur used to have a couple of buddies who'd cut holes in the ice and jump in. I think it's crazy myself, but some folks still do it."

If Brendan Millar was dumb enough to want to do it, Dani figured, then why should she stop him? "Oh, all right. Tell him it's okay."

Long after the school day had ended, Dani thought about her conversation with Lou.... All these months, and she still had the same old rush of emotion just hearing his name. The thought of him could make her knees go weak.

She wished she could say she'd forgotten him, but she hadn't. Not a single day went by that she didn't hope he'd call her and tell her he couldn't live without her. Instead, she'd gotten a phone call asking her if he could use the sauna. Why didn't he just call her himself?

That question continued to nag her until finally, on the last day of class before the holiday break, she bought a round-trip ticket for Minneapolis. All the way to the airport she asked herself why she was doing this. The only answer she could think of was that she needed closure. For endless days she'd clung to the hope that he was going to come back into her life. She would not be able to move forward until she saw him face-to-face and heard him say it was over.

Snow was falling when she arrived in Minnesota. Once more she rented a Ford Explorer, but this time she didn't make the mistake of driving at night. The trip on the icy roads was challenge enough in the daylight.

She didn't stop in Hidden Falls but went straight on to the resort. Although the road had been plowed, the wind was blowing, creating drifts of snow in the open areas. It was with a great sigh of relief that Dani arrived at the resort. Hers was the only car parked outside, however.

The first place she looked for Brendan was in the sauna. Trudging through the deep snow, Dani made her way to the wooden building. She pulled open the door, but the room was cold and empty. So were the shower and changing room.

A glance toward the lake told her there were no holes cut in the ice. The only indication that anyone had been at the resort was the path shoveled between cabin number two and the half-moon. She followed it, then knocked on the cabin door. There was no answer. She tried to open it, but it was locked. She had no keys.

As she headed back to her car, she saw a tiny movement across the lake. Squinting, she realized it was a cross-country skier. She watched as the figure came closer and closer.

About a hundred feet from shore, the figure called her name.

It was Brendan. She watched him approach until he was right in front of her.

"Did you bring your skis?" he asked.

"No, I didn't bring my skis!" she snapped irritably.

He released his boots from the bindings and leaned the skis and poles upright against the cabin. "Come on in. I'll make us something warm to drink."

"How come the door's locked?" she asked as he fumbled with the keys.

"Are you complaining?" He pushed open the door and gestured for her to go inside. Once they'd taken off their winter gear, he made them each a cappuccino. "See what electricity can do?" he said with a grin as he handed her a cup. "Make yourself comfortable and I'll get a fire going."

"You don't look surprised to see me," she said as he spread kindling in the fireplace and she took a seat on the couch.

"But I am. I hoped you'd come, but I knew what I was competing against."

She frowned. "What are you talking about?"

"Your life in California."

"Maybe you're forgetting whose idea it was for me to go back," she told him, her voice rising.

"You didn't wait for me. I said I was coming back, that we had unfinished business." The fire suddenly burst into life, the dried wood crackling and popping like the tension between them.

"But you didn't come back. I waited for a week. And then when you finally called, you acted as if you didn't care about me at all," she accused.

"It was a stressful week. I had to call you from Joe's office, and there were always people there." He hesitated for a moment, his expression troubled. "By the time I was able to leave, what do I find when I get here? You'd gone without a word. At least you could have left me a note."

"I did. I said that you could call me when you were ready to finish our business."

He shook his head. "I didn't get that note...." He paused. "So you didn't get tired of waiting for me?"

"I did get tired, and when you treated me as if I didn't matter..."

"You always mattered," he said.

"Well, it was pretty hard to tell. What was I supposed to think? You were with your mentor and working in the church and all, so I just assumed—"

"I'd had another change of heart and decided to return to the priesthood?"

She nodded.

"If that's the case, why did you come here?"

"Because..." She hesitated. "Because we need closure."

He laughed.

"What's so funny?"

"You flew two thousand miles, drove another 250 in near blizzard conditions to tell me we need closure?"

"Why else?"

"I was hoping you'd want to tell me that you felt the same way I did—that our time apart has proved one thing. We belong together."

Dani's heart began to thump madly. "You want to pick up where we left off?" She made it sound as if it was an absurd idea.

"No," he said. "I'd rather start over, because I think the Brendan Millar standing before you today is a much better prospect for a husband than the one you knew during the summer.'' The look in his eyes was familiar. It was the one that made her skin tingle.

She swallowed with difficulty. ''What makes you think I'm looking for a husband?''

''Just wishful thinking on my part, because I think I've found the woman I want to spend the rest of my life with.''

He spoke with such tenderness she could sit still no longer. She rushed into his arms and kissed him long and hard. When it was over, he pulled the two of them onto the couch, cradling Dani in his lap.

''I'm sorry I couldn't give you what you wanted this summer,'' he said, resting his forehead against her hair. ''But until I knew just who I was, it wouldn't have been fair.''

''Are you saying I fell in love with a stranger?''

''No, but when I left the seminary, I really didn't know who I was. I needed to figure out why I'd entered the seminary in the first place.''

''And now you know?''

''I think I do. My mother wanted me to be a priest, and Father Dorian was like a father to me, so I grew up thinking that was my vocation. After high school, I started college, knowing that as soon as I finished, I'd enter the seminary. But then Caroline came along.'' He sighed. ''I was married at twenty and a widower at twenty-two.''

''What happened to her?'' Dani asked softly.

''She was killed in a car accident,'' he replied, ''the day after our second wedding anniversary. It seems rather ironic. You see, I was working as a truck driver, making long hauls. That was something that drove her nuts, because for one thing she hated to be alone, and she was convinced that it was too dangerous an occupation and that I'd die in an accident."

Dani nodded. "And then she was the one who..."

"Yeah. Six blocks from our apartment. She was on her way to the grocery store. She swerved to avoid hitting a toddler who'd wandered out into the street. Doing that, she crossed into the oncoming traffic." He shook his head. "She died so a child could live."

"Oh, Brendan. That's so sad," she sympathized.

"Her life was sad, Dani. Unlike you, she didn't have parents who loved her."

"But she had you."

His laugh was without mirth. "Yeah, she had me."

"Are you saying you didn't love her when you married her?"

"Not the way I should have," he stated honestly. "And I know I never made her happy. This summer when I said I felt like a kid who'd fallen in love for the first time and didn't know what to do, I was speaking the truth, Dani. What happened between us was so good, so satisfying, so intimate.... I never had that with Caroline."

"You don't need to tell me this if you don't want to," Dani murmured.

"Yes, I do. It's something I've been thinking about a lot lately. Actually, ever since we made love the first time. My physical relationship with Caroline was not a satisfying one. No matter how hard we tried, we couldn't seem to find the magic. I thought it was my fault, thought I'd married her for all the wrong reasons."

"Why *do* you think you married her?"

"Because I thought I could save her from a life of poverty and abuse. At the time, I didn't realize that was the reason. She was beautiful, had a big heart and she needed me. We met when we were only nineteen, and both of us wanted to be out of the projects. Together we thought we could leave behind all the problems that had plagued us as children. Neither one of us realized that until we fixed what was broken inside us, together we wouldn't be a healthy, happy couple.''

"I think you're too hard on yourself. From what Jodie said, Caroline thought you were the sun, moon and stars."

"Keep in mind that Jodie was only six or seven at that time."

"Kids can sense when people are happy or unhappy. And every marriage has its share of problems," she said on a positive note.

"It wasn't long after we were married that we realized we'd made a mistake, but we were both determined to make the marriage work."

"I thought you must have loved her so deeply you knew life would never be the same without her, so that's why you entered the seminary."

"She *is* part of the reason. Because we'd had such an unsatisfying sexual relationship, I saw it as another sign that I should have become a priest. I figured that if I could be celibate in a marriage, I could certainly do it as a single man. All my life, people had told me what a fine priest I'd make. I decided to find out."

"And did you?"

"Yes. I realize now that I entered the seminary for the wrong reasons. Partly because it's what I was expected to do, and partly because I wanted to be successful as a man."

"You can be a successful without being a priest."

"Yes, but I never really had a chance to find that out

for myself.'' He sighed. ''That's why I came to Sacred Lake.''

''And you met me,'' she said with a grin.

He kissed her to leave her in no doubt he was delighted he had. ''Which was totally confusing. I fell in love with you, yet I didn't feel I had a right to be in love until I figured out exactly who I was and what I wanted.''

''And now you know?''

''Yes. All I've ever really wanted to do is help people. And I can do that without being a priest, something the job at the youth center has taught me.''

''Are you teaching school?''

''Only temporarily. I'm a sub. What I'd like to do is get involved in a program I've been hearing about from some of the social workers.''

''What kind of program?'' Dani asked.

''To prevent teen pregnancy. It's been shown that when teens are involved in community-service programs, pregnancy rates are dramatically reduced among the participants. If we could get the local at-risk teens to volunteer in nursing homes and preschools, maybe we can give them a sense of their future, help them achieve their goals.''

''It sounds promising,'' Dani said. ''It would also go hand in hand with an idea I've had for the resort.''

He looked at her quizzically.

''Actually I've been thinking about this for a while, but I wanted it to be my surprise to you. I'd like to make The Last Place on Earth a place for unwed moms. It was something Jodie said to me about never having been to a resort before. I know this isn't the easiest place to get to, but don't you think it would make a nice retreat for pregnant teens?''

"I think it's a great idea. Does this mean I won't have to move to California to be with you?"

She clasped her hands around his neck. "I was hoping I could convince you to be a member of the staff."

"Give me the job application and I'll sign on the dotted line. This is the one place on earth I want to be."

EPILOGUE

"HOW DO I LOOK?" Jodie pirouetted nervously in front of Dani.

"Very nice. Are you going to be okay?"

Jodie nodded, but Dani wasn't convinced. The sound of tires crunching on gravel announced the arrival of their visitors.

"That must be the Grangers." Dani extended a hand to Jodie, who placed her sweaty one in her aunt's. "This is it."

When they stepped out into the bright July sunshine, they saw a dark-haired couple climb out of a minivan. A moment later, the woman reached into the back seat and plucked a baby from the child seat. Her husband helped a little girl climb out and took her by the hand.

"Welcome to The Last Place on Earth," Dani said, leading Jodie down the steps to greet them. "I'm Dani Millar and this is Jodie Fisher."

The Grangers introduced themselves, but it was the little girl clinging shyly to her father's pant leg who garnered all the attention. Steve Granger urged the dark-haired five-year-old forward and said, "Chryssa, can you say hi to Dani and Jodie?"

"Hi!"

"You have a pretty dress," Jodie said, stooping to talk to the little girl.

"My mommy made it," she said proudly.

''Well, you are very lucky to have such a nice mommy,'' Jodie told her, then gave Roberta Granger a smile.

''Come and sit at the picnic table,'' Dani urged everyone. ''Jodie made some cookies and lemonade.''

The Grangers stayed for an hour, visiting, laughing, sharing stories. When Roberta and Steve buckled their two children back into their seats, Dani thought she saw a sheen of tears in Jodie's eyes. Not long after the mini-van disappeared down the gravel road, Jodie sat on the wooden swing where five years ago she'd contemplated the most important decision of her life.

''You okay?'' Dani asked as she sat down beside her.

''Mmm-hmm. She's beautiful, isn't she?''

Dani covered Jodie's hand with hers. ''Just like a princess.''

'HAVE I DONE something wrong?' Angie persisted, wishing Taylor would emit a sense of camaraderie instead of holding an impenetrable reserve.

'Not at all,' he assured her. 'I would say a lot of things right. You seem to be fitting into our little Outback community very well. I've heard only good things about you.'

'They're nice people,' she said sincerely. Only the Maguire family kept her shut out of their hearts.

'Yes,' he agreed. 'Though I appreciate it's taken considerable effort from you. It is a world away from what you're used to.'

The control Angie had been exerting over her feelings snapped. He wasn't as blatant as his aunt in his prejudice against her but she'd felt it coming through every word he'd spoken and she didn't deserve any of it.

'Don't judge me by your wife!'

His jaw jerked. A flicker of some dark emotion destroyed the steady power of his probing gaze.

'No two people are the same. If you don't know that, you're a man of very limited vision. So I come from the city as your wife did! That doesn't stop me from being an individual in my own right.'

She straightened up, proudly defiant, furiously angry with the situation. 'I'm *me*. Angie Cordell. And it's time you took the blinkers off your eyes, Taylor Maguire.'

Then she whirled away from him, too agitated by the explosive expulsion of her emotion to keep facing him.

The storm outside hadn't yet eased. There was nowhere to go. She stopped at the window, staring blindly at the torrential rain. The thundering on the roof was almost deafening but it wasn't as loud as the silence behind her.

'You want me to go, don't you? You've given me a month's respite and now you want me to leave and channel my energies somewhere else.'

'I didn't say that, Angie.'

'You were working your way around it.' Bitterness at his tactics spewed the suspicion. 'Do you have your first choice of governess waiting in the wings?'

'No. I said I'd give you a chance.'

'Have you?' She swung around to face him. 'Have you really, Taylor?'

He hadn't moved. He didn't move now except to make a gesture of appeasement. 'Angie, I was merely trying to ascertain how you felt.'

'Then let me tell you your cynicism was shining through every word.'

He frowned, shook his head. 'I didn't mean to hurt you.' The blue eyes fastened on hers with devastating sincerity. 'I truly did not come in here to take you down or suggest you leave.'

Her heart jiggled painfully. He might be speaking the truth but the judgements were still there, the judgements that ruled his attitude towards her, that kept her shut out of his life, denied any real sharing with him, denied his confidence and trust. She didn't know why it meant so much to her but it did. It did. And the need to fight for justice from him was as much a raging torrent inside her as the rain outside.

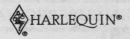

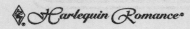

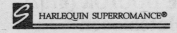

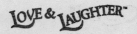

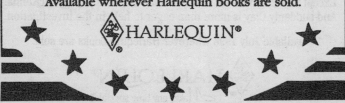

MEN *at* WORK

All work and no play? Not these men!

April 1998

KNIGHT SPARKS by Mary Lynn Baxter

Sexy lawman Rance Knight made a career of arresting the bad guys. Somehow, though, he thought policewoman Carly Mitchum was framed. Once they'd uncovered the truth, could Rance let Carly go...or would he make a citizen's arrest?

May 1998

HOODWINKED by Diana Palmer

CEO Jake Edwards donned coveralls and went undercover as a mechanic to find the saboteur in his company. Nothing— or no one—would distract him, not even beautiful secretary Maureen Harris. Jake had to catch the thief—*and* the woman who'd stolen his heart!

June 1998

DEFYING GRAVITY by Rachel Lee

Tim O'Shaughnessy and his business partner, Liz Pennington, had always been close—but never *this* close. As the danger of their assignment escalated, so did their passion. When the job was over, could they ever go back to business as usual?

MEN AT WORK™

Available at your favorite retail outlet!

COMING NEXT MONTH

#794 COTTONWOOD CREEK • Margot Dalton
Home on the Ranch
Someone has been skimming profits from Clay Alderson's
ranching operation, and now the government has sent an
auditor to check the books. Ms. J. C. McKenna is all business.
Which means Clay is going to have to fight the attraction he
feels for her. Especially since she considers *him* the prime
suspect.

#795 THE WANT AD • Dawn Stewardson
When April Kelly sees a personal ad asking for information
about Jillian Birmingham, she knows she's in trouble. What
she doesn't know is why Paul Gardiner placed the ad or how
much *he* knows about her past. When he tells her he has
information that can liberate her from that past, she knows
she has to take a chance…maybe even trust him.

#796 HIS BROTHER'S BABY • Connie Bennett
9 Months Later
The two brothers were as unalike as brothers could be.
Now the one Meg Linley loved with all her heart is dead,
and the other wants custody of her unborn child. And what
Nick Ballenger wants, Nick Ballenger gets…*usually.*

#797 FALLING FOR THE DOCTOR • Bobby Hutchinson
Emergency!
Dr. Greg Brulotte has it all. He's a successful ER surgeon
living the good life. He loves his job and his death-defying
hobbies, and he loves women. But when the doctor becomes
a patient after a debilitating accident, he learns about the other
side of life—and about the other side of nurse Lily Sullivan.